FRACTURE

A CURVY GIRL ROMANTIC SUSPENSE

F-BOMB: CURVY VIGILANTES
BOOK 8

MARY E THOMPSON

FRACTURE

F-BOMB: Curvy Vigilantes, book eight

Ebook ISBN: 978-1-953879-47-9

Print ISBN: 978-1-953879-48-6

Audiobook ISBN: 978-1-953879-49-3

 Created with Vellum

F-BOMB: CURVY VIGILANTES

Say hello to the Curvy Vigilantes, a group of plus-size women who protect their city. They have no training, but they don't need it. All they need is the desire to right wrongs and to protect the ones they love... and maybe some help from the men strong (and smart) enough to fall for these kick-ass curvy women.

F-BOMB: CURVY VIGILANTES
Forsaken (subscriber exclusive)
Fury
Framed
Feign
Fierce
Fatal
Fear
Flee
Fracture
Faith

SUBSCRIBE NOW AT MARYETHOMPSON.COM

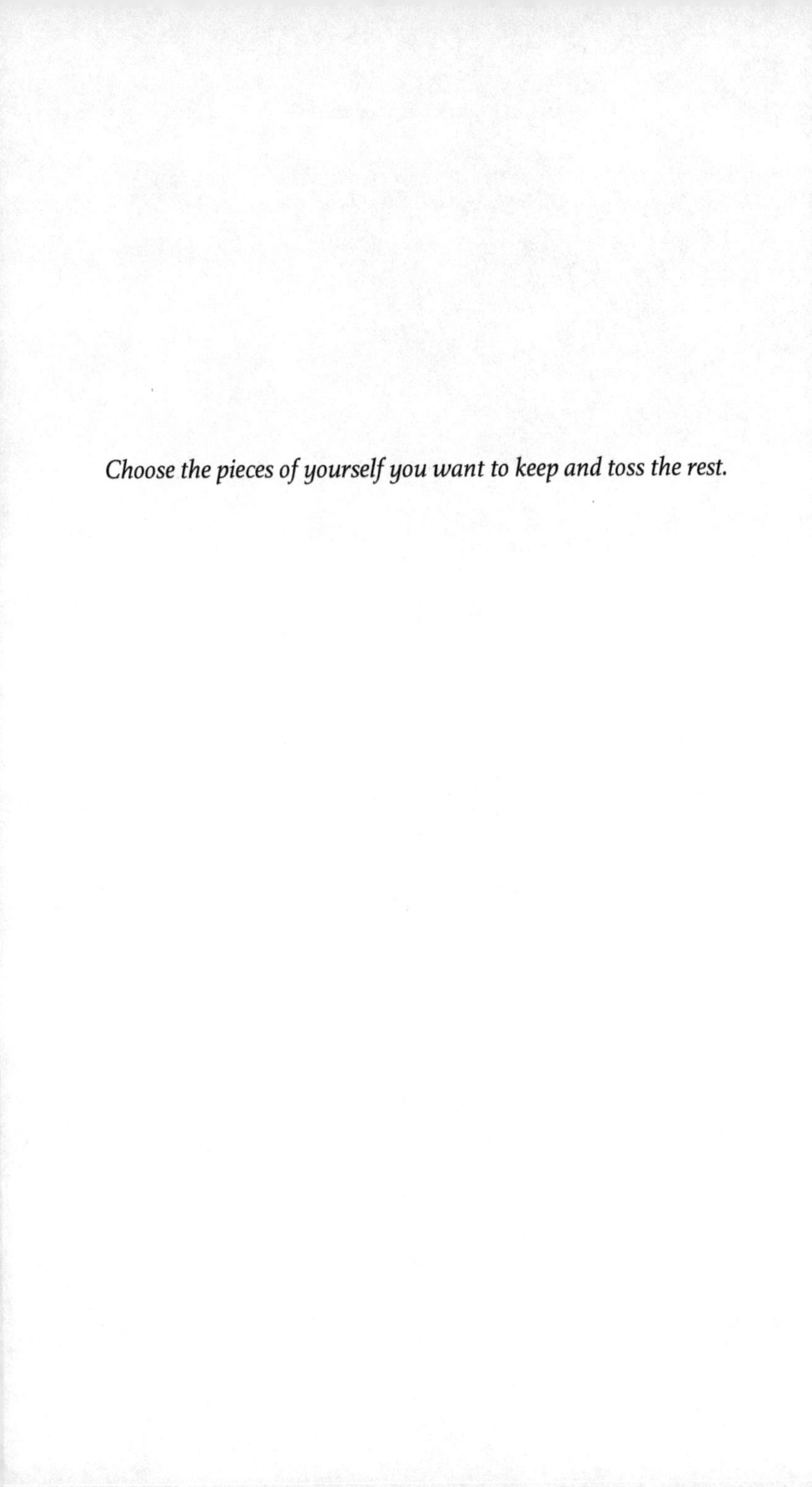

Choose the pieces of yourself you want to keep and toss the rest.

1

VINNIE MORGAN IGNORED THE PHONE BUZZING ON HIS HIP AND continued down the deserted hallway. Something wasn't right. His gut told him he needed to investigate, and he never ignored his gut. Not when it was so loud.

Three days. It had been three days since anyone had heard from Lorelei Sloane. The badass woman who was in charge of the biggest investigation his city had ever seen hadn't been out of touch with her team since it was created.

Going missing at her partner's wedding wasn't more of a comfort. Especially when Vinnie heard she was meeting with a contact. Not that it surprised him she would take off during a social event for work. There was no doubt in his mind she would have at least checked in afterward.

In Vinnie's line of work, people didn't go dark. Not when they were on a case. Not without someone knowing where they were. Sure, the gorgeous woman in charge could have shacked up with someone after the wedding, but for three days? That didn't feel right to Vinnie. He'd seen her in action. He knew her type. The type that would stop at nothing to get the job done and put the bad guys away.

He was the same type. It was why he was plucked from the force and invited to join SWAT. A decision he never once second guessed.

Vinnie's heart pounded as he drew closer to the door. If he broke in, he could surprise a woman who was perfectly fine. If he ignored that fear, he could find anything.

No one was in the hallway. Not a sound came from behind any of the doors. Either they were expertly sound-proofed or no one was home. A high-end place like Lorelei Sloane's apartment complex could have been either. But it made Vinnie aware of every creak the floor made as he moved toward her unit.

The door was closed. It didn't appear to have been forced open at any point. The trim was intact, and the door wasn't damaged. But something still wasn't right.

Vinnie tried the knob. Locked. He jiggled the door a little and could tell the deadbolt wasn't engaged. A single woman living alone in a big city would never lock her door-knob only. Especially not a woman with her training.

He knocked softly, hoping he was wrong about every-thing and Agent Sloane would open the door and tell him he was being paranoid and a creep. He waited, holding his breath so he didn't miss a sound from the other side of the door. None came, and Vinnie pulled out his lock-picking kit.

Less than ten seconds later, he had the door open and his suspicions and fears were confirmed. Lorelei Sloane laid on her couch in the living room. She'd been badly beaten. Her beautiful face was marked with cuts and bruises. Her clothing was all in place, but she was not okay. She was far from okay.

She was barely alive.

Vinnie snatched his phone just as the buzzing started up

again. He swiped to answer, not caring who was calling him. "What?"

"Where the hell are you?" his boss barked.

Yeah, Vinnie might have skipped town. Against orders. He would be lucky if he wasn't fired. Except he had good news. Sort of. "I found her."

"Who?" Damien asked. Vinnie had his boss's attention now.

"Lorelei Sloane. She's in her apartment in Boston. We need an ambulance here now. Head trauma, bodily injury." Vinnie swallowed roughly as he took in the bloody clothes and bruises appearing on Lorelei's dark skin. He knew if he could see them, they were worse than they appeared. And so was she.

Noises in the background told Vinnie that Damien was notifying everyone that Lorelei Sloane was alive and where she was. Vinnie put his phone on speaker and set it down so he could hear if Damien asked more questions.

Vinnie probed her skull, checking for fractures.

She groaned and opened her eyes. Deep brown pools stared up at him.

"You're safe now," Vinnie whispered.

She appeared to nod, then drifted off again.

"Hey, wake up. Stay with me."

Her eyes blinked open again, slowly, like it was taking all her effort to open them.

"There you go. Do you know where you are?"

The pinch between her brows said she either thought he was insane or she had no idea where she was. Either was possible. She opened her mouth, then winced and slammed her eyes shut again.

"Lorelei, look at me. I need you to stay with me. Help is on the way."

She drew a breath, one that stopped in the middle with another wince.

Vinnie laid her head back on the couch and ran his hands over her sides. At least a few broken ribs. She wormed away from his touch, telling him where she hurt the worst. He held his breath and slid his hands over her hips to her legs. She didn't fight him until he touched her right ankle, which he realized was bent at an awkward angle.

"Fuck," Vinnie whispered.

"Paramedics and police should be there any minute," Damien said.

Vinnie sucked in a breath and looked back up at the woman he'd been watching for months. The woman who led a multi-agency team without hesitation. She was strong and smart and capable.

And she was broken.

She opened her mouth again, a whisper of a word coming out.

Vinnie moved back to her head again and saw the marks around her throat. It could have been hands or it could have been something more. It didn't matter what it was, she was going to have a hard time talking for a while.

"I'm not going to let anyone else hurt you, Lorelei. You're safe now."

She nodded, the move jerky like it hurt. Her eyes filled with tears.

All Vinnie wanted to do was scoop her up and hold her, but he didn't know what other injuries she had. That and they'd never actually spoken, so him being in her apartment was more than a little fucked up.

Voices outside grew louder, then the squawk of a radio echoed in the hallway.

"In here," Vinnie called, drawing the attention of the people heading toward them. "I haven't cleared the apartment."

Two officers walked in first, guns drawn. They nodded to Vinnie, then spread out to search the place. Both called out clear and came back into the living room as the paramedics entered.

"Can you tell us what happened here, Mr. Morgan?" one of the cops asked, clearly aware of the overall situation from Damien.

Vinnie shook his head and watched the paramedics work. "I wish I could. I showed up a few minutes ago and found her like this. She's been missing for three days. People were here two days ago, but there was no sign of her. She's an FBI Agent."

"It's pretty clear someone wanted her dead."

"Yeah. The people she's been investigating. We just don't know who that is."

"We'll get a crime lab out here. Hopefully, we'll find something. Are you local?"

Vinnie shook his head. "No, sir. I live in Niagara Falls, New York. Where she's been for the last few months, running the investigation."

"That's a long way from here."

"Yeah. These people are smart."

"Too smart."

Vinnie nodded. Unfortunately, that was accurate.

"Your name is Lorelei Sloane. You are an FBI Agent," the woman said.

Lorelei nodded, the slight movement making her brain

feel like it was full of eggs. Raw ones that had no shape and would make you sick.

Which was how she'd spent the last day.

"Okay," Lorelei whispered. It was the best she could do with the damage to her throat.

"Do you remember anything about who attacked you?"

Lorelei groaned, sending a bolt of pain through her throat. She jerked at the feel and sent more pain through the rest of her body. Tears welled up in her eyes, but she refused to let them fall. She was not going to show her pain.

"Do you need more meds?" the menacing man in the corner asked. He was up and out of his seat, hurrying to her side.

The nurses said his name was Vinnie and he came in with her, but Lorelei didn't remember him. Not that it was a shock, since she didn't remember any damn thing.

"I'm fine," she hissed.

She was being a bitch to everyone. She fucking hated feeling like she was incapable of doing something, and at the moment, she was incapable of doing everything. She couldn't go to the bathroom alone. She couldn't sit up. She could speak or think or remember anything.

All she wanted to do was cry and scream and remember who she was and what happened to her.

"Maybe we should do this another time," Vinnie suggested firmly.

The woman sighed heavily. She glared at Vinnie, but he didn't blink. She looked back at Lorelei and flipped her tablet closed. "Fine. I'll be back tomorrow."

"Thanks," Vinnie said in a tone that suggested he was less than grateful.

Lorelei watched the woman walk out of the room. She knew there was a reason she was there, but everything was so mixed up that she didn't know what it was. "Who was that?"

Vinnie moved to the chair next to the bed. "That was Alexis Waterford. She's an FBI Agent in your old office. She said you didn't work together, so you only met a handful of times, but she is trying to find whoever attacked you."

Lorelei nodded, trying to pretend she followed any of that. She'd been told over and over again that she was an FBI Agent, but she wasn't even sure what that really meant. Since she woke up the day before with Vinnie hovering over her, she hadn't recognized anyone or anything. It was all foreign to her, including the woman in the mirror.

The doctors said it was because of the assault. She'd been beaten so badly she didn't recognize herself, but shouldn't she recognize something? Her eyes, her hair? Something?

For all Lorelei knew, it was a stranger staring back at her.

The only thing she was sure of was that Vinnie was one of the good guys. She couldn't explain how she knew that, but she did. He saved her. He protected her. He hadn't left her side since she woke up.

A knock on the door made Vinnie tense. He moved around the bed to check whoever was at the door before opening it.

"Vinnie Morgan?" a man asked.

"Yes, sir. I'm sorry—Oof," Vinnie said.

The machine Lorelei was connected to beeped quickly with her panic. Someone hit Vinnie or did something to knock the words out of him.

"Thank you," the other man whispered.

What did that mean?

"Happy I made it in time, sir," Vinnie said.

Who the hell—?

The curtain separating Lorelei from the men slid to the side, and they both stepped back into view. Lorelei's gaze slid down Vinnie, cataloging him to make sure he wasn't harmed.

Satisfied her protector was okay, she looked at the other man. Blond hair, blue eyes. White. There was something... maybe... familiar about him, but Lorelei wasn't sure what it was.

"Holy fuck. Are you okay?" He moved toward her quickly, crossing the space before Lorelei could say anything.

She recoiled when he reached out to touch her, and he pulled back.

"Sorry. I should have asked where your injuries are. I was just going to touch your hand," the blond man said.

"Who..." She looked from him to Vinnie, then back to the blond man.

"This is Adam Johnson. He's your partner. At the FBI," Vinnie said.

Lorelei looked at the man.

He held her gaze for a moment, then turned to Vinnie. "Why are you telling her who I am?"

"She doesn't remember anything from before yesterday. Who took her, from where, where she was held. And she doesn't remember who she is. You're the first one to show up that she should know, but clearly she doesn't know you either."

Adam looked at her, his face going soft.

"Nope," Lorelei said. "No pity. Fuck that. Get out if you're going to look at me like that."

Adam snorted. "Well, they didn't knock your personality out. We just have to help you remember everything else."

"We?" Lorelei asked.

Adam nodded and gestured to the door. "Raina is here. My wife. You were at our wedding before you went missing. And Karli, your cousin, is here with her boyfriend, Cole."

"Cousin?"

Adam nodded and looked at Vinnie. "Is it okay if the others come in?"

Vinnie nodded. "As long as everyone gives her space and time to process. Maybe start with her cousin?"

"Okay. Thanks."

"I'm here, too, you know," Lorelei snapped at them. She didn't like people making decisions for her.

"You are, but if you don't know me, chances are you're not sure what the doctors have said about visitors and recovery. I'm asking the person in the room who has an intact memory."

Lorelei scowled at both men. She wanted to be indignant, but they weren't wrong.

Adam walked out, saying something to someone in the hallway before coming right back in. He held the shoulders of a Black woman with dark hair like Lorelei's, same tight curls and dark brown eyes. She had full lips and red circles around her eyes.

"Oh, my God," she whispered as she moved toward Lorelei. "I'm so happy you're alive."

"Me, too," Lorelei said. She stared at the woman who must be her cousin and tried to remember her. Just like Adam, she was familiar, but her mind wasn't letting her access any of her memories.

"Adam said you don't remember anything."

Lorelei looked at Adam, once more trying to place him. She kept scanning the room and found Vinnie. "I remember Vinnie."

Karli looked at the man. She tilted her head and smiled. "I don't remember Vinnie. Have we met?"

Vinnie shook his head. "No, ma'am. I'm on a SWAT Team in Niagara Falls. We've been called in for support a few times. I heard about your cousin's disappearance and couldn't let it go."

"Wait, we didn't know each other before?" Lorelei asked. The nurses said he came in with her. Didn't that mean they had some kind of history?

Vinnie shook his head. "No. Not well. We've met, but we'd never spoken until yesterday."

"Well, shit. I thought I knew you." Her memories were shot, but Vinnie was someone she didn't doubt was supposed to be there. He protected her. Made sure she wasn't pushed too hard. Never left her alone unless he veri-fied the ID of whoever walked into the room.

But he was a stranger.

Lorelei looked at the man who said he was her partner. "Wait. How do I know you're all here to keep me safe and not to hurt me again?"

"Look at me, Lorelei," Vinnie said. He sat down in the chair next to her bed. "You know I'm not going to let anything happen to you. You know I'm here to protect you and help you and keep you safe. You might not know me, but you know that."

Lorelei looked at the man and nodded slowly. The beeping of her heart rate monitor slowed as she stared at him.

He was right. She wasn't afraid of him. He wasn't a threat. He was the one who saved her. And he was protecting her in ways she didn't even realize. Making sure she was given time to rest and not pressured to reveal things she didn't know.

He was her guardian angel.

"Wow," Karli whispered from Lorelei's other side. "I've never seen you calm down that quickly."

"Same. You're good for her, Vinnie," Adam said.

Vinnie didn't look away from Lorelei as he spoke. "She's good for all of us. I'm just lucky that I get to be around her for a little while."

Lorelei's body tingled at his words. Desire? Maybe. Appreciation? Definitely. "Thank you."

Vinnie nodded at her. "I'm not leaving unless you tell me you want me to. And if you do, I'll be right outside making sure no one ever hurts you again. I promise you that."

Lorelei sucked in a breath. She might not remember anything about her life before she woke up, but she knew, without a doubt, no man had ever made her a promise like that. And no man had ever made her feel like she didn't have to do it all. Like she could lean on someone else and know she wouldn't fall.

It was a damn good feeling. Because with Vinnie by her side, Lorelei knew she'd find answers. All the answers.

2
____

Vinnie watched Lorelei speak to her cousin. The confusion on her face when Karli said something Lorelei didn't remember was enough to make Vinnie want to throw everyone out of the room so Lorelei wasn't under anymore stress, but it wasn't his place. He wasn't her boyfriend or husband or even her partner.

Vinnie glanced at the man who'd been by Lorelei's side for years and found Adam Johnson staring at him. When Adam jerked his head toward the hallway, Vinnie nodded.

"Where are you going?" Lorelei asked, the heart rate monitor beeping faster as soon as Vinnie stood.

"I'm going to speak to Adam and whoever else is waiting outside that door to see you and assure them all that you're okay and tell them you might not be ready for a large group of people. If you're okay with that." Vinnie paused, holding eye contact with Lorelei until she nodded.

"Are you coming back?"

"Absolutely."

Lorelei nodded again, then turned her focus back to Karli.

Vinnie felt like he was walking into the lion's den, but he understood why there would be questions. Lots of them.

Adam stepped out ahead of him and looked up and down the hallway. He nodded to the two men standing guard, then jerked his head to an empty break room across the hall.

Vinnie followed the other man, hating that his heart pounded at the prospect of getting his ass handed to him by a man who, for all intents and purposes, outranked Vinnie.

Adam closed the door behind them, and Vinnie stood at attention, preparing for the lecture.

"Thank you," Adam said, surprising the hell out of Vinnie.

"Sir?"

Adam waved his hand. "You don't have to call me sir. I'm not in your command. And I am going to make sure you are not reprimanded for this."

"Why would you do that?"

Adam let out a shaky breath. He ran his hand over his face and shook his head. Emotion filled his blue eyes, emotion that showed Vinnie just how much Adam cared for Lorelei. "She'd be dead if it weren't for you."

"I was only doing what I thought was best."

"And you were right. When Raina, my wife, and I heard Lorelei was gone, we panicked. We started making calls in the middle of our reception. We had everyone we knew looking into her disappearance. For days, we waited for news. We thought she was gone. Vanished like so many others who were never seen again."

"They wanted someone to find her."

Adam nodded, his face twisting with pain. "They did. But I imagine they wanted it to be after she was dead. Which was what would have happened if you hadn't gone looking for her. So, thank you. And I will do everything to make sure you don't lose your job or have even one mark on your record as a result of this. And if that doesn't happen, if my word isn't enough, I guarantee you I will find a new place for you. My cousin is one of the F-BOMB owners, and they're always looking for good people."

"Thank you, sir," Vinnie said, appreciating the support. He didn't care what happened when he left town in search of Lorelei. All he cared about was finding the woman who was working harder than the rest of them to find the people who were destroying their city.

"The team at her apartment said there was nothing left behind. Nothing that would say who brought her there. Did you see anything?"

Vinnie shook his head. "No, sir. I noticed her doorknob was only locked on the bottom, not the deadbolt, and picked the lock. As soon as I was inside, I saw her and did what I could to judge her injuries. That was when my boss called and sent the police."

Adam sucked in a breath and nodded. "That's what we were told. Your prints were on the doorknob but nowhere else in the apartment, so they immediately ruled out you as a suspect."

"I was a suspect?" Vinnie asked. That surprised him.

Adam shrugged. "You were the one who found her. You know how these things go. Guilty until proven innocent."

Vinnie snorted. If that wasn't the truth. "So, this was about confirming my story?"

Adam shook his head. "No. This was about me thanking you for saving the life of one of the most important people in my world. After my wife, my sister, and my parents, sometimes before, it's Lorelei. She's saved my life more times than I can count, and I've done the same for her. I wouldn't have

Raina if it weren't for Lorelei. I wouldn't have any of the good things in my life. I love her like family, and to me, she is family. So this is about me saying thank you, and asking if you'll stick around."

"Stick around, sir?"

"She trusts you. She's never responded the way she did when you were right there. She's going to need help going forward. Not just because of her injuries but mentally, she's not the same person she was before this."

Vinnie started to interrupt, but Adam held up a hand.

"She will get back, but she doesn't know me or Karli, and I'm sure she's not going to know anyone else."

"She doesn't even know herself. I overheard her in the bathroom asking who she was. She was alone, so I know she was talking to herself."

Adam closed his eyes and drew a breath. "For whatever reason, probably because you were the first person she saw, she feels like she knows you. I want to ask your boss if you can be temporarily assigned as her personal protection. If you are willing to do it. If you're willing to be that person for her. Until she's back to herself."

"Yes, sir. Of course. I will do whatever it takes for her to feel like herself again."

"Thank you. Can I call you Vinnie?"

"Of course, sir."

Adam breathed a smile. "Again with the sir."

"Sorry, sir. Habit."

"I understand. But if you're with Lorelei like you're going to be, you're going to have to see me as an equal. These people don't see rank." Adam nodded his head toward the hallway, where four people were talking. Adam lifted his hand when one of them noticed him, then the group moved toward the break room Adam and Vinnie were in.

"Is this him?" one woman asked.

Adam nodded and reached his arm toward the woman. "Vinnie, this is my wife, Raina. That's Karli's boyfriend, Cade, and more friends, Jessica and Braden. When we heard Lorelei was alive, we got here as fast as we could."

"Thank you for finding her," Raina said. "I don't know how we can repay you."

"Just doing my job, ma'am," Vinnie said.

"Did he just call me ma'am?" Raina asked, glaring at her new husband.

"Duty requires it. He saved Lorelei."

Raina growled and glared at Vinnie. "Please call me Raina. It's so much better than *ma'am*."

"I'll do my best."

Raina smiled at him. She drew a breath and let it out slowly. "Can we go see her?"

Before Adam could reply, Vinnie stepped forward. "Lorelei is very tired and confused. She's been through a lot, and she needs a minimum level of stress right now."

Raina looked at Adam, then back to Vinnie, then to Adam. "What am I missing? Do we know you? Do we know him? Why are you the one in charge right now?"

"I apologize, ma—Raina. Lorelei went through hell. She doesn't know who she is. She is scared and overwhelmed and confused, and Adam's asked me to stay and keep her safe."

Raina's brows shot up. Before she could argue, Adam spoke up.

"Lorelei is responding to Vinnie. He found her, so she trusts him. When he speaks to her, she calms down. He's the only person she is relaxed around right now, so it's important we all listen to him."

"But he doesn't know her. Does he? Do you? Do you know Lorelei?"

Vinnie shook his head. "No, ma—Raina. I don't. We've never spoken before this. I was on the SWAT Team that helped bring in Trevor Davis, and I've been called in for some of the other things happening, but Lorelei doesn't know me. Traumatic brain injuries are complicated, and most people who suffer from them take a while to figure things out. When one person imprints on them, it's encouraged for that person to be their buffer. Their contact. I have no intention of keeping any of you from seeing Lorelei or from negatively affecting her at all. I only have her best interests at heart."

"And you think the best thing for her is rest?" Braden asked.

Vinnie met his gaze and nodded. "I do. She will need lots of help. She will need every single one of you to be there for her. I know you're all anxious to see her tonight."

"We thought we lost her," Jessica whispered.

"I understand. And I know it's important to all of you to see for yourself she's alive. I will ask her if she's up for visitors, but I reserve the right to throw you all out as soon as I suspect she needs a break."

"We can respect that," Cade said. "We're not going anywhere. We will be around to do whatever Lorelei needs."

"I'm sure she'll appreciate that. She'll need a lot of help. But her recovery needs to be on the doctor's timeline so she has the best chance at healing."

Raina snorted. "You definitely don't know her if you think she's going to wait for anything."

"I've seen her in action. She's the strongest woman I've ever had the privilege of working with. I have no doubt she will push the doctor's orders and will be back at it before she's supposed to be because Lorelei Sloane is not the kind of woman you can keep down. But that also means she's at risk for setbacks. If she ignores what the doctors say, she's at greater risk and could never fully recover."

"He's right," Braden said. "We learned a lot about TBIs in our training. Lorelei is going to hate it, but she will need to take some things slow." Braden turned to Adam. "We trust him?"

Adam nodded. "Without a doubt. I've read his whole record, and it's impeccable. He's on SWAT because he's damn good at what he does. Never even one mark on his record. There's no doubt in my mind he's the only one Lorelei will listen to, too."

"I find it hard to believe she'll listen to anyone," Jessica said.

"You'd be surprised." Adam turned to Vinnie again. "Will you go back in and see how she's doing and if she's up to anyone else seeing her?"

Vinnie nodded, moving through the group with the awareness that it was an excuse for them to talk about him without him in the room. Not that they had any trouble talking about him while he was there, but he didn't want to know what else they were going to say.

Besides, being away from Lorelei, even for fifteen minutes, made him anxious. He wanted to see for himself that she was okay.

LORELEI STARED at the door when Vinnie walked out. She felt like a piece of her was missing without him by her side. She couldn't explain it, but she figured that was part of her injury. Another thing she couldn't explain.

"How are you really doing?" the woman in the chair asked. Karli. Her cousin.

Lorelei didn't know what to say. She didn't know what she was supposed to feel like. "I'm okay," she settled on, knowing it was a benign answer that would likely appease her cousin.

Karli pursed her lips. She was familiar, like the woman Lorelei saw in the mirror, but any memory of the woman was out of reach. "Want to tell me about the hottie who found you?"

"Back off," Lorelei blurted.

Karli smirked. "So you do like him. I thought so. The way you looked at him told me. You always wore your expressions on your face. You learned to hide them over the years, and the training, but I could always read you."

"You're wrong. And Vinnie is just doing his job. He found me because I was missing."

Karli's brows went sky high. "You don't know, do you?"

"I thought we established I don't know a damn thing."

Karli snorted. "Sorry. And true. But about Vinnie. He didn't come here because he was ordered. His boss is pissed. He left. Didn't tell anyone where he was going or what he was doing, just came here because some instinct told him to."

"I thought he was sent to find me."

Karli shook her head. "Nope. He came on his own."

"But he saved me. He helped me. He's... he's police, right? Isn't he?" The machine beeped faster and faster. Lorelei struggled to breathe properly. Everything hurt, like she was trapped.

Who was she supposed to trust? Who was really there to help her? To make sure everything was okay? Was she even who they said she was? What if everyone was lying to her?

"Lorelei," Karli said. "You're safe. Vinnie is safe. He's police. He worked with you in Niagara Falls. I was just saying he didn't come find you because he had to. He came because he wanted to."

The beeping slowed down, but it was still fast. It was still hard to breathe. Panic seized her. Was she safe? Would she ever be safe? Who was telling the truth?

"Lorelei," Vinnie said, his voice breaking through the haze of fear that settled over her like a blanket. "Look at me, Lorelei."

She struggled to find him, but he let her search on her own, not forcing her gaze to his until she was ready to find him.

"There you go. Breathe with me. In. Out. Slow. In, two, three. Hold. Out, two, three. In. Out. Are you okay?"

Brown eyes with a golden ring around the center. Dark brows drawn low over those eyes. Wrinkles marred his skin at the edges, like he was a man who enjoyed life, even though he saw the worst it had to offer.

"She panicked when I told her you weren't ordered to come find her. That you came on your own," Karli explained.

Vinnie closed his eyes, stealing the comfort from Lorelei. He swore under his breath, then opened his eyes and caught her gaze once more.

He was a stranger. Everyone told her that. Even he told her that. But she knew him. She knew she could trust him. She couldn't explain it, but looking into his eyes, Lorelei knew she'd never been safer in her life than she was with him in the room with her.

"You're okay now," Vinnie said. "I will tell you anything you want to know. You can have Adam or Karli investigate me. Whatever makes you feel safe."

"You do," she said without thinking about how it sounded.

His lips lifted on the edges like her answer made him happy. "Offer still stands. Anything you want to know, I'll tell you."

"Did you really come here without being ordered?"

Vinnie nodded. "I did. And I might lose my job for it, but it doesn't matter to me because you're alive. You're safe. That was worth it."

"They can't do that. Why would they do that?"

"I defied orders. I left the state without telling my boss. They don't like that. Even though I was not working, I was technically supposed to be on call and available."

"Did someone else get hurt because of me?"

Vinnie shook his head. "No. I didn't miss any calls. But I would have, and I knew I would, and I was willing to take the risk. Finding you was more important to me than anything else."

Lorelei sucked in a breath, her throat stinging with the move. She winced, and Vinnie noticed, immediately backing up and grabbing her water.

Lorelei hadn't realized how close he was until he wasn't. He held her hand and hovered above her, blocking everything else from her view.

She sipped the water he offered, the cool liquid soothing her throat.

"Better?"

She nodded. "Yes. Thank you."

"You're welcome." He set the water down, then looked at her again. "I came in to see if you were up for more visitors, but it looks like maybe you're not."

Lorelei closed her eyes. If she said no, she would hurt the feelings of whoever was out there waiting to see her. Any of them could trigger something. A memory. Something that would help her figure out who the hell she was and what she was doing when she disappeared. "It's fine."

"Are you sure?"

She nodded. "For a few minutes."

Vinnie nodded, then lifted his gaze to Karli. Lorelei hadn't even realized Karli was still in the room. "Will you let them know they can come in, but only for a little while? Please?"

Karli nodded and moved to the door.

Lorelei took another moment to study the one and only person she trusted. "Thank you for saving me."

Vinnie smiled, and something settled into place for Lorelei. Something she couldn't define. "You're welcome." He squeezed her hand, giving her strength and courage to face the people who walked in the door.

More strangers who were supposed to be friends. One by one, they approached her. Having been told what was going on, they each moved to the edge of the bed and introduced themselves, then stepped away, not reaching for her or anything.

Lorelei didn't realize she needed that until Karli was at her side again. Karli had her arm around a man Lorelei had zero memory of, even though she was sure she should know him. He was dating her cousin. Why wouldn't she know him?

But he was a stranger.

"We're just so happy you're okay," one woman said. Raina maybe? There were too many names.

"When the doctor says you can leave, Dawn said you can stay with her. Or at one of her houses. Unless you want to stay with one of us," Jessica said. Lorelei was pretty sure that was Jessica.

"Okay," Lorelei agreed. She had no idea who Dawn was or why she would stay with her, but maybe by the time she got out of the hospital, some of her memories would come back.

"We know this is a lot," Adam said. "You will be able to decide everything when you're ready."

Lorelei nodded, looking for Vinnie. He'd moved out of the way while the others spoke. It was clear he wasn't a part of the group. He didn't speak when the others did. He didn't add to the conversation. He didn't even really seem to know them.

But he was the one Lorelei wanted to hear from. The one she wanted to know.

His presence made her feel safe. But he was the only one who hadn't offered to let her stay. She'd have to change his mind about that.

3

———

Sweat dripped from Lorelei's forehead. Fear swamped her. Anger, frustration, acceptance.

She was going to die.

Another punch landed on her ribs. Another crunch that told her a rib was broken.

Breathing was harder, like being held underwater. But different because there was plenty of air, it just hurt like a son-of-a-bitch to draw it into her lungs.

"What do you know about Trevor Davis?" the man barked.

Lorelei spit at him. She was not going to give up anything. She couldn't. If she told them what she knew, they'd kill her source. Hell, they probably would anyway, but Lorelei couldn't live with herself if she could have stopped any of it.

"Bitch!" He backhanded her, her cheek exploding with pain from the ring he wore on his pinky.

She was going to be sick. She shouldn't have gone on her own to meet her informant, especially for the case she was on, but she'd done it before and didn't want to pull anyone away from the reception.

"Lorelei!" a man shouted.

She looked up at the man who'd slapped her. His lips weren't moving.

Who was calling her name?

Pain ricocheted through her body.

"Lorelei!" That voice. It was familiar. She knew who it was. Maybe? He was safe. He wouldn't hurt her.

"Wake up, Lorelei. You're safe. I'm not going to let anyone hurt you again. Come on. Open your eyes."

She blinked her eyes, prying them apart. The vision in her head vanished the moment her eyes opened.

"What?" she tried to speak, but the word barely came out as a whisper.

"You're safe, Lorelei. You're okay. I got you." He repeated the words over and over again.

His scent wrapped around her. His words calmed her.

It was a dream. It wasn't real. She was okay. She was with Vinnie. She was safe.

Sleep claimed her once more, and Lorelei didn't fight it. The soft beeping slowed with her breathing, and she held on to Vinnie and slept.

VINNIE WAS glad he wasn't connected to one of the monitors. It would still be screeching, like it did when Lorelei had her nightmare.

Nightmare. Such a shitty word. She wasn't having a bad dream. She was reliving the hell she went through.

It had been five nights since she was admitted to the hospital. Five nights of Vinnie sleeping when he could, mostly in tiny snippets. He barely left Lorelei's side. She panicked when he wasn't there, and every night, she woke up with a nightmare.

She never remembered them in the morning. He asked her the first morning, and she looked at him like he was insane. Since then, he did what he'd done that first night and climbed into bed with her and held her when the nightmare struck.

She never spoke during her nightmare. He wasn't sure if that was because she was scared, hiding, or refused to answer any questions. Probably the last one knowing Lorelei.

Not that he gave himself that much credit. He still barely knew the woman. No matter how many nights he held her in his arms and breathed in her scent and calmed her with his body.

The doctor told him it was likely because he found her. Just like Vinnie assumed. The imprint of him on her memory was temporary. Once she got all her memories back, she would no longer need him in her life.

It was a painful blow, but one he understood. Lorelei didn't need him. He was there to help with her recovery, not to be her partner, in work or life.

With her settled again, Vinnie finally relaxed. His heart rate slowly lowered, his body accepting that the threat was over. After five nights of very little sleep, he needed to get what he could. In the morning, Lorelei was leaving the hospital.

THE BAG of clothes sat on the foot of the bed, unfamiliar items pouring out of it. Lorelei wanted to reach for her favorite clothes, for something that made her feel strong and powerful and beautiful. Something that made her feel like the woman everyone around kept saying she was.

But she still didn't remember her.

The doctors said she would. Eventually. But Lorelei wasn't the most patient woman. She wanted to remember now.

"What do you want to wear?" Karli asked.

Her cousin. Lorelei knew Karli was her cousin because she'd been told every day, but she hadn't conjured up any memories of the other woman. Something that was clear on her face whenever she walked into the dreaded hospital room with hope in her gaze.

Lorelei wouldn't lie, but it was tempting just to avoid that look of disappointment that followed the hopeful one.

"I don't know," Lorelei answered. Nothing felt like her. The clothes were as familiar to her as everything else in her life. Karli said Lorelei had been mostly living in Niagara Falls for the last few months. Did that mean the clothes were left behind in her Boston apartment? Ones she never wore, so they were left behind?

They were fucking clothes. Why was it so damn hard to choose something to wear?

She lifted her gaze to Vinnie and nibbled on her lip. What would he want to see her in? He was the only one who didn't make her feel like he was waiting for her to do something. He was just patient and approving.

He moved toward the bag and rifled through it. He pulled out a pair of panties that looked silky and sexy and sinful. His cheeks turned red before he shoved the panties back into the bag.

"Give me those," Lorelei said, reaching her hand out to Vinnie. "I need something. I need all of it. I can't be shy right now."

Vinnie held her gaze, then lowered his and pulled the panties back out of the bag. He handed them over, not throwing them at her, but waiting for her to grab them before he let go.

Lorelei touched the soft fabric, running her hands around the edges and finding herself imagining modeling them for Vinnie.

Whoa. Where did that come from? She couldn't even remember if she'd had sex, but she was overcome with the desire to pop her amnesia cherry with Vinnie.

She sucked in a breath, then balled up the panties and shoved the dirty thoughts away.

Vinnie handed over a pair of cotton shorts, ones that looked endlessly comfortable. He grabbed a teal tank top, then pawed through until he found a brown bra that matched Lorelei's skin tone.

"I'll wait outside," Vinnie mumbled, making a beeline for the door before Lorelei could thank him for finding her clothes.

The soft click of the door told Lorelei he was in the hallway, and the air Karli sucked in told Lorelei she wasn't the only one who found that interaction more than a little hot.

"Wow. I mean... damn."

Lorelei looked up at her cousin and found it impossible not to grin at the look on Karli's face. "What?" Lorelei laughed.

"That was... Hot as fuck. Is something going on with you two?"

Lorelei shook her head. "No. He's just helping me. He's a good guy."

"He's a really good guy if he's going to pick out panties for you and not ask you to model them."

"I was kind of hoping he would," Lorelei blurted.

Karli tipped her head back and laughed loudly. "I love it! Okay, yeah, you're liking this protector thing."

Lorelei's mood soured at the thought. "I don't want a protector."

"No one does, hun. But sometimes you need someone who's going to put you above everyone else in the world and make sure you have exactly what you need."

"Is that what…"

"Cade?"

Lorelei nodded. Details were fuzzy. "Yeah, sorry. Is that what Cade does for you?"

Karli nodded, her eyes taking on a dreamy quality that said she was head over heels for her boyfriend. "He does. When we met… he was the only one I trusted to keep me safe. Sort of like you are with Vinnie."

"He's not the… Okay, fine. I don't know why, though. Are you sure I didn't know him before?"

Karli shook her head. "He said you never spoke. Adam doesn't know him. I really don't think you knew each other. Besides that, if you did, it was in passing and not nearly as well as you knew Adam or me. The connection you feel has to be what the doctor said and because he found you."

Lorelei nodded, trying to keep all the data together. It was a lot. "I guess."

"Do you want me to help you get changed?"

Lorelei looked at the clothes and knew there was no way she could do it alone. "Are you sure? Are we that close?"

Karli grinned. "If you're asking if I've ever seen you naked, the answer is yes. But admittedly, it's been a few decades."

Lorelei snorted. "I have a feeling it's too soon to ask Vinnie to help me get my clothes on."

"You need to ask him to help take them off."

Lorelei scoffed.

Karli laughed. "You know you were thinking it."

Lorelei chuckled because yeah, she was.

Karli helped Lorelei get her panties over the cast on her right leg and up to her knees, then held Lorelei steady while she stood and pulled the panties up under her hospital gown. They repeated the process for her shorts.

"How do you want to do this? I don't think you can make that clasp work," Karli said.

Lorelei shook her head. "I guess you're getting a look at my boobs. Sorry, cuz."

"Is it weird to say I'm thrilled to be able to do this because it means you're still alive?"

Lorelei smiled at her cousin. Even though she couldn't remember their past, she knew Karli was a good person. Cade, too. They both refused to go back to Niagara Falls without Lorelei. They got a hotel room near the hospital and were with Lorelei from the beginning of visiting hours to the end. The only time Vinnie left the room was when Karli was with Lorelei.

She wasn't alone. She had people who were making sure she was okay.

"Stay seated like you are. Lift your gown so I can get the bra around you and secure the clasp. You can try to get it into place." Karli moved around the bed to the back so Lorelei didn't have to move again.

She nodded, lifting her hospital gown out of the way while Karli looped the bra around Lorelei's stomach. It wasn't too tight, but after days of not wearing a bra, and five fractured ribs, it wasn't comfortable either.

"Are you okay?" Karli asked.

"I will be, but that's just different. It hurts like a bitch."

"What can I do?"

Lorelei shook her head. "Nothing. I just have to heal. It's not going to be fun until I am."

Karli was still while Lorelei inhaled slowly and exhaled again. She did it five or six times before the pain was tolerable.

"Okay. Let's see if we can get these girls in the sling. I don't think I can do it myself. If you want to call a nurse, I won't be offended."

"Oh, please. I can lift a boob or two. Drop your gown and we'll make it work."

Lorelei eased the gown from her body, the rush of cold air on her bare flesh lifting her nipples to peaks. She moved to get her arms into the straps of her bra. Karli held the strap away, guiding Lorelei's arm through the strap. Together they eased the strap up and Lorelei positioned her breast in the cup.

Karli moved to the other side just as someone knocked on the door. Before either of them could say anything, the door opened and Vinnie walked in.

"Are you—Shit!" He slapped his hand over his eyes. "I'm sorry. I should have waited. I'll be back." He ran into the door trying to back out of the room with his eyes covered, then closed his hand in the door.

Lorelei looked up at Karli, and both women burst out laughing.

"Did you see his face?" Karli asked. "He looked like a tomato."

"Oh, don't make me laugh. Ow. That hurts. And my boob is still hanging out."

Karli choked down her laughter. "Sorry. Okay, let's get you into your bra so we can let your guard dog back in."

"He's not my guard dog." The thought made her smile.

"Uh huh."

With her bra in place, Karli helped Lorelei pull the tank top over her head. When she was dressed and settled on the bed again, Karli opened the door to let Vinnie in.

"Are you sure?" Vinnie asked before he walked into the room.

Karli said something Lorelei couldn't hear.

Vinnie grunted a response, then moved from the door into the room. His gaze was glued to the floor. "I apologize for not waiting until you said I could walk in. I should have thought it would take you a while. I'm truly sorry."

"Vinnie." She waited until he looked at her. "It's okay. They're just boobs."

He choked on his next breath, and his cheeks went even redder. He nodded and moved around the bed, keeping his distance.

Lorelei smiled at Karli, and they both laughed softly.

Another knock on the now open door brought the doctor into the room. "I see you're ready to go. Have you made your plans for where you'll be for the next few weeks?"

Lorelei shook her head. The doctor dropped that bomb on her the day before, when they talked about her getting the hell out of the hospital. Dr. Jones said Lorelei could not be alone for longer than an hour or two for at least two weeks, maybe longer if she wasn't improving beyond that. Besides the memory, her broken ribs were going to restrict her from doing most basic functions alone until they were mostly healed.

Dr. Jones pursed her lips and raised her brows. Then she slid her gaze to Vinnie.

He crossed his arms and met the doctor's gaze.

"Lorelei can't be alone. She has to have someone with

her for the majority of time for the next two weeks. If that can't be arranged, she needs to go to a rehab facility—"

"I'll do it," Vinnie blurted. He uncrossed his arms and moved toward Lorelei. "If she's okay with that. If you'd rather stay with Karli or Adam or any of the other people in Niagara Falls, I don't want you to feel like you can't."

Lorelei exhaled slowly. "I'd rather stay with you. If you're sure it won't be an inconvenience."

"We all live in the same area," Karli told Dr. Jones. "I'm available to help out, and so are the others, if Vinnie has to work or needs a break from this one." Karli winked at Lorelei.

Lorelei rolled her eyes. "I'm sure everyone will need a break from me."

"I'm good," Vinnie said, his tone rough, growly, like he was frustrated.

Lorelei looked up at him. She might not remember who she was or the last time she had sex, but she knew what that look on his face meant. She knew what he was thinking. And she was thinking the same thing.

"Okay, so now that that's settled, your discharge orders. No strenuous activity for ten days. That means no sex." She glared at Lorelei, then Vinnie before continuing. Karli just laughed. "No carrying anything over five pounds. Use your spirometer at least four times every day for a month or longer, depending on how you're healing and feel. If you're continuing to improve in a week, you can start other activities for ten to fifteen minutes at a time. Normally, I'd suggest walking, but with your broken ankle, that's not a great option. Find something that gets you up and moving a bit, though. You can slowly increase that and add in some minor strenuous activities, but don't overdo it. If you try to do too much too fast, you risk a setback. With your amnesia and head injuries, a setback is a major risk, so please go slow."

Lorelei nodded, keeping her gaze locked on Dr. Jones and refusing to look at Vinnie. She could not think about avoiding sex with him or that would be the only thing she wanted.

Hell, it was starting to become the only thing she wanted. After remembering who she was.

"We'll make sure she follows orders," Karli assured Dr. Jones. "Thank you for everything you've done."

Dr. Jones smiled at Karli. "You're welcome. I'm glad things are going well. It's a true testament to how strong Lorelei is that she's done so well with her progress." She moved to Lorelei. "Thank you for what you do. I've read up on who you are, and the world needs people like you out there. I'm sorry for what you went through, but I have no doubt you will regain your memory and get right back out there and make the world a better place."

"Thank you, Dr. Jones."

Dr. Jones smiled and put her hand on Lorelei's shoulder, squeezing gently. "I'll get your paperwork signed and you'll be good to go. Someone will be in with a wheelchair to take you out. If you have any issues, please get in touch. Otherwise, I'll send all of this to your primary care for followup."

"Thank you."

Dr. Jones smiled at Karli and Vinnie, then let herself out of the room.

Lorelei looked at the two people who'd been there for her more than anyone else in the last week. She wouldn't be getting out of the hospital if it weren't for the two of them. "Thank you both for being here. For helping me."

"Nowhere else I'd rather be," Karli said.

Vinnie just nodded, his gaze unwavering, just like his support.

"I'll go have Cade pull the SUV around to the front. Are we going to your apartment here first to get your stuff?"

Lorelei nodded even as fear welled up inside her.

"Okay. We'll see you outside in a few." Karli waved and walked out, not even realizing Lorelei was panicking.

But Vinnie did.

"Shit," he breathed.

Before Lorelei could process what he was doing, he'd climbed into bed with her and wrapped his body around hers. His arms held her close, but not tight enough to hurt. He whispered in her ear.

"I got you, Lorelei. You're safe. No one's going to hurt you."

Lorelei closed her eyes and let his words and body soothe her. Her breathing slowed, and the panic drifted away. It was like magic.

"How did you... how did you do that?"

His chest rose with the breath he sucked in. He held it, then let it out slowly. "I've been doing that every night since you were admitted. You're having nightmares, and the only way for you to sleep is if I hold you."

"Are you kidding me?"

4

VINNIE KNEW HE WOULD HAVE TO TELL HER ABOUT THE nightmares eventually. And about holding her. But he hoped he would be able to tell her in a way that didn't create more panic.

From the look on her face, he missed the mark.

"I've been having nightmares?"

Vinnie nodded. He eased away from her, releasing her slowly. He didn't want to, knowing letting her go immediately after a panic attack could send her right back into the spiral, but she was angry, and he knew better than to hold on tight to a woman who wanted to hit him.

"And you..." She swallowed roughly. "You just crawl into bed with me and hold me?"

"I shouldn't have touched you without your approval. I apologize. I won't do it again."

"That's not... Okay. Thank you." Lorelei looked conflicted.

She wasn't the only one. Vinnie hated himself for ever touching her. For thinking it was okay, even though he knew it helped her. He never should have done it. He didn't have the right, and he was an asshole for putting his hands on a woman without her consent.

It didn't matter that there was nothing sexual about it, or that he only did it to calm and soothe her, he violated her trust and her body. He was wrong to do it.

A knock on the door stopped him from saying anything else. An orderly pushed a wheelchair into the room and asked if Lorelei was ready to go, completely oblivious to the tension in the room.

Lorelei smiled at the man and let him help her into the wheelchair.

Vinnie grabbed her duffle bag and crutches, then his own bag, and followed them out into the hallway.

A nurse met Vinnie outside the door and pulled him aside. "Her paperwork. So she has a copy in case she needs it."

"Thank you," Vinnie said.

"You're welcome. I hope she feels better."

"Me, too."

Vinnie forced his lips into a smile for the nurse, then followed Lorelei and the orderly to the elevator. The two of them chatted the entire ride down, talking about life in Boston and their favorite places to eat.

Vinnie hadn't left the hospital since Lorelei was admitted and had nothing to add to the conversation, so he kept his mouth shut.

Cade and Karli were at the door when Lorelei was wheeled out. Karli helped get her into the backseat of an SUV, then thanked the orderly for his help. Cade went around to the driver's side and got in.

"Are you coming with us?" Karli asked.

"I have my SUV here. I drove it to Boston when I came to find her."

Karli shook her head. "I'm so sorry. I never even thought about how you got here. Lorelei said something about driving back. Is she planning to ride with you?"

Vinnie shrugged. "We haven't spoken about anything. I'm not sure of her plans."

"Would you be willing to let Cade and I ride with you? Or maybe just me? The six of us came out here together, but Jessica and Braden took Dawn's plane home when he had to get back to work. Dawn offered to send it back for us, but I don't think Lorelei can fly with her injuries. I'd really like to stay with her."

"Whatever is best for everyone," Vinnie said. He wasn't there to ruffle feathers. He'd already inserted himself in their world enough.

"Are you going to the apartment with us?"

Vinnie nodded. "I'd planned to. Unless you think I shouldn't."

Karli was shaking her head before he finished speaking. "No, I think it would be better if you're there. I don't know how she's going to do."

"She panicked after you walked out."

Karli looked at the car, then the hospital. "Just now?"

Vinnie nodded.

Karli took a step toward him and crossed her arms. She chewed her lip. "I didn't realize. Should we not go?"

"She needs to face it. She needs to feel safe in her home again."

Karli thought for a second, then nodded. "You're right. I agree. We'll wait for you before we go in, though."

"I'll be right behind you." He started to walk away, then realized he had Lorelei's things. "Do you want to take these?"

Karli reached for the crutches. "She'll need these, but

we'll figure the rest out when we get there. Maybe bring her bag up so she can decide what to take to Niagara Falls and what to leave here?"

Vinnie nodded, then jogged toward his SUV. Cade pulled away, but when Vinnie made it to the street, Cade was waiting for Vinnie to follow him to Lorelei's apartment.

Vinnie turned up the radio and tried to push away his guilt. What he did was unforgivable. Lorelei deserved better. He would ask if she wanted to stay with Karli with the knowledge he'd been inappropriate with her. She probably would. He'd accept it, even though he'd hate it.

Vinnie parked next to Cade in the parking lot outside Lorelei's apartment. It was hard to believe it'd been less than a week since he first set eyes on the building. Old brick, a dozen stories tall, and full of dark secrets he never imagined.

Vinnie met the others on the sidewalk with Lorelei's bag slung over his shoulder. Karli was talking to Lorelei, so he nodded at Cade, and the four of them moved toward the building.

At the door, Adam and Raina were waiting for them. Hugs were exchanged between the women, then their group of six went inside.

The three women led the way down the hallway. Cade and Adam talked, following right behind the women. Vinnie walked along at the end, separate from the rest of them. He wasn't a part of their group before, and he wouldn't be for long. Especially after what he confessed. Lorelei would get her memory back and not need him. Not want him in her life. There was no reason to get deeper in with the others.

Karli unlocked Lorelei's door and let everyone in. The chatter quieted as soon as they were inside the apartment.

Once Vinnie made it in, he understood why.

The couch where he found Lorelei was still covered in blood. The discarded bandages and supplies the paramedics used littered the floor. It was obvious something bad happened in that space.

"Lore," Karli breathed.

Lorelei looked at her cousin. She drew a breath, one that everyone else in the room echoed, and closed her eyes. "Let's just get this over with."

Karli and Raina led Lorelei to the bedroom. Cade and Adam looked at the blood and the rest of the apartment, then turned to Vinnie.

"Thank you, again, for finding her. Looking at this, and knowing the condition you found her in, we were close to losing her," Adam said.

"I'm glad it didn't come to that." Vinnie wasn't a hero. He was just lucky he got to her in time.

"So are we," Cade agreed.

The three men started picking up the trash in the living room. Adam seemed to know his way around the apartment, retrieving a trash can and bags without having to search for anything.

"What should we do about the couch?" Cade asked, looking between Adam and Vinnie for an answer.

Vinnie shrugged.

"The Lorelei I know would probably say clean it. Keep it as a reminder of what she survived. You can't stop her," Adam said, chuckling.

"She's not like her cousin," Cade said. "Karli would demand it was gone. She wouldn't want the smallest reminder."

"Like living in the apartment where Tonya was killed?" Adam asked.

Cade nodded.

Vinnie didn't know the details of the story, but he knew enough to understand Tonya was the woman murdered because she was mistaken for Karli.

"I can't even imagine. Raina's the same. She'd say burn it," Adam said.

Cade laughed. "That sounds like a good plan to me. But I guess we need to ask her."

Adam nodded, and the three of them kept cleaning up the rest of the apartment.

The three women returned with two suitcases and one duffle bag. Vinnie looked at the volume of stuff and wondered how she didn't have more.

"It's too much, isn't it? I shouldn't have packed that second suitcase," Lorelei said, glaring at one of the bags.

"I figured you'd have more," Vinnie said without thinking.

Everyone froze.

Lorelei snorted. "I guess I don't have a lot of stuff. At least, not a lot that feels like me right now. Maybe if I knew who I was or felt comfortable in what I have, but I just don't know."

"Do you have your guns?" Adam asked.

Lorelei patted her hip, then pointed to a suitcase. "I have a safe with one in it, and I'm carrying."

"You're carrying now?" Cade asked.

Lorelei shrugged. "I might not remember it, but it felt natural. Like I was—"

A noise at the door had all of them turning. Before anyone could say anything, the door swung open and revealed a short, gray-haired woman.

"What the hell are you doing here?" Lorelei barked, gun

drawn and trained on the trembling woman's chest. "I asked what you're doing here! Why are you here?"

The woman's eyes were huge. She dropped her handbag and the tote she carried, hands flying up.

"Lorelei!" Adam barked, moving toward her. He took a step between Lorelei and the woman, breaking Lorelei's focused attention. "Lorelei! Look at me. Listen to me. That's Anabelle. She's your housekeeper. She's supposed to be here."

LORELEI STARED AT ADAM, trying to piece together what Adam was telling her.

"Ms. Sloane?" Anabelle whispered from the door. She hadn't moved since the door opened and she had a gun pointed at her.

Adam reached for Lorelei, and she realized he was reaching for the gun.

Lorelei handed it over to him, leaning back against the wall behind her. She pulled a gun on an innocent woman. A woman who had no right to be treated like she was wrong.

Adam handed the gun to Vinnie, then faced Anabelle. "Lorelei was attacked last week. She has no memory of who she is or who anyone else is. I know if she knew what she was doing, she never would have done what she did."

"Thank you, Mr. Johnson. Is she okay?"

Adam nodded and moved to the side so Lorelei could see Anabelle.

"I'm so sorry. I didn't know. I..." Lorelei couldn't say anything else. She turned and thunked her way to the bathroom as quickly as her crutches would carry her.

Voices raised behind her, but Lorelei couldn't go back.

She couldn't believe she thought carrying a gun was a smart move. That she would know who was a threat and who wasn't.

That wasn't why she wanted it. As soon as she picked it up, she felt better. Safer. Like she wouldn't end up beaten and half-dead and unable to stop whoever stole her memory.

She felt stronger. But it was a false strength because if Adam hadn't been there and Lorelei had pulled the trigger, she would have hurt a woman who was no more guilty than Lorelei was herself.

She couldn't be trusted.

Someone knocked on the bathroom door, and Lorelei hoped it was Vinnie before she heard Karli's voice.

"Are you okay?"

Lorelei laughed mirthlessly. "No. I can't believe I just did that."

"Anabelle is okay. And she understands. She's only worried about you and if you're going to be okay. She's very sweet."

Lorelei let out a breath. "I wish I could say I know, or that's why I hired her, but fuck, I don't know a damn thing." Lorelei pounded the countertop.

"Open up, cuz."

Lorelei hesitated, but unlocked the door to let Karli in.

"You can't be blamed for this. I know it sucks and you want to be yourself again, but you're not there yet."

"What if I never get there?" Lorelei whispered, meeting Karli's gaze in the mirror. The question had been on her mind since she was told she had amnesia. She desperately wanted to know who she was, to remember her past, but what if she never did? What if everything before Vinnie woke her up was gone forever?

"Then you become whoever you want to be."

"What do you mean?"

"I mean, you start over. You choose who you want to be. You get to create your reality, your life, however you want."

"Is that what you would do? You would reinvent yourself?"

Karli shrugged. "I don't know. The idea has some appeal. We get tied down in the choices we made years ago. Careers, friends, home. We get to a point in life where we look around and say how did I get here? But you have a choice to go somewhere else. No one would blame you if you never came back to this apartment. If you left the FBI. If you made all different choices with your life. But only you can decide what's right for you. And what's right now might be different than what would have been right before."

Lorelei drew a breath and nodded. She didn't know what was right for her. Then or now. She was confused and overwhelmed. The only thing she did know was she did not need to be carrying a weapon.

"Will you and Cade take my guns?"

"Of course. Or Adam can. He's probably more comfortable with guns."

Lorelei nodded. "Okay. I just know I can't risk shooting someone innocent because I don't know who they are. Shit. I need to apologize to a woman I have no memory of and tell her I'm an asshole."

Karli chuckled. "She won't think that. She cleaned Adam's apartment for years, too, from what he said. It sounds like she's a very nice woman."

"That's good. Makes me happy I didn't shoot her."

"I bet she agrees."

Lorelei snorted and shook her head. "Okay, let's get the hell out of here. I can't be in this apartment any longer."

"Let's go."

Lorelei followed Karli out of the bathroom. All conversation stopped in the living room when they walked in.

"Ms. Sloane, I am so sorry I scared you. Are you okay?" Anabelle asked, rushing to Lorelei but stopping before she reached her.

"It's my fault. I'm sorry I don't know you. I wish I did, but I guess they all filled you in."

"Yes, yes, and I am so sorry. If I'd known, I never would have just walked in."

"If I'd known you existed, I would have called you, but, hell, I could have someone else who's about to walk in and I wouldn't know it. Not knowing who I am or who anyone else is sucks."

"You will get your memory back, Ms. Sloane. You will be yourself again."

"I hope so. Thank you for being so sweet, Anabelle. I am so sorry I panicked."

Anabelle shook her head, then stopped when Lorelei moved forward and hugged her. Anabelle patted Lorelei on the back.

"I've never hugged you, have I?" Lorelei asked as she pulled back.

"No, Ms. Sloane. You aren't very..." Anabelle looked around the room as though judging if she could say what she was thinking.

"Affectionate," Adam provided.

Anabelle nodded. "Yes, that's a good word. You're always very nice, and I never have to ask you to pay me. You're very generous, which I appreciate. But you're not warm and fuzzy."

Lorelei saw Karli raise her eyebrows and smiled. "Maybe I should change that."

Anabelle and Adam hid a chuckle with a cough, and Lorelei glared at her partner.

"Stop laughing."

Adam held his hands up in defense.

"I don't want to be someone who holds back their emotions. That doesn't feel like me." Lorelei looked around the room at the people who all knew the old her. The woman she couldn't remember.

Except Vinnie. He said they hadn't spoken before. Which version of her would Vinnie like?

No. Lorelei wasn't going to change who she was for a man. She was going to be the version of her she wanted to be. Like Karli suggested.

"I think it's time we get out of here," Lorelei said.

"I will clean the couch, Ms. Sloane. It'll be like nothing happened."

"Don't worry about it, Anabelle. I'll have someone get rid of it. I don't want it here. I don't want to ever see that couch again."

"Are you sure, Ms. Sloane?"

"Yes. And I think you should call me Lorelei."

"Lorelei?"

"Yes. If I call you Anabelle, you should be calling me Lorelei."

"Yes, Ms. Sloane."

Lorelei smiled at Anabelle.

Anabelle chuckled. "I will try. Is there anything else?"

Lorelei looked around at the apartment she didn't remember. At the place she came to and only felt safe because Vinnie was there. She didn't want to be there. She couldn't imagine going back there, living in that apartment knowing someone dumped her body there to let her die.

"One more thing. I'm moving."

The others in the room gasped, but Lorelei ignored them.

"I don't know if I'm going to find another apartment in Boston or move somewhere else, but I can't be here. I would appreciate it if you would keep this place in the same excellent shape you've kept it in so far, and I will make sure you know well in advance when it's sold, but I can't be here."

"I don't blame you, Ms... Lorelei. I wouldn't want to be here either if I were you."

"Do you feel safe being here, Anabelle? Are you okay being here?" Adam asked her.

Anabelle nodded. "It's a safe building. I know it's okay. And my husband knows where I am at all times. If he doesn't hear from me, he will send a search party."

"Are you sure?" Lorelei asked.

Anabelle moved to Lorelei and grabbed her hand. "I am fine. I am happy to take care of this place for you. I'm just happy you are safe. You are alive. I will get rid of the couch. Don't worry about that. It will be good."

"I can't—"

"You focus on getting healthy. I will take care of this. I will let you know how much it costs, and I will be here to let someone in. You need to be well so you can get back to kicking ass and protecting the world."

Lorelei snorted. It didn't sound like who she was now, but she couldn't deny she liked the idea of it. "I'll try."

"Good. Keep in touch."

"You, too. Please."

"Yes. I will. Be careful. Take care of her, Adam."

Adam nodded. "I will. We all will."

Anabelle hugged Adam, then gushed over Raina for a minute before they all filed out of the apartment and left Anabelle to her work.

They made it down to the parking lot before Lorelei realized each of the men was carrying one of her bags. "I'm sorry you're all taking care of me."

"That's why we brought them," Karli teased. "But we do need to figure out how you're getting back. Vinnie said he has a vehicle and some of us could maybe ride back with you in that."

Lorelei's gaze snapped to his.

He nodded once, not giving anything away.

She wanted to talk to him about what he confessed before they left the hospital, but they hadn't had a moment alone. "I—"

"If you'd feel more comfortable with Karli and Cade, I understand," Vinnie said.

Lorelei shook her head. "No, but I need to keep my leg propped up on the seat. Do you have a backseat?"

"Ooh, I forgot about that," Karli said. "Maybe I should go with you two, and Cade, you drive home with Adam and Raina."

"I really don't want to be stuck with the newlyweds," Cade teased.

Adam kissed Raina soundly, dipping her back before bringing her upright and smirking at Cade.

"Exactly," Cade said. "You don't think you can sit in the back with Lorelei?"

"Let's go see. Vinnie, where did you park?"

Twenty minutes later, they had a plan. Adam and Raina were going to take a few days for a mini-honeymoon on Cape Cod. Karli, Cade, Vinnie, and Lorelei were going to drive Vinnie's SUV back to Niagara Falls.

Together.

Yay.

5

———

LORELEI'S SCENT FILLED VINNIE'S SUV. SHE WAS IN THE SEAT behind him, next to Karli. Cade sat up front. And talked. Cade carried the entire conversation. Vinnie just tried to keep the vehicle between the lines on the road.

"Do you mind stopping sometime soon?" Lorelei asked, her voice small, anxious.

"Are you in pain?" Vinnie asked, not letting anyone else get a word in. He moved to the right lane. An exit was coming up.

"A little."

Vinnie checked the clock on the dash. "You can have another pain pill in about five minutes. I'll stop now and we can get you something to eat so you're not taking it on an empty stomach."

"Thank you."

Cade went back to talking. He was trying to tell Lorelei all about their group of friends. The people they all spent time with in Niagara Falls.

Vinnie knew some of the names, and some of the situations, but he didn't know most of the people. He was a little surprised when Cade mentioned Marcus Patrick. He was Vinnie's mentor, a man he considered it an honor to know, and an even greater honor to have on his side.

Vinnie kept his mouth shut about knowing Marcus, not wanting to put the police captain in a situation where he wasn't comfortable. If Cade and the others didn't know Marcus and Vinnie knew each other, Vinnie wasn't going to out the relationship.

Or the reason he met Marcus more than two decades ago and how Marcus saved Vinnie from a very different life.

Vinnie pulled off the interstate and found a fast food place. All four of them got out of the vehicle, Lorelei a little awkwardly.

"Are you okay?" Vinnie asked her.

She nodded. "Yeah, just sore. It's not easy to keep my leg propped up, and it's kind of tight with Karli there."

"She insisted on coming with you."

Lorelei nodded, forcing a smile that didn't meet her eyes. She closed her eyes and took a breath. She let it out slowly, coughing at the end.

"Do you need to use your spirometer? How long has it been?" Vinnie moved to the back of the SUV and opened the hatch. Karli and Cade's things were mixed with his bag and Lorelei's luggage. He didn't think to put Lorelei's stuff on top, or to find out which bag had her pills and her medical supplies.

"I'm okay, Vinnie. I'm sorry I needed to stop."

Karli stepped in before Vinnie could reply. "You're the one we're all here for. You don't need to apologize. We don't mind. If you need to stop every two hours, we will. If you need to stop every thirty minutes, we will. It's all good."

Vinnie nodded his agreement. He didn't care if it took a week to make the seven-hour drive from Boston to Niagara

Falls. He'd do whatever he needed to do to make sure Lorelei was comfortable.

"I hope I can make it longer with a painkiller. I should be okay," Lorelei said.

Vinnie found the bag of her things from the hospital in the top of the duffle bag. He pulled it out, then zipped the duffle again. "We should keep this stuff up front. So she can use it when she needs to."

"Good idea. I didn't think about that before." Karli nodded, then swung her gaze to Lorelei. "Let's go use the bathroom and get food, then we'll get back on the road."

Lorelei nodded and followed Karli and Cade to the restaurant.

Vinnie trailed behind them, the bag of meds in his hand. Cade held the door for everyone to go in. The two women went to the bathroom first, and Cade pulled Vinnie aside.

"I don't think we're going to make it back today. Should we look for a hotel?" Cade asked.

Vinnie nodded. "Probably. We got a late start, and a road trip isn't easy when you're not injured."

"Yeah. What I'm afraid of is she's going to argue. She doesn't like to be weak or incapable."

"Are you asking if I'll take the heat for it?"

Cade shrugged. "She isn't likely to argue if you say you're getting tired and want to stop for the day."

Vinnie nodded. "I don't mind doing that. Maybe another hour or two?"

"That's probably good. Then we're about halfway and can take our time going the rest of the way tomorrow."

"Works for me. They're coming. Something quick and we can grab dinner when we stop next?"

Cade reached for Karli and nodded at Vinnie's question.

"We're thinking something small here and stop in an hour or two for dinner. You guys okay with that?"

"Perfect. You know I'm always up for something to eat," Karli said, tilting her chin up for a kiss Cade didn't hesitate to give her.

Twenty minutes later, they were back on the road. Cade continued his conversation, and Vinnie watched Lorelei in the rearview mirror.

By the time they stopped for dinner, Vinnie wasn't having to make things up when he said he was exhausted and didn't want to drive any longer.

"Don't stop because of me," Lorelei said, seeing through the ruse Cade tried to pull.

Vinnie shook his head. "It's been a long few days. I think it's good for all of us to get some sleep tonight and to start fresh in the morning."

"I'm sorry," Lorelei said.

"What are you sorry for?" Karli asked.

"Because you've all been worn out because of me. Coming out here. Driving back. Away from home and jobs and whatever else you have going on. Other people in your lives." Lorelei didn't meet his gaze when she spoke, and Vinnie wondered if she was trying to find out if he was single.

No. He couldn't go there. He couldn't think about it. He already crossed a line with her. He wouldn't do it again.

"Well, we're here for dinner. Let's eat, then we can find a hotel," Cade said.

They filed out and into a local restaurant that had great reviews online. The hostess led them to a booth, but Vinnie stepped in and asked for a table since Lorelei was on crutches and sliding into a booth wouldn't be easy.

Cade and Karli sat on one side of the table, with Vinnie

and Lorelei on the other side. He propped her crutches against the wall behind them, out of the way of the foot traffic, then made sure she was okay before he sat next to her.

He should have let her ride back with Cade and Karli. Then he'd already be home and away from the temptation that was Lorelei Sloane.

Their server came over and took drink orders, leaving them with a list of specials and a few recommendations to consider.

"I'm getting tired, too," Karli said after they ordered dinner. "This was a good place to stop."

"We need to see if there are hotels available," Cade said, pulling out his phone. "Oh, the place we passed on the way here has space. How do we want to do this?"

It was the question Vinnie had been dreading since Cade mentioned stopping for the night.

"I wonder if they have a suite with a few rooms. Something where we could stay in the same space," Karli suggested, looking at Cade's phone with him. "What about this one?"

Cade tapped the screen, then nodded. "Yeah, that should work. Two bedrooms plus a living room and kitchen. I'm going to go ahead and book it so we can just go there and check in."

Vinnie was partly grateful they didn't ask his opinion and partly annoyed. Two bedrooms plus a living room. He didn't have the money for a place like that, but he would figure it out.

Vinnie didn't say much through dinner. He focused on his food and silently observed Lorelei. She seemed increasingly uncomfortable as they sat there, but he wasn't sure if it was pain or something else. All he knew was he was ready to get the hell out of the restaurant by the time the check came.

"We got this," Cade said, grabbing the check before Vinnie or Lorelei could object.

"You don't have to do that," Vinnie argued.

"You're driving your own vehicle and taking us back. The least we can do is cover your expenses on the way," Cade told him without looking up from his wallet. "That means we're paying for the hotel, too."

"No. I can't accept that." Vinnie was not a charity case. Not anymore. He paid his own way. He didn't rely on others to support him.

Karli reached over and grabbed his hand. Vinnie looked at her and saw all the emotions she'd kept hidden for days. "When Lorelei went missing, I knew something was wrong. It wasn't like her to disappear. But I don't have the skills to do anything about it. I'm an art therapist, not an investigator or anything like that. I barely slept. I was borderline insane." Karli drew a breath and let it out, her emotions spilling over and a tear racing down her cheek. "When we heard you found her, I nearly collapsed with relief, even though she wasn't okay. She was alive. And that's because of you. It doesn't matter to me that Lorelei doesn't know who I am, I love her. She was my best friend when we were little. Life took us in different directions and we haven't been as close in the last few years, but she's family. Losing her was unimaginable. And because of you, it wasn't a reality. So, us paying for a few meals for you and a hotel room for all of us to stay in and your gas and whatever else is not charity. It's gratitude. It's not much in the big picture, but it's us saying thank you for not giving up on her and for doing what you did and bringing her back to us."

"And if you ever need anything, we hope you'll think to

call and ask us because this isn't enough. There's no limit," Cade added.

Vinnie wanted to argue, but he understood it. He'd felt that same level of gratitude before. He still did. It was something that never went away. Something you never lost. When someone changed your life, you never forgot it. "I'm happy I arrived when I did."

"So are we. Now, no more arguing, we're paying. Cade's good for it," Karli teased.

Cade just shrugged. "Business is good."

Vinnie had never been on the receiving end of gratitude, but it felt good. Even better knowing Lorelei was safe, and he'd never let anything happen to her again.

LORELEI LOOKED at her cousin differently after Karli's declaration. To hear the emotion in her voice, and to see it, told Lorelei her relationship with Karli was another thing she wanted to change. Karli and Cade dropped everything to be there for Lorelei. They stayed, they were riding back with her instead of flying, and they were paying for everything.

Lorelei never considered the cost of their trip until that moment. She had no idea if she had money or credit cards somewhere, or where her handbag was or anything. She was just rolling through life without a thought to how she was going to pay for things.

Or a thought to what her disappearance did to the people who cared about her. Karli told Lorelei her parents had passed years ago, explaining why no one arrived saying they were her parents, but there was other family. Karli asked them all to give Lorelei time and space, but Karli didn't stay away. She pushed aside her fears and pain and sat by Lorelei's bed every day, helping her change and eat and use the bathroom and do everything.

It was a level of safe Lorelei needed. A level she only felt with Vinnie.

Vinnie.

Lorelei looked at the man next to her and wondered what drove him to find her. There were others looking for her. Karli said someone had checked her apartment the day after she disappeared. But Vinnie didn't give up. He kept searching. And he found her.

Vinnie didn't say much through dinner, only responding when someone asked him a question directly. After dinner, he drove them back to the hotel. Cade went inside to check them in while Karli helped Lorelei out of the SUV and Vinnie collected their luggage.

Cade came out with two keys and handed one to Vinnie, then picked up half the luggage. He led the way inside, past the desk to the elevator to the right of the lobby.

The suite Cade booked was huge. Each of the two bedrooms had a king bed and a private bathroom. The living room, kitchen, and dining room were all part of one open space. A balcony looked onto the Hudson River.

Lorelei was drawn to the balcony and the view. She pushed open the door and let the warm evening air wash around her as she hobbled outside. The noise of the city and the voices inside the room faded away as Lorelei stared at the water.

Why was she drawn to it? Why did she want to see it? She tried to figure out if there was anything familiar about it, but her mind was maddeningly blank.

"Are you tired?" Karli asked, joining her on the balcony. "It's beautiful out here."

Lorelei nodded. "Yeah. Um, I'm okay. I'm starting to hurt a little so I'll probably stay up until I can take another pill, then try to sleep. I wish I could shower."

"Maybe we can tie a bag around your cast?" Karli suggested.

"That's what Dr. Jones said."

"Want me to find something? I'm sure the kitchen has something. Maybe a trash bag?"

Lorelei nodded. "Thank you."

Karli turned to go back inside, but Lorelei grabbed her hand.

"And thank you for being here for me. Paying for all of this. Giving up your time and being away from work and everything. I know I don't remember you, but I know all of that is huge. And it means a lot to me."

"You would have done the same for me. You did when I was missing. You came to find out what was going on, and you stayed. You were chasing a lead on who's behind all the shit that's been going on when you disappeared."

Lorelei sucked in a breath. Something was trying to break through. A memory or a thought or something.

But just as quickly as it snuck up on her, it vanished.

"Did you remember something?" Karli asked.

Lorelei shook her head. "Something was there, but I... no. I'm sorry."

"Why are you sorry? You can't control it."

Lorelei smiled at her cousin, knowing it was true even though she wanted to control it. She wanted to tell her brain to come back. To remember. To be her again.

"I'll go look for a bag and some tape. Then you can shower."

Lorelei nodded, turning back to the view. Lights flashed in the distance. Cars raced by on the street below. The bellow of a boat echoed all around. Something was familiar, but Lorelei didn't know what.

Karli came back a minute later with a trash bag and a roll of tape. The two of them went to the bathroom in the room where Lorelei's things were.

"How do you want to do this? Do you think you can get your clothes off around the bag?"

Lorelei looked down at her cast and knew the answer was no. "Maybe I can take off my underwear and put my shorts back on, then it'll be easier so I don't mess up the tape."

"I was thinking the same. Let me know when you're ready for me to come back in."

Karli left Lorelei alone to change, which Lorelei did as quickly as she could. She was sweating by the time she called Karli back in, unable to take care of her top and bra on her own.

"I hate that you're in this much pain," Karli whispered.

"I'll heal. I'm alive and have the opportunity to."

"Thanks to Vinnie."

"Yeah."

Karli bagged and taped up Lorelei's cast. Karli started the shower and helped Lorelei get her bra off before leaving the bathroom so Lorelei had some privacy to finish undressing and take her shower.

Lorelei used her crutches to get close enough to the shower to use the bars on the wall. She put her back to the water and hopped into the shower, doing her best to keep her cast out of the direct stream. The handicap bar on the wall allowed her to keep her balance while the water ran over her body and soothed some of the aches she had.

The longer she stood there, the more tired she felt. The day took more out of her than she realized. Days stuck in a hospital bed meant she didn't do much. Her energy levels were low, but she wasn't putting out any either. Sitting in a vehicle wasn't taxing, but it was more than she'd been doing.

And she was worn out.

Lorelei washed herself and used the shampoo Karli gave her to clean her hair. When she was done, she turned off the water and Karli came back in.

"Do you have your towel?"

"No. I can't reach it."

"I'll grab it and bring it over. I should have thought of that before. Sorry."

"We're figuring this out together."

Karli chuckled and draped the towel over Lorelei's back. Karli helped Lorelei move away from the water on the floor and dry off. "I found some clothes that should be okay for you to sleep in. Do you want to go to the bedroom and get dressed?"

Lorelei nodded and yawned. She wrapped the towel around her body and used her crutches to move to the bedroom. Karli used another towel to dry the bag, then removed it from Lorelei's leg before helping her into her clothes.

When she was dressed, Lorelei swung her feet up onto the mattress. She winced when she tightened her muscles and her ankle let her know she was still injured. Six to eight weeks in a cast was going to be tough. "How in the hell am I going to do this for two months?"

"It'll get easier. And I'll come over every day to help you. Or you can live with Cade and me. That offer will always be open."

"I know." Lorelei felt guilty for choosing to live with Vinnie instead of her cousin. Especially after what Karli said at dinner.

"I need to stop trying to talk you out of staying with Vinnie. I apologize. You feel a connection to him. Aside from the obvious attraction, you trust him. There's nothing wrong with that. I'm not going anywhere. And I'm thankful he's willing to stick around and make sure you feel safe."

"Me, too." Lorelei chewed on her lip. "Is it weird he's the only one I feel completely safe with?"

"No. Not at all. You've been through something traumatic, and your brain is protecting you. Vinnie is a good man."

"Okay." Lorelei's eyes were closing.

"Do you want your painkiller?"

"Yeah. I almost forgot." Lorelei made a move to get up, but Karli told her she'd bring it in.

Karli came back with one pill only. "I don't want you to get up during the night and forget you took it, so the rest are out in the kitchen."

"Okay. Thank you."

"You're welcome. Get some sleep."

Lorelei nodded, falling asleep before she could ask where Vinnie was going to sleep, and if he would stay with her.

6

———

"What do you mean she's alive?" the boss asked. "That was not what I told you to do. You were supposed to find out what she knows, who she told, and take care of her."

"I did. I thought I did. She was almost dead when I dropped her at her apartment. I don't know how the hell she survived," Benjamin said. He toyed with the stupid ring he wore on his pinky. A sure sign he was nervous.

The boss scowled. This never would have happened if she were a man. They always followed her father's orders to the letter. But with her, they thought close was good enough.

She drew her gun and fired it past Benjamin's head, not giving him time to react until the bullet sank into the wall behind him.

Benjamin's eyes went wide. He knew what that shot meant. And that he wouldn't get a chance to avoid the next one.

Bringing him up as her second was a risk. But she was running out of people she could trust. They all turned out to be spineless fuckwads instead of reliable soldiers.

"Almost isn't good enough," she snarled at him.

"Understood."

"Just because she said she didn't tell anyone what she knows doesn't mean she won't now."

Benjamin shook his head, moving forward with a smirk. "She doesn't remember a damn thing. Amnesia. Doesn't even know who she is."

"Well, at least you did something right."

Benjamin's grin fell. "Someone had to be there right after I was. I took care of her boss."

"Is that how you want me to take care of you?"

Benjamin took a step back. "No. I will handle the agent. And anyone else she told about you."

"You better, or the next shot won't hit the wall first."

Benjamin glanced back at the hole in the wall. He nodded once, then turned and headed for the door.

As soon as it was closed behind him, the boss sank to her chair. She wasn't safe. That fucking agent knew her name. She knew too fucking much. And Benjamin let her live.

"Nina!" The boss stood and stomped her way from the office to her attached suite. It was one of many, and the one she spent most of her time in. Also, the one where her best friend stayed. "Nina!"

"Are you okay?" Nina came around the corner, hurrying to the boss's side. "What happened?"

The boss sank into the oversized chair next to the fireplace. A fire smoldered, enough to crackle and give off the scent but not so much to heat the already warm room in the middle of summer. "Agent Sloane is alive."

Nina sucked in a breath. "She is?"

The boss nodded and burrowed deeper into the chair. "Benjamin fucked me over. He was supposed to take care of her. He never would have done it if my father was in charge."

"Your father isn't in charge. You are."

That was what she loved about Nina. Nina always made her smile. Reminded her of what she was capable of. "You're right. He's not here."

"And everyone knows you are in charge, and that you are more than capable of handling anything. You've proven that."

She sat up straighter and smiled. "I have. Damon and the cops, Trevor, the girls who ran. None of them lived to tell their stories. They learned their lessons."

Nina nodded. "You take care of us. There's no reason anyone would want to leave here."

The boss looked up at Nina. Her beautiful red hair and those gray-green eyes that couldn't lie if her life depended on it. Nina had been her confidant for years. The one person she could count on to always be there for her and always tell her the truth.

"I love you, sis."

Nina smiled. "I love you, too."

They weren't sisters, but it felt like they were. If she'd had a sister, she imagined it would be the same relationship. Someone she took care of, someone she gave everything to, someone she made sure was happy and safe and loved.

The boss sighed. "I always feel better after talking to you. Do you want to watch a movie? It's been a long day."

"Sure. What are you in the mood for?"

"You pick. But nothing happy. Those movies about people falling in love with their brother's friend or some stupid shit make me sick. Things like that don't actually happen. Not to people like us. We have to rely on each other."

Nina nodded and turned to grab the remote. "A classic?"

The boss chuckled and got up from her chair. "A classic sounds good."

She sat out on the couch next to Nina as the opening credits started. They both raised the footrests at the same time, then chuckled and leaned toward each other.

Nina's hair smelled a little funky. It had been a while since the boss gave her extra shower time. She was usually with the rest of the girls and only got a shower before she was supposed to meet with someone, but the boss had been pulling Nina out of the rotation more lately. She needed her.

The movie played, and as the main character smiled through her first kill, the boss felt herself relax. It was a good night for murder. It always was.

THE SUITE around him settled down, and Vinnie knew he had to report in to his boss. Damien had been more than generous letting Vinnie stay in Boston as long as he did, but slow rolling the trip home and then letting Lorelei stay with him might push his boss over the edge.

It was late, but Vinnie knew Damien would answer.

"Are you going to be at work tomorrow?" Damien asked in lieu of a greeting.

"I'm not in Niagara Falls yet."

"Where the fuck are you?"

"A hotel in Albany."

"I hope this is a personal expense because I didn't authorize it."

Vinnie shook his head. "It's being handled."

"What the fuck does that mean?"

"It means I'm still with Lorelei Sloane and her family.

Her cousin and the cousin's boyfriend wanted to ride back with Lorelei and found out I had my personal vehicle. Asked if they could all ride with me."

Damien snorted, then burst out laughing.

Vinnie listened to his boss laugh for a solid minute. He knew better than to interrupt him.

"You got yourself in the middle of a fucking show, didn't you? Damn. I have a job for you. Tomorrow. We're supposed to be on shift. I was counting on you being here."

Vinnie looked around the expensive suite that made him feel like he was out of place. He wasn't a high-level kind of guy. The motel around the corner with the busted sign and cage around the front desk attendant was more in his price range. Not the suite overlooking the water with the valet parking and all glass entrance.

"I didn't know I was going to get roped into driving them all back. Or that Lorelei wouldn't be able to sit in the car for long. She needed to stop every hour or two at the most."

"Are you going to make it back tomorrow? To be on shift the next day?"

"Yeah, but—"

"Good... but what?"

"She's staying with me. Until she's healed."

"Are you fucking..." Damien drew a long breath and let it out slowly. "You have a job, Vinnie. One you worked your ass off to get. What the hell is going on?"

"You know this is important. That she's important."

"Yeah, I do. Everyone knows. But not everyone left the fucking city to go find her like you did."

"I..." Vinnie couldn't explain what drove him, but Damien was human. He would understand a connection. "She's a friend of a friend. And she knows something. She has to, or this wouldn't have happened. It's all connected. If she disappeared forever, what she knows is gone, too. We might never find out what's going on."

Damien sighed again. "I know. I get it. What I don't know is how I'm going to cover your shifts for however long you're out. A week or two we'll manage, but five or six more weeks?"

"The others said they could stay with her. Her cousin and friends. I will be back to work, just not this shift."

Damien exhaled again. His patience was running thin. "I want to tell you to get your ass back to work and let the FBI fucking deal with their shit, but I know that's not the right call. And I've never gotten a call from the FBI saying you deserve a medal or some shit. We all know this is important."

"It is," Vinnie said, thankful Damien wasn't arguing.

"Okay. I'll figure it out, but I expect you to check in and keep me updated on how things are going and when you'll be back."

"I will. Thanks, Damien. It means a lot."

"Yeah, well, hurry back. And if you could find a replacement for your shifts, it would mean a lot to me, too."

"I'll see what I can do. She's got some powerful friends."

"She sure does. Powerful enemies, too."

"Unfortunately."

"Get some sleep. We'll talk soon."

"Thanks."

Vinnie hung up the phone and let out a breath. He wasn't sure how that was going to go, but no one in law enforcement in Niagara Falls thought this was a small thing. They all understood the magnitude of Lorelei Sloane going missing and not remembering anything about who she was or what she was doing when she vanished.

Damien wanted the hell to end as much as the rest of them.

Vinnie turned the TV on in the living room and stretched out on the couch that was a little too small for his five-ten frame and accepted that he wouldn't get much better sleep on the couch than he did for almost a week in the chair at the hospital.

But at least Lorelei was well enough to be released. It was progress.

Tomorrow, they would make more progress. Getting home. Hopefully.

SHE LAUGHED. He was a fucking idiot. He told her everything. And he was too fucking stupid to realize she was getting information out of him.

"What the hell are you laughing at, bitch?"

"Is that the worst you can do? Call me a bitch? I've been called that since I was a teenager."

He scowled. Dark hair, dark eyes. That ring. She knew the ring.

Her cheek. He hit her with the ring. It hurt.

She tried to pull her arms up to press her hand to her cheek, but they didn't move.

"You're not worth another word," he said after a minute.

He wasn't very smart. And it came through whenever she insulted him. Or when she turned his questions around and got the information she needed from him.

"That's fine. I have all I need from you."

"What the hell are you talking about?"

"You've given me so much information. I really appreciate the help."

"The fuck I did. I didn't tell you a damn thing. You said you already knew it all."

She smiled. "I lied."

Rage filled his gaze and filtered into his body. He grew bigger in seconds, like the rage actually inflated him. He punched her face and ribs, the breath pouring out of her and not enough filling the empty spaces he created inside her.

Numbness took over, the pain too intense to process it. Protection. She understood it. She also understood he was going to kill her.

Maybe taunting him was a bad idea. Damn her mouth and always wanting to get the better of someone. She knew better. But it was funny to see the look in his eyes when he realized she played him.

He didn't stop hitting her until she wheezed, a funny sound exiting through her body. Then he laughed. Loudly and for a long time.

She was tied to the chair she was in, unable to move. Her body slumped to the side, her hands locked in place and keeping her from falling over. Her feet were bound the same way.

She fought to breathe, air rushing from her in gasps and pants that did little to fill her lungs. Everything hurt. Her entire body screamed in pain.

He kept laughing.

At some point, he stopped. She wasn't sure if he stopped or she passed out, but the sound stopped. Then everything hurt again, like it was fresh. Something hit her ribs, and she screamed. The pain was so intense she thought she was going to be sick.

She bounced. A car? Something. She was hot, sick, and couldn't breathe. She wasn't going to survive, and all he was going to do was laugh.

She was in and out of consciousness, trying to figure out where she was, but she couldn't piece enough together. He was driving her somewhere. It seemed like it was taking a long time, but it could have been a few minutes.

"Too much to drink," he said.

She groaned, trying to figure out what he was talking about. They were moving again. Walking. Sort of. He was half-dragging her.

Inside. They were in a hallway. Going toward a door.

Her apartment. He was taking her to her apartment. She could wait him out, then get help. Call someone. Run.

He unlocked her door and ushered her inside. She tripped, nearly falling. She had no strength. No energy. She had to fight back. Get away. Get help.

"You're not going to get help," he said.

Had she spoken out loud, or could he read her mind?

"No, if you go anywhere, you might tell someone what you know. And that would be really bad."

She stumbled again, tripping over her own feet.

He lifted her. Her arm was thrown over his shoulders, giving him all the advantage. They got almost to the couch, and she tripped once more.

With her body half on the ground, he lifted his foot and stomped on her ankle.

The crunch was almost as bad as the pain that made her head spin. She tried to scream, but all her other injuries stopped her from making any noise. Bile rose in her throat, but she choked it back. Throwing up would hurt more.

"Now you can't run away. No one is going to find you. And everything you know will die with you. Nice knowing you, Agent Sloane."

He dropped her on the couch and walked out, closing

the door quietly and leaving her alone with her pain to keep her company.

A door closed somewhere, and she opened her mouth to yell. Instead of mind-numbing pain, a sound came out. A shout that woke her up.

"A dream," she breathed.

Lorelei looked around the strange room. Darkness surrounded her. Panic settled in as her eyes adjusted and her memory came back.

Hotel.

Karli and Cade.

Vinnie.

Lorelei drew a deep breath. It hurt, but not as badly as it had in the dream she had.

Her dream.

There was a man. A man who beat her. He wanted information from her. But she played him.

Lorelei closed her eyes and tried to remember what he told her. It was there. Stuck in her mind. In her dream, she knew it. She knew all of it.

But awake, outside her dream, she still didn't know anything.

Lorelei got out of bed and nearly fell on her face. "Crutches." Tears sprang to her eyes. He stomped on her ankle to make sure she didn't get help. But help came anyway. Vinnie found her.

But he wasn't there now. He held her every night and kept the nightmares away. He protected her, kept her safe, made sure nothing hurt her, even her own broken mind.

But she was alone. Vinnie was only there when she didn't know she needed him so much. Since he told her about the panic attacks, he hadn't helped. He pulled back. He left her alone.

She hobbled to the bathroom and propped the crutches against the wall. She used the handicap rails to lower herself to the toilet and emptied her bladder, then pulled herself up and replaced her clothes. She hobbled to the sink and washed her hands, then went back to her bed.

She didn't want to know what happened. She didn't want to remember. She knew there was more, but it was too painful. Too hard. She wasn't strong enough to face it.

Lorelei sat up in bed and stared at the walls. Going back to sleep would risk having another dream. Remembering more about what happened to her. She shook her head and pulled her good leg to her chest. She wrapped both arms around her knee and watched the door.

She wasn't going to be caught off guard again. She couldn't. She had to be strong and protect herself. Especially if Vinnie was done protecting her. She was on her own.

7

———

Vinnie woke up instantly. The sound of Lorelei crying out was already a part of him. A piece he both knew without thought and hated with every fiber of his soul. He ached to go to her, to hold her and soothe her and help her sleep once more.

But he couldn't.

He promised himself he wouldn't touch her again without her permission. She knew about the nightmares and panic attacks. He didn't tell her the way he wanted to, but he told her. And she didn't ask him to continue. So he wouldn't.

But it still killed him to lie on the too small couch and listen to her fight the terror in her mind. A whimper and a gasp, a muffled cry.

He sat up and ran his hands through his short hair, tugging at the ends. He wanted to block the noise, but he couldn't. He deserved to hear her suffer. She wasn't alone, even if she didn't know it.

Movement in the bedroom told him she was awake. A

steady thump confirmed her crutches. The toilet flushed, water ran, then the thump led Lorelei back to her bed.

Vinnie didn't move. He hated himself for sitting still as much as he hated himself for touching her in the first place. She deserved to be treated with respect and in a way she was comfortable with. He crossed that line.

When the noise in her room stopped, Vinnie forced himself to lie down again. He stared at the ceiling of the suite and wondered how he was going to survive weeks of Lorelei Sloane in his tiny apartment. He didn't think through that part when he offered to let her stay. He lived in a one-bedroom apartment with one bed and one bathroom. It was tiny, almost too small for him alone sometimes. And he was going to be sharing it with a woman who drove him out of his mind crazy without even trying. A woman who tempted him with her every move.

A woman he had to resist, no matter what.

Lorelei Sloane was someone who mattered. She was going to stop the hell that ruled Niagara Falls. She was smart and strong and not looking to get tied down to a man who had nothing to offer her.

Vinnie needed to remember that. Her cousin was involved with a private investigator who could afford a suite without a second thought. Lorelei's friends were cops and firefighters and not hurting for money. Karli casually mentioned Dawn Patterson had flown them out to Boston on her private plane.

Vinnie wasn't at their level. He never would be. He was there to do his job, then leave her to do hers.

That was it.

A door opened at the front of the suite, and Vinnie sat up. He'd stripped off his shirt overnight, but he reached for it and tugged it over his head as the thud of crutches drew closer.

"Oh, sorry. I didn't realize you were out here. Did I wake you up?" Lorelei asked.

Vinnie shook his head. "You're good. How are you feeling? Can I get you anything?"

She kept going, making her way to the chair on the other side of the couch, closer to the balcony. She looked wistfully at the balcony, then sat. "I'm good. I just needed to get out of bed."

"Did you... Um..."

She looked over at him, her brown eyes telling him the answer to the question he started to ask. No, she didn't sleep well. "I'll be fine."

Vinnie nodded. He knew she would be. She was too strong not to be. He opened his mouth to apologize for not being there, even though he knew she didn't want him there, but before he could say anything, another door opened.

They both turned to watch Karli approach. Her hair was tied in a silk scarf, and she wrapped a matching robe around her body as she moved toward them. "Morning. I thought I heard you come out here. Hey, Vinnie."

"Morning," Vinnie said.

"I didn't mean to wake you," Lorelei said.

Karli rubbed her eyes. "All good. I wanted to be up when you got up. How did you sleep?"

"Good," Lorelei lied.

Vinnie didn't correct her.

"Good. I was hoping being out of the hospital would help you. Our bed was really comfortable. Vinnie, I'm sorry you ended up on the couch. I didn't know there were only two beds when Cade booked the room. We should have gotten you another one."

"I was fine," Vinnie said. The kink in his neck argued with his words, but he wasn't going to tell Karli that.

Lorelei smirked at him. But she kept his secret just like he kept hers.

"What time do you want to get on the road?" Karli asked.

Vinnie shrugged. "Whenever you guys want to go."

"The earlier the better," Lorelei said. "Since I have to stop so much, it's probably best if we leave early."

"I'll go wake Cade up. He didn't budge when I got out of bed," Karli said, shaking her head.

"It's fine. We need breakfast and time to get things packed up. He doesn't have to get up now."

"Is it okay if I use the bathroom in your room to shower?" Vinnie asked Lorelei.

"You didn't have a bathroom to use?" Lorelei asked.

Vinnie shook his head. He wasn't worried about it, but he wanted to shower before they got on the road. He hadn't had much more opportunity to clean himself up in the last week than she had. The nurses took pity on him and showed him where there was a bathroom with a shower, so he used that most days, but he always rushed through. To take his time would be nice.

"Yes, of course. Feel free. Karli and I will be fine without you."

"Thank you." Vinnie grabbed his duffle and headed toward Lorelei's room. As soon as he stepped in, her scent hit him in the face and propped up his cock. He hurried through before one of the women saw the effect on his body, closing the bathroom door but leaving the bedroom door open in case Lorelei needed something.

The bathroom was even worse. It smelled like her, but

also not like her. Vinnie paused and drew a deep breath, regretting the move as soon as he did.

He was hard as fuck and about to come just standing there.

He yanked his clothes off in a frantic rush and turned the shower on. He got in before the water was warm and wrapped his hand around his neglected dick. He'd been holding Lorelei every night and worrying about her every day, and he wanted her. Bad.

He hissed at the feel of his hand on himself. One stroke, and his knees nearly buckled. He groaned and put his hand on the wall to support himself, then fisted himself hard.

It wasn't going to take long. He pictured her lips when she smiled at him. He inhaled her scent. He imagined the feel of her hand wrapped around him.

His forearm hurt from the fast, punishing strokes he used. His breath rushed out of him. He ducked his head under the water, letting the heat fuel him. His entire body tingled. His balls tightened. His throat closed up.

He exploded. Thick ropes of cum flew across the shower and hit the wall with a splat. He grunted, trying to hold back the sounds he wanted to make. He pumped his dick harder, more, faster, making sure everything left him.

Every inch of his body throbbed. He felt like he'd gone ten rounds in the ring instead of five minutes in the shower. He was worn out, and not as relieved as he'd hoped he'd be.

"Fuck," he whispered. It should have helped, but all it did was make him want her even more. He closed his eyes and saw her. He breathed and smelled her. He moved and felt her.

He was so damn screwed.

Vinnie rushed through the rest of his shower, soaping himself up and rinsing off and growing hard again. He debated taking care of the problem again, but it would take too long. He would be fine. It would be fine. He could control himself.

He hoped.

By the time Vinnie made it back to the living room, Cade was up and Karli was in the shower. When Cade and Karli swapped placed, Karli took Lorelei to her bedroom to change and pack so they could leave.

They grabbed breakfast and got back on the road, Vinnie behind the wheel and Lorelei right behind him once more.

Two hours in, they stopped so Lorelei could stretch and get some fresh air. Another hour after that, they stopped again. Cade said they were only ninety minutes from Niagara Falls, and Lorelei said she'd try to make it in one trip.

Twenty minutes from Cade and Karli's house, Lorelei started shifting in her seat. Vinnie watched her in the rearview mirror, wondering if she was okay.

Karli talked, oblivious to Lorelei's discomfort. Cade continued the conversation with Karli. Neither of them seemed to notice Lorelei was in need of another stop.

Vinnie saw a sign for a rest stop and hit his blinker.

"You okay?" Cade asked.

Vinnie nodded. "Can't make it. Sorry. Need to stop at the bathroom real quick."

"Oh, okay," Cade said.

Vinnie looked at Lorelei in the mirror. She smiled at him. He made the right call.

THE STOP WAS ONLY a few minutes, but it made Lorelei feel so much better. She hated making them all stop so many times, but she was uncomfortable. Sometimes it was pain, others just stiff. But she hated it. When they made it to Cade and Karli's house, Lorelei nearly cried in relief.

"Are you sure you don't want to stay with us? We have plenty of space," Karli said.

Lorelei got out of Vinnie's SUV to stretch, again, and shook her head. "I'll be fine with Vinnie. I know you don't understand, and I can't explain it, but I feel like that's the place I need to be."

Lorelei glanced at Vinnie. He was unloading Karli and Cade's things from the back of his SUV. He and Cade were talking too quietly for her to hear what they were saying, but if Lorelei had to guess, it was about her.

"Vinnie knows how to get in touch with me. Adam said the FBI is going to issue you a new phone. Once you have that, we'll make sure you have a way to contact all of us. And when you're up for it, we'll all get together so you know all the people I've been telling you about for a week."

Lorelei breathed a laugh. "That sounds good. Thank you for everything. It was above and beyond."

Karli shook her head and stepped closer to hug Lorelei. "Not even close. I love you, cuz. I am so happy you're back and you're going to be okay. Call me if you need anything."

Lorelei nodded. "I will."

Karli hugged Lorelei tight, then stepped back and smiled. Karli's eyes were a little misty, but she ducked her head and moved toward Cade. He put his arm around her shoulder, then shook Vinnie's hand and waved to Lorelei.

Lorelei stood next to the SUV while Karli and Cade went inside. She knew she should feel something, but she wasn't sure what she felt. Affection? Appreciation? Yes to both. But she didn't feel the loss of her cousin the same way she did when Vinnie left the room. Lorelei trusted Karli and believed she was honest, but when Karli walked away, it wasn't the same visceral reaction Lorelei had to Vinnie walking away.

"Are you sure you don't want to stay with them?" Vinnie asked after a minute.

Lorelei looked up at him. She didn't know how long she'd been staring at Karli's house thinking about Vinnie, but with the man right there, she knew without a doubt she was making the right choice. "No. If you're okay with me staying with you, that's what I'd like to do."

He nodded. "Can I help you get in?"

Lorelei nodded. Getting into the SUV wasn't easy. She had to sit on the seat, then scoot herself all the way to the other side since she couldn't lift her leg, or fit it on the floor of the backseat.

"Would the front be better? I'm about ten minutes from here."

Lorelei shook her head slowly. "I'm not sure. We can try it."

"I don't want to hurt you."

"You never would. I know that."

Their gazes collided and clung. Lorelei's body felt warm, warmer than the summer afternoon should have made her feel. It wasn't the sun. It was the man who was staring at her like she was special. Like she was more important than the woman she used to be.

A car driving by revved their engine and broke the spell that locked Lorelei and Vinnie together. He cleared his throat and reached for her crutches. "This is easier. You know you can do it. We'll work on the front seat when you're not so worn out from driving all day."

"Sounds good." Was her voice always so breathy? God, she sounded like she was trying to talk him into her bed. Did she have a bed? Where was she living? She had an apartment in Boston, but Karli said Lorelei was staying in a hotel in Niagara Falls. Should she go there?

Lorelei ignored the thought and let Vinnie help her get into the backseat of his SUV. He took the crutches once she was on the seat, then waited for her to move herself to the other side of the vehicle before he set her crutches on the floor next to her and closed the door.

He took a minute before he walked around the SUV and climbed into the driver's seat. He pulled away from the curb without a word and navigated the streets Lorelei would swear she'd never seen before in silence.

Vinnie pulled into an apartment complex nine minutes later. He wound through the buildings until he made it to a lot toward the back and turned in. He found a parking spot near the building entrance and turned off his Bronco.

"I don't have an elevator. Or a spare bedroom. Or a lot of things. I probably should have told you all of this before you decided to come here. I can take you back to your cousin's if you want me to. Or somewhere else. Wherever—"

"I want to be with you," Lorelei admitted. "You make me feel safe. I... I know you don't know me and I pushed myself into your life, but—"

"You didn't push. I did. And I'm sorry for that. I'll grab our things and we can go up." He was out of the vehicle in the next second, slamming the door so hard it jolted Lorelei's shoulder.

He was pissed. Dammit. She made the wrong choice. Again.

He threw their duffles over his shoulders and grabbed each of her suitcases.

She didn't like that she couldn't help, but it was all she could do to get herself around.

Vinnie opened the door for her and grabbed her crutches, holding them until Lorelei made her way across the vehicle and could get out. He led the way to the door and opened it for her, then led the way up the stairs to the third floor of the building.

Lorelei was breathing heavily by the time they made it to his door, but she didn't want him to know. She drew slow, deep breaths to hide how hard she was panting.

Vinnie noticed anyway. "I should have told you about the stairs. And everything. I'm sorry. We'll get everything straightened out tomorrow. Let you rest tonight."

Lorelei just nodded, letting him have the excuse to get rid of her.

Vinnie let them in, and she moved out of his way so he could bring in all their luggage.

She took in his apartment while he carried everything to what she assumed was the bedroom. The place was small, but clean and comfortable. A gray couch dominated the living room, with a smaller matching chair to the side and a massive TV on the wall opposite. A wooden coffee table sat in front of the couch with coasters and remotes on the top. A blanket was thrown over the couch like someone had just tossed it there.

Space that Lorelei assumed was a dining room was instead full of free weights with a treadmill in the middle of the room. The light fixture was hooked up at the ceiling instead of left to hang low and risk hitting Vinnie every time he walked by.

The kitchen was behind the dining room, the three spaces creating an L-shape. Cabinets lined both sides of the galley kitchen, with appliances breaking up the yellow wood stain that made her think the kitchen was old.

"It's small, and it's kind of crappy, but—"

"It's neither. And I appreciate you letting me stay here."

Vinnie nodded. "Let me show you around. Obviously, living room, kitchen, and the dining room I don't use. I eat on the couch since I live alone. Bedroom and bathroom are back this way if you want to follow me."

Lorelei wanted to ask if someone else had ever lived with him. If he was single or if there was another person in his life. But she didn't.

His bedroom was roughly the same size as the living room. A king-size bed took up almost the whole space. He lifted her suitcases onto the bed, blue sheets and a white comforter making the room look brighter than it was with only one lamp on.

The bathroom was... tiny. Lorelei had no idea how she was going to take a shower in that little bathroom. Without handicap handles to help her get in and out. *Shit*. She never thought about that.

"It's all small. I know. It's not anything like your place."

"I was left to die in my apartment. I don't have a lot of fondness for it right now."

"Lorelei."

She swallowed roughly and turned to go back to the living room. "I know you don't want to babysit me. I'll be fine if you have to go do something. See someone or whatever."

Vinnie followed her to the living room, shaking his head. "I already checked in with my boss, so I'm good. I have to go to work sometime, but he's agreed to let me have time to figure that out. So I can be here with you."

"I don't want you to put your life on hold because of me. We're strangers."

Vinnie took a step back like what she said bothered him. He nodded sharply. "You're right. But I agreed to let you stay here, so I'm going to make sure you're okay. Are you hungry? I was going to order some food and I'm guessing you're going to want to get some sleep."

"Sure, sounds good." It didn't. None of it sounded good. But she didn't know what else to say to the man she didn't know anymore than she knew herself.

8

———

What the fuck was he thinking, offering to let her stay with him? Vinnie kicked himself all through a completely awkward dinner and after Lorelei excused herself to go to bed. He heard her shifting in his bed and knew she wasn't any more comfortable than he was.

He'd make it better tomorrow. He had to.

Vinnie finally fell asleep somewhere after midnight. His sleep was fitful and broken, a cry waking him sometime before the sun lightened the shades on his windows.

It had been ten days since she disappeared. A full week since he found her. And her memory was still not back. What did that mean?

Vinnie spent his spare time over the last week researching memory loss and what the recovery would be like. When he wasn't looking at Lorelei, he was thinking about her and wondering how he could make her feel better. How he could help her be herself again.

A text popped up on his phone from Marcus and a smile lifted Vinnie's lips without a thought.

Are you up for breakfast? I heard you have a guest.

I'm up. Not sure if my guest is. I'm assuming you know all the details by now.

Yeah. Frannie has been champing at the bit to rush over to your place and mother Lorelei.

Sounds like Frannie. She's been helping people since I met her.

She's an amazing woman. So is your guest. Let us know when you guys are up for company. We can come to you or meet somewhere. Whatever is easiest.

With her crutches, I think leaving as little as possible is best. Probably taking her to Karli and Cade's later.

I thought she wanted to stay with you?

I don't think she really understood what she was asking.

You and I both know people in crisis moments aren't always rational from the outside.

Yeah, I guess.

Have you asked her what she wants?

I don't think she wants to hurt my feelings.

She's definitely lost her memory if that's the case. She never worried about that before.

She's not the same.

Even if she had her memory, she wouldn't be.

True.

Let me know when you're ready. We'll bring food to you.

Thanks, Marcus.

You're welcome. It's been too long anyway.

Vinnie nodded. He couldn't remember the last time he saw Marcus outside of work. It had been way too long.

Less than an hour later, Lorelei was up. Her first stop was the bathroom, then she made her way out to the living room. Vinnie sent Marcus a text that Lorelei was up, then folded his blanket and returned it to the back of the couch. His suitcase was tucked into the corner of the living room, out of the way so Lorelei could move around without tripping on it.

"Good morning," she said. Her voice was soft, still sleepy.

"Morning," Vinnie managed, his rough with desire and thoughts of caring for her.

"Your bed is very comfortable."

That was not the image Vinnie needed to start his day. He was already battling a hard-on, and thinking about her in his bed was not going to help the fight. "I'm glad you slept well." He stood and walked to the kitchen. Coffee would help.

"Not really, but it was comfortable."

"More nightmares?"

She nodded.

Vinnie scooped ground coffee into the drip machine

he'd had for a decade. He grabbed the carafe and filled it with water, then dumped the water in and started the machine. "Did you take a painkiller this morning?"

"I did. And I did my breathing thing." She shook her head.

"Still hurts?"

"Yeah."

When did his kitchen get so damn small? With her at the entrance, he felt closed in. Not trapped because she wouldn't do that, but like he couldn't breathe without sensing her. Without wanting to pull her closer like he did in the hospital and inhale her scent and wrap himself around her and hold her close until she relaxed into him.

He missed that.

She took a step toward him. "Vinnie?"

He swallowed. "Yeah?"

"Can you... I mean, will you...?"

The look in her eyes went straight to his dick. Desire, trust, faith. All things she couldn't have for him. All things he had in her and was projecting. All things that were so wrong when she didn't know who the hell she was or who he was.

He imprinted on her. That was all it was. Like a scared child who latched on to the person who found them, Lorelei was scared and didn't understand herself why she wanted to be around him. She admitted that. She didn't want him.

He was the one with an issue controlling his emotions. Controlling the raging need pulsing through his veins.

He needed to get the hell out of there before he did something he couldn't take back, or let her do something she didn't really want to do.

"I'll be right back," he blurted, squeezing past her and running to the bathroom.

Lorelei watched Vinnie run and closed her eyes against the pain. She missed the man from the hospital. The one who held her and made her feel safe. This man was distant.

She tried asking if he had someone in his life the night before, but he didn't answer the question she was afraid to ask. If he had a significant other, no wonder he was acting weird. She should have just stayed with her cousin.

Lorelei stared at the coffeepot as it puffed and popped and dripped coffee. Lorelei had no idea how she liked her coffee. Or if she liked it. The hospital brought some, but it was not her favorite. The scent of it made Lorelei think she liked it. The sharp jolt combined with the smooth depth of it. She wanted to like it, but maybe it wasn't her thing.

Maybe she'd never know what was her thing.

A knock on the door startled her. It wasn't her home, but Vinnie also didn't mention anyone was coming. It was possible it was Karli and Cade, but wouldn't Vinnie have mentioned that?

Vinnie came rushing back, ignoring her before he went to the door and threw it open wide. He grinned at the older couple on the other side, opening his arms to hug the woman.

Parents? They were white, but they didn't really look like him. Not that it was the sole determinant of family, though.

The woman glanced past Vinnie and found Lorelei watching them. Her eyes went soft as they slid down Lorelei's body.

"Frannie," Lorelei said.

The woman's eyes went wide. She pulled back from Vinnie. "Did you tell her my name?"

Vinnie shook his head. "You know her?"

"I..." Lorelei didn't know. The woman wasn't familiar, but for some reason, she knew her name.

"It's okay, Lorelei. We know it's going to take a while for you to remember anything." Frannie came closer as Vinnie hugged the man who'd come with her. "We brought breakfast. And creamer. Vinnie said he didn't have any."

Lorelei nodded and let the woman hug her.

"How are you feeling?" Frannie asked softly.

Lorelei shrugged.

Frannie laughed softly. "To be expected. Do you want to sit? I can get you a cup of coffee. I know how you like it."

"You do? I don't."

Frannie chuckled. "That's okay. You'll remember everything eventually."

"What if I don't want to?" Lorelei breathed, the question making everyone in the room stop.

Frannie was the one who spoke first. "It would be nice if we could choose."

Lorelei nodded and let Frannie guide her to the couch. Frannie sat next to her and nodded to the man. "That's my husband, Marcus Patrick. Marcus is the local police captain. You've been working together. He and Vinnie have known each other for longer than I've known Marcus."

"Oh, um, okay." Lorelei didn't know what to say.

Frannie chuckled. "I bet you've gotten a lot of information over the last week. Names and events and a lot that you don't know."

Lorelei nodded.

"It's not easy." Frannie looked at Marcus. "We should eat. I'm starving."

"Of course." Marcus replaced Frannie on the couch and offered his hand to Lorelei. "I know there are a lot of people offering you help, but I hope you'll accept my offer of the same. If there's anything you need or want to know, please reach out. Vinnie knows how to get in touch with me."

Lorelei nodded at the older man. He gave her the same sense of calm that Vinnie did. In a different way, but she knew Marcus was someone she could count on and trust. Someone who wouldn't lie to her or manipulate her. And someone who would be brutally honest with her. Which was why she had to ask him...

"What's the chance the man who took me will be found?"

"Man?" Vinnie barked, rushing back into the living room with Frannie right behind him. "Do you remember something?"

Lorelei nodded, avoiding meeting Vinnie's gaze. "Last night and the night before, I had nightmares that woke me up. Both nights I remembered a man."

"Can you tell me anything about him?" Marcus asked.

"He was mean. And he wanted to know what I knew about something."

"Do you know what he was asking about?"

Lorelei shook her head. "No. I can't ever remember details."

"You only started having nightmares two nights ago? When you left the hospital?" Frannie asked.

"She had them before," Vinnie answered.

"But you never remembered anything?" Frannie asked.

Lorelei looked up at Vinnie. "He helped me. He calmed me down and let me go back to sleep."

Frannie looked between them, then at Marcus. "Um, what does that mean, exactly?"

"When she would wake up, I would hold her. That's it, I promise. I know it was a violation to do it, and I know I shouldn't have, but the first night she had a nightmare, I worried she was going to hurt herself. She was thrashing around and fighting. I thought she would make everything worse, so I started talking to her. She calmed down a little, but not enough. I held her hand, but she was still frantic, so I held her. As soon as she was in my arms, she settled. Her breathing eased, and she went back to sleep." Vinnie closed his eyes and shook his head. "I know it was wrong, Frannie. I know it crosses a line. She never gave me permission to put my hands on her, and—"

"It appears to me you're the only one beating yourself up, Vinnie. Correct me if I'm wrong, Lorelei, but it sounds as though you were sleeping better and feeling better when he took those nightmares away." Frannie raised one eyebrow at Lorelei and waited for an answer.

Lorelei bobbed her head just enough to nod. "I didn't know until I had a panic attack, and Vinnie... It made me feel better to have him close."

"Then it sounds like there's nothing to forgive, Vinnie." Frannie reached for his hand. "You didn't do anything intended to harm Lorelei. You were protecting her. Sometimes our memories are the worst thing to get protection from, and you were able to give her comfort and care when nothing else did. Stop beating yourself up for it and accept what she's telling you. She's not angry at you."

Lorelei shook her head. "I'm not. I never was. I was shocked, but not mad."

"I'm... Okay," Vinnie said.

"To answer your original question," Marcus said, "we won't stop until we find the man who did this to you. And whoever he's working for."

"Working for?" Something tingled in her mind.

Marcus nodded. "We know there's a boss, but we don't

know who it is. I'm guessing the man who took you isn't the boss. It's unlikely he would expose himself."

"He meant for me to die. He broke my ankle in my apartment. Said he couldn't have me leaving to get help."

"You remember that?" Frannie gasped.

Lorelei swallowed roughly and nodded.

"Oh, honey, I'm so sorry." Frannie set a mug of coffee in front of Lorelei, followed by a plate of the most delicious and fluffy looking cinnamon rolls. "Eat. Drink."

Lorelei nodded and did both. The other three joined her, the sounds of breakfast being enjoyed outweighing the worries in Lorelei's mind.

The coffee was good, and the cinnamon rolls were even better. By the time she finished, she was stuffed and feeling better than she had in days.

"Vinnie, come for a walk with me," Marcus said in a clear ploy to leave Lorelei and Frannie alone.

Vinnie looked at Lorelei, as if asking her before he left.

Lorelei nodded. "I'll be fine."

"Okay." Vinnie followed Marcus outside, locking the door behind them.

"Karli and Raina have been in touch with me. Jessica visited when she and Braden got back. I know he had to come back to work, but she hated to leave."

"I understand. Everyone has a life. Things they need to do."

"Yes, but we're all here for you. And worried about you. I know Karli and Raina told you about all the others. When you're ready, we all want to get together. But for now, I have something for you."

Lorelei waited as Frannie reached into her handbag. There was a moment of panic when Lorelei wondered if she was wrong to trust Frannie, but then Frannie pulled out something small and black and handed it over.

"What is this?" Lorelei asked as she accepted the... "A mask?"

Frannie nodded. "When I was in my twenties, I worked at a nightclub. The dancers all wore masks like this one. I know, weird, but I saw a woman killed on my walk home one night. I set out to find who killed her, and when I confronted him, I wore my mask. It was... maybe a way to hide who I was, maybe something else. But it made me feel strong. Like I wasn't alone. Like I could do anything."

"A mask did that?"

Frannie breathed a laugh. "Hard to believe, I know. A few years ago, I gave a mask to another woman who needed to feel strong and know she wasn't alone. And another, and another. Your cousin Karli has one, Raina has one, Jessica has one."

"And you want me to have one?" Lorelei asked. She turned the mask over in her hands. It was simple. Plain black with a little sparkle in it like it was dropped in glitter and washed, but some stuck in the fabric. The loop to go around her head was tight, and the mask itself was soft. There was no way a mask would make a difference.

"I know it doesn't seem like much, but the women who have them call themselves the Curvy Vigilantes. We've been fighting the same fight as you for a long time. You were the one leading the charge on the legal side, the one who was getting us closer to finding the answers we've been looking for."

"You never found who killed that woman?" Lorelei asked.

Frannie shook her head. "I did, but it was a long time after. And he answered to someone else. We don't just want justice for one person, we want it for all the women who've been hurt, killed, or targeted by this organization. Including you."

Lorelei shook her head. She was a *victim*. She hated the word. It made her feel powerless. Like she wasn't good enough to do something about the man who attacked her.

"You know my name, but do you know what I do?"

Lorelei thought for a minute, then shook her head. She wasn't sure how she knew Frannie's name, but it was all she knew about the woman.

"I own and operate a women's shelter. Domestic violence survivors in many cases. Women who have nowhere else to go. Who feel like you're feeling right now."

"How do you know how I'm feeling?"

Frannie patted Lorelei's hand. "I've gotten very good at reading people over the years. You're feeling alone, scared, confused, and maybe like you hate that you are a victim."

Lorelei shrugged. She couldn't deny any of it, but she didn't want to admit it either.

"I've felt all those things. So have the women who've come through Shelter in the Storm over the years. We don't like to use the word victim because it has negative connotations. It sounds like something happened to you that you couldn't stop. We prefer to call our guests survivors or fighters or just guests. We help women figure out what's next for them. And that means letting go of the things that held them back. For you, I have a feeling fear is a big thing right now. Those dreams, nightmares, are making you want to not sleep or making you want to not remember."

Lorelei nodded.

"I can't imagine how hard it is to relive what you went through. But your memories are important."

"I know. Because I know something."

Frannie shook her head. "No. Because they're a part of you. Your memories tell you about your first love, your family, the people you choose to spend time with. Memories define us in ways that we can't explain. They make us who we are, and that's why you're drifting right now."

"You think it's a mistake to lean on Vinnie? Because I didn't know him before."

Frannie chuckled. "Not even a little. Vinnie is a good man. A great man. He's someone I would trust with my life if I ever had to. He's smart and kind and trustworthy. And that you know that without knowing him says there's a part of you that's working how it should."

"I almost shot my housekeeper," Lorelei admitted.

Frannie shrugged. "You're going to remember some people and not others. You're going to trust some instincts and not others. You can't control how that happens. All I know is you're not alone, Lorelei. You don't have to be. There are people who want to be there for you, and who will be there for you. Probably before you're ready, but it's because we care about you and want to see our friend back."

"Thank you," Lorelei said. There was no pressure with Frannie. It wasn't the same as Karli or Adam, where Lorelei felt like she was letting them down because she couldn't remember them. Frannie accepted what Lorelei knew and didn't know and trusted she would remember what she needed when the time was right.

"Take it slow. Talk to Vinnie, if he's your safe person. And if you feel better with him by your side, ask him to be there. He's beating himself up, and the only one who can get him to stop that is you."

"I will. I wouldn't be here without him, and I am beyond grateful to him. I owe him my life."

"You owe no one anything. You are strong on your own. But you can show him your gratitude."

Lorelei's cheeks heated. "What do you mean by that?"

Frannie's brows went up, and a smirk lifted her lips. "What do you think I mean, Lorelei?"

Lorelei chuckled, shaking her head at Frannie.

Frannie leaned over. "He's a very attractive man, isn't he?"

Lorelei snorted. "You're trouble."

"The best ones are, my dear. Including you."

Lorelei drew a breath, one that hurt her lungs but reminded her she was alive. She was trouble. For the people who wanted to hurt her and others. She wouldn't rest until she stopped them.

For good.

9

———————

"You look like shit," Marcus said, shooting a side-eyed glance Vinnie's way.

Vinnie snorted. "Gee, thanks. It's nice to see you, too."

Marcus shook his head and grinned. "It's always nice to see you. But you and I both know this is above and beyond. What's going on with you and Lorelei?"

"Nothing. I promise. I kept my hands in safe zones. I didn't do anything that—"

Marcus stopped him with a hand on his shoulder.

Vinnie stopped talking and looked up at his mentor, the man who saved his life and made him the person he was.

Marcus set his other hand on Vinnie's other shoulder, his full focus on Vinnie. "I would never, never, assume that of you. You're one of the most upright and honest men I've ever known. I wasn't asking about that. I assure you."

"I just..." Vinnie paused to find the right words. "I never meant to upset her."

"It sounds like you did the opposite of upsetting her. It sounds like you were the reason she got any sleep the first week. But you've pulled back. Why?"

"She didn't know." Vinnie exhaled, relieved to have someone he could be honest with. "God, when I found her..." Vinnie drew a breath. He could still see her. He pushed down the emotions he felt when he walked into her apartment, but they were right there, beneath the surface. He hadn't had a chance to feel them until right now.

"I can't imagine how painful it was for you," Marcus said softly. "Are you okay?"

"She was the one hurt."

Marcus chuckled. "And seeing her hurt can be painful. There's nothing wrong with that. I've seen all those women hurt, and it's been painful for me. Them and so many others."

Vinnie nodded. Every month, he donated to Frannie's shelter. It was a dream of hers and took her a long time to make it a reality. Vinnie was proud to have helped and to continue helping, even if it wasn't much, and to know his money was going to a good cause.

"Lorelei is a strong woman. She's not someone who ever let others see when she wasn't strong. It sounds to me like she's letting you see that version of her, and that's a powerful thing."

"Yeah," Vinnie agreed. "It is. It's... Damien called right when I walked into her apartment, right when I found her. I just acted, checking her and letting him know where I was so real help could arrive."

"You're not real help?" Marcus asked with a smile.

Vinnie chuckled. "Medics. People who could stabilize her and actually save her life."

"You saved her life," Marcus said without a trace of humor. "If you hadn't arrived when you did, she would be dead and we'd all be trying to figure out what she knew that they killed her for."

Vinnie shivered at the thought. Lorelei Sloane not on earth anymore would be a tragedy. It ached to even imagine it.

"You care about her." Marcus wasn't asking, he was seeing the truth Vinnie didn't want to admit.

He nodded anyway. He'd never been able to keep anything from Marcus. "I know it's ridiculous. And I'm not going to do anything. I would never."

"Vinnie, I've already said I trust you. I know you're not the kind of man who's going to take advantage of a woman. But you are the kind of man who's going to pull back when you should be leaning in."

"What do you mean?"

"I think she needs you. She trusts you. She asked to be here. You have yourself convinced she should be with her cousin, but she doesn't know Karli. She knows you."

"No, she doesn't. I'm the guy she saw when she woke up, so she thought she knew me."

"No, Vinnie. That's not it at all. You're the guy who made her feel safe. The one who told her you'd make sure she was okay. Who protected her from her memories and her pain and who gave her back a piece of herself that she couldn't get any other way."

"What piece?"

"Her sanity. Her faith in her instincts. For a woman like Lorelei, who's lived so long by her instincts, it's the same as her sanity."

Vinnie sucked in a breath. Marcus was right. Vinnie had been beating himself up for touching Lorelei, but the reality was he helped her.

"On top of that, you have the skills to keep her safe. You're trained in this kind of thing."

"But shouldn't she be with someone who can devote all

their time to her safety? Damien is already making noise about me needing to be back at work."

"I'll take care of Damien. I'll assign an officer to the SWAT team for this week. Next week, too, if you want. As long as you want to be away. I know this case is important to you, too."

Vinnie nodded, thinking through his options. "It is important. Maybe more now. I can't see leaving her, but I also can't walk away from my job forever."

"Talk to her about it and see what makes the most sense. Maybe she'll want to get out after a week and you can go back to work and let her stay with Karli or Frannie or someone."

"How the hell did she know Frannie's name?" Vinnie asked. He'd been wondering about that.

Marcus laughed. "My wife is a constant surprise. I guess I shouldn't be shocked someone remembers her when they don't even know themselves."

Vinnie snorted. "True."

They walked a little longer, the silence comfortable and safe for Vinnie. It had been since the day he met Marcus. The day the beat cop caught Vinnie shoplifting and gave him two choices. Go back and apologize to the store owner or go to juvie.

Vinnie knew the right answer, and because Marcus gave him time to think about it, Vinnie made the right choice. A choice that meant he took responsibility for his actions and apologized when he messed up.

"You know you're not the same kid who stole that sweatshirt when you were a teenager."

Vinnie breathed a laugh. "I was just thinking about that. I don't know where I'd be if another cop picked me up that day."

"It doesn't matter because it didn't happen that way."

Vinnie stopped and looked out at the parking lot of his apartment complex. Beat-up cars and rusted junkers filled most of the spots. Vinnie hadn't leveled up very well, but he knew what he was doing with his life mattered.

"If you weren't here, she wouldn't be either."

Marcus's quiet words were a punch to the gut. One that knocked the breath out of Vinnie. "That's..." He drew a breath and let it out slowly, internalizing the truth of it. "Thank you for always being here for me."

Marcus chuckled. "I should be the one thanking you right now. A lot of people have you to thank for bringing her back."

"Do you think she'll get her memory back?" Vinnie blurted. He wasn't sure which answer would make him feel better, but he wanted to know.

Marcus shook his head. "I don't know. I hope so. Do you hope so?"

Vinnie laughed. "You're not supposed to be able to read my mind."

Marcus grinned. "Then maybe you shouldn't make it so easy to read your mind."

"She's going to leave as soon as she remembers who she is."

"Maybe. Maybe not. She seems pretty comfortable with you. She's not the same person she was. She's... softer. Lighter."

"It's the amnesia. Lorelei Sloane is a badass. She's not going to be broken down by this."

"Maybe not, but that doesn't mean it won't change her or that she won't come back wanting to be different. Karli told Frannie that Lorelei isn't the same. She's friendlier and kinder. She's more like the version Karli remembers from when they were kids."

"You think losing her memory has given her back a part of her she lost?"

Marcus shrugged. "I'm not a psychologist, so I can't say, but don't we all become a little jaded after a while? A little less optimistic and happy?"

"I don't think I was ever optimistic or happy."

Marcus snorted. "Then maybe you need some joy in your life."

Vinnie looked up at his building without thinking.

"Or maybe you've found someone who brings you joy and you need to accept that you're allowed to have her in your life."

Vinnie shook his head. "She doesn't want me. Not really. I'm safe, but how many women have you heard say 'I fell in love with him because he was safe'?"

Marcus laughed. "Well, maybe they don't say it like that, but I promise you, the ones who've left Shelter in the Storm definitely felt that way when they found someone new."

Vinnie ran a hand over his jaw, feeling the stubble from not shaving that morning. "I don't want her to be with me because she's afraid of not being with me."

"Then maybe you should let her be safe with you and not worry about what happens after she gets her memory back."

Vinnie nodded, but he still hated the idea. But she wasn't his. She wasn't his before she lost her memory, and she wasn't his after. His place in her world was temporary. And he had to be okay with that.

SHORTLY AFTER FRANNIE and Marcus left, someone showed up with a package for Lorelei. She was anxious about it until Vinnie realized he had a text from Adam saying the FBI was going to send Lorelei a new phone and computer so she could get back into her files.

She wasn't ready. She didn't want to go back to everything. But she knew if the others had the answers, they would have already found whoever took her. She had to do it.

Vinnie went to take a shower while Lorelei used the temporary password Adam texted so she could get into the phone and computer.

As both loaded all her files, Lorelei wondered about the things Frannie said. About Vinnie and not being alone.

Lorelei got the feeling she was used to doing things alone. That she didn't let others in very often. She couldn't figure out that feeling. Vinnie was there. Karli was there. Adam was there. It was obvious she wasn't alone, but they all seemed almost surprised by the way she acted around them.

The shower turned off and Lorelei realized she'd been staring at the bathroom door the entire time Vinnie was in the shower. Her body flushed hot. Desire spiraled in her belly. It didn't matter that she was injured and not allowed to engage in any strenuous activities, she wanted to do all of them with Vinnie.

The bathroom door opened with a billow of steam obstructing her view of him for a second before he walked out of the bathroom with only a towel wrapped around his waist.

She gasped, but thank God he didn't hear her. Or if he did, he didn't react.

A second later, the bedroom door closed, and she breathed again.

"Damn," she whispered. He was gorgeous. Defined muscles and dark hair all over his chest. Even his feet were sexy.

Could she have an orgasm without it getting too strenuous?

Lorelei shook her head at herself. She could not be thinking about that. She needed to focus on who tried to kill her.

Vinnie came back to the living room and busied himself in the kitchen while Lorelei stared at her new phone. She assumed it would be easier for her, but it was confusing for her battered brain. There were apps that she didn't know how to use and phone numbers for people she'd never heard of. She needed someone to tell her what everything meant. What was important.

A glance toward Vinnie said he wouldn't be of any help. He was on his phone and not paying her any attention.

Lorelei thought about calling Adam, but he was still on his honeymoon, and interrupting that was a bad idea.

She was just getting the courage to ask Vinnie to help when he announced he had to run out.

"You're leaving?" she blurted. She didn't like the idea of being alone.

"I'm only going downstairs to get groceries. I don't have anything here since I was gone for a week. I put in an order and the driver will be here soon."

"They don't bring it upstairs?"

He shook his head and stuffed his feet into sneakers. "I said I would meet them downstairs. I'll take my keys so you don't have to worry about the door being unlocked. I'll be back in a few minutes."

"Okay," she breathed, not feeling okay in the slightest.

Vinnie let himself out without a glance in her direction.

If that didn't sting...

Lorelei stared at the door, listening to the lock engage, then to Vinnie's steps carrying him away from her. She tried to breathe normally, but she was panicking. The same as she did when she woke up from her nightmares and he wasn't there.

Fear was a fucked up thing. She didn't remember so much of what happened to her, but her body knew she was alone. She had no help, no one to protect her or help her or save her.

"There's no one coming," the man said in the nightmare that morning. Taunting her. Reminding her she had no one.

And there she was again, no one around to help. Broken ankle that would stop her from running away.

Her ribs hurt like they hadn't been healing for a week. Her lungs screamed for air. Her brain felt like the blows to her head were fresh.

Footsteps echoed in the hall, and a few seconds later, the key engaged in the lock. Vinnie or a stranger? Did someone pretend to be the driver and take Vinnie? Come to finish the job they started with Lorelei?

The door swung open, and Vinnie appeared. He glanced her direction, then turned away. He locked the door and carried the grocery bags to the kitchen, ignoring her and the panic she was sinking into.

Lorelei forced herself to breathe, drawing in deep breaths to slow her racing heart. She picked up the spirometer and breathed into it, using her panic attack as a motivator to get better.

Vinnie put the groceries away, then retreated to the bathroom. Again.

Without a word. Again.

That was not going to work for her.

As soon as he came out, she pushed herself off the couch and blocked his path to the kitchen. His apartment was small, and there were only so many places he could hide.

He stopped when he saw her in his way. He looked around her, like he was going to move past her, but she put out a crutch to block him.

"What the hell is wrong with you?" Lorelei demanded.

"What are you talking about?"

"I'm talking about you avoiding me. Keeping your distance from me. Not touching me or talking to me or being in the same room as me. Where's the guy from the hospital? The one who held me when I had a panic attack? The guy who held my hand so I didn't freak out? Where's that guy?"

"I'm right here, Lorelei." He sighed, still not meeting her gaze.

She shook her head. "No. No, you're not. You're some other guy. Some guy who's a stranger. Some guy who wants to be a stranger."

"You have no idea what I want. And I am a stranger. You don't know me."

Lorelei laughed, the sound foreign and rusty. "You really think I don't know you? Hell, I don't know myself, but I know you. You're the one who's acting like you can't wait for me to be anywhere but here. Maybe I should grant you that wish and get the hell out of here."

"You're not going anywhere," he growled.

She moved past him to his bedroom, the one that had all her things in it. She picked up a shirt and threw it in her bag.

"What do you think you're doing?" He was at the door to his room.

"I'm leaving. I can call Karli to come get me."

"You're not leaving."

"Why not?" She spun to face him, ignoring the pain in her head with the quick movement. "The guy I chose to stay with isn't the same one who's standing in front of me. That guy made me feel safe. Like nothing would happen to me."

"I took advantage of you."

"No, you didn't."

"Yes, I did! When you had those panic attacks, you didn't know I held you. I violated your privacy, your personal space. I never should have touched you."

She shook her head. "We talked about this. I haven't slept since I left the hospital because I keep having panic attacks. I wake up every night, wishing you were with me. Wishing you were holding me and telling me I was safe. I'm tired and wound up and so damn—" She rolled her lips in to stop the next words from leaving her mouth.

"So damn what, Lorelei?"

She glared at him. The challenge in his gaze pushed her to answer him. "So damn horny I'm about to lose my mind. Which is pretty tough to do since my mind has already taken a hike."

"Lorelei."

"Just let me leave, Vinnie. Let me pack my stuff and get out of your life. You don't have to take care of me anymore."

He moved into the room, stopping right next to her. He grabbed her wrist and plucked the shorts from her hand. "You're not going anywhere, Lorelei."

"You've made it clear you don't want me here. You offered because you felt some sense of obligation or something, but now you regret it and want me to leave. I'm not going to force myself on you."

"I want you here. More than I should."

"What does that mean?"

"It means I'm a selfish asshole who offered to let you stay because not being in the same room as you made me feel like I was missing a piece of myself."

She sucked in a breath. Part desire, part relief. "What?"

He cupped her jaw and tilted her face up to meet his gaze. Desire burned in his brown eyes. "Tell me not to kiss you, Lorelei."

"What if I want you to kiss me?"

He didn't give her a chance to say anything else. His lips came down on hers hard, stealing the breath from her.

She lifted her arms to wrap them around his waist, pulling him close. She nearly cried with relief, with desire.

He pulsed against her stomach, and she moved closer, needing to feel the proof that he wasn't just telling her what she wanted to hear.

She whimpered, and he pulled back.

"Did I hurt you?"

She shook her head. "No. More. Please, more."

10

———

Vinnie was going to hell. A hell of his own making. How was he going to resist her? The doctor said nothing strenuous for ten days. He was already about to burst. Another week would kill him.

"Please," she breathed, and he was done.

Resistance wasn't an option. Claiming her was the only thing he could think of.

His lips came down on hers again, crashing against her mouth and demanding of her. He parted her lips and devoured her, his mind lost to the temptation of Lorelei. A temptation he'd resisted for far longer than he thought possible.

She whimpered and pressed herself closer, then sucked in a sharp breath and pulled back.

"Ow," she breathed.

"Are you okay?"

She nodded, but the grimace on her face said otherwise. "I forgot about the ribs."

Vinnie smoothed the hair back from her face so he could look at her. Her curls were soft and stiff at the same time. Like all of her. A little bit pliable and a little bit resistant. "I shouldn't have pushed you."

She breathed a laugh. "I think I was the one pushing."

Vinnie grinned. "Are you okay?"

She nodded, breathing slow and easy. "I guess kissing you is a strenuous activity."

Vinnie snorted. "I lost my mind a little there. I have been resisting you for far too long."

"I thought we didn't know each other before."

He shook his head. "That didn't mean I wasn't drawn to you. I don't skip out on orders and go AWOL for just anyone."

"You're in a lot of trouble, aren't you?"

He shook his head, not wanting her to blame herself for his choices. "It's all okay. My boss knows you're important. It might have been a different story if I hadn't found you, but I did."

"And I'm very grateful for that."

"Me, too." Vinnie was quiet for another minute, trying to find the words to ask what he needed to know.

"Just say it," she said with a long exhale.

"Do you still want to leave?" he asked.

She shook her head slowly. "I never wanted to leave. Did you kiss me to keep me here?"

"No. I am not manipulating you. If you want to leave, I will drive you to Karli's. But I don't want you to go for the wrong reasons."

"What are the right reasons?"

"If you don't feel safe here. Or comfortable. Or would rather be with someone else, someone you know better."

"None of that is true. I wanted to leave because I'm putting you out. I'm in your way and messing up your life. It's not fair of me to ask so much of you."

"I invited you here because I couldn't stand the thought of you being somewhere else. I invited you here because I'm selfish and couldn't imagine walking away from you."

Lorelei smiled up at him. "I didn't want to go anywhere else. I know my memory isn't right, and I know I can't really trust myself right now, but I feel safe with you."

Vinnie sucked in a breath and reached for her. He stepped closer to her so she could lean on him. He kissed the top of her head and held her. "I am going to do every-thing in my power to keep you safe."

"I know."

Vinnie drew a deep breath, peace settling inside him. She was safe. And she trusted him. That was all he could ask for at the moment.

Her hands wandered, and his body responded, telling his brain her safety wasn't the only thing he wanted. He wanted her.

Bad.

"Lorelei," he groaned.

"Don't tell me no." She leaned back and looked up at him.

He couldn't deny her. He couldn't deny himself. He leaned down, closing the distance between them again and pressing his lips to hers. He banked his desire, holding back the feral side that wanted to throw her on the bed and ignore the warnings from the doctor. The warnings that would mean she was in pain.

She whimpered and licked his lips, seeking entrance.

He opened for her and thrust his tongue along hers.

She gasped, then sighed, like that was what she needed. Her fingers gripped his shirt at his waist and tugged up. The first brush of her hand against his skin nearly had him leaping out of his flesh.

She spread her fingers wide and slid them up his back. She dragged her nails across his spine, and he swore his eyes would have rolled back in his head if they weren't already closed.

He let his hands slide to her hips, holding her in place for him to grind his erection against her. She moaned in his mouth and dug her nails into his back. She pressed her body closer to his, wincing when she tried to support her weight on her broken foot.

"Dammit."

"On the bed," he growled. "Spread your legs."

She hurried to listen to him, scooting across the mattress and parting her thighs for him. "Wait. I'm still dressed."

Vinnie ignored her attempt to get up again and crawled over her. "I'm not strong enough to resist you if your clothes come off. One more week, Lorelei. Then we can talk."

"But—"

Vinnie covered her body with his, keeping his weight off her entirely so he didn't hurt her ribs, and stopped her argument with his lips on hers.

She drew a shaky breath and responded to his kiss with hands in his hair, pulling him down.

He withdrew enough to whisper, "Your ribs. I can't lay on you."

"Dammit," she blurted.

Vinnie chuckled. "We can take this slow."

"I don't want slow. I want an orgasm."

Vinnie kissed her softly, notching himself between her thighs. He stroked against her as he licked her tongue.

She sighed happily, a shaky breath leaving her as he withdrew.

Vinnie thrust against her slowly, keeping his pace and his

kisses on the safe side of frantic. If he lost touch with himself, he'd hurt her. And he couldn't risk that. He rubbed against her body, finding the spot that made her gasp and the spot that made her sigh and the spot that made her moan.

"Is this okay?" he whispered against her lips.

"I haven't had an orgasm like this since high school."

Vinnie pulled back. "Do you remember something?"

Lorelei shook her head and laughed. "No. Maybe a feeling. No concrete memory, though." She moaned softly. "Don't stop?"

"I won't. Unless I hurt you."

"You won't." She lifted her good leg, propping her foot on the bed and opening herself up wider.

Vinnie gritted his teeth and recited team stats in his head. She felt good. Too good for rubbing together with all their clothes on. Too good for a grown-ass man.

"Vinnie." Her breath hitched. A wince had him pausing, but she dug her nails into his skin, and he knew stopping would almost be worse than continuing.

He pushed his body higher, giving her more space to breathe, and thrust harder. He watched her face twist, pain and pleasure fighting in the tightness of her lips and the pinch around her eyes.

Then her lips parted, and a gasp escaped her. "Vinnie," she sighed, her body shaking as the orgasm filtered through her.

It wasn't enough. He knew it wouldn't be enough. But it was more than nothing. And with practice and patience, he would learn what she needed.

"Thank you," she whispered, blinking up at him. "Best orgasm I can ever remember."

Vinnie snorted, rolling to the side before he fell on her

with his laughter. "My manhood feels like it's being questioned with that comment."

She shook her head and looked over at him. "Not even a little." She looked down, avoiding his gaze. "Thank you."

Vinnie reached for her hand and brought her fingers to his lips. "You're welcome."

She gasped when he licked her knuckles. "Don't get me started so soon. I might never let you out of this bed."

"I might not have a problem with that."

She breathed a laugh, then shifted her hips. "I should get up and use the bathroom. Maybe change."

"I'll go start dinner. If you're hungry."

She nodded. "Starving."

Vinnie grinned at her tone, then rolled out of bed. He made sure she was okay, then carried himself to the kitchen, ignoring the pulsing in his pants.

A week couldn't end soon enough.

LORELEI GLARED at the computer on the coffee table. Ever since it arrived a week ago, it had been mocking her.

Day one it was easy to ignore because she told herself she was focused on Vinnie. The orgasm he gifted her with that day was head-clearing in a way she never expected. Not that she knew what to expect, but she was ready for an orgasm.

Days two and three were easier than day one. Vinnie was being sweet and kissing her and got his hands on her in a very, very good way. He was cautious and careful and refused to let her touch him. He said he was worried he'd hurt her if he didn't keep himself firmly in check, but that only served to make Lorelei want to push him even more.

He didn't let her.

Days four, five, and six were a dance. Vinnie and orgasms or the computer. Her focus was locked on one or the other. Lucky for her, Vinnie took his task seriously.

But now it was a full week later, and Vinnie had to go to work. Leaving Lorelei alone with the computer.

"Karli will be here soon," Vinnie said as he rushed around his apartment, getting ready for work.

Lorelei had taken over his home. Her clothes were everywhere. Her things blended with his. It looked like she'd been there far longer than she had. And her presence was making it harder for him to get ready for work. He'd cleared out a drawer for her and moved some of his things aside in the closet so she could unpack her suitcases. It was sweet, and made her heart squeeze, but he'd opened her drawer at least three times when he was gathering clothes for after his shower.

He refused to walk out of the bathroom in a towel. Not after the way she devoured him with her eyes and he nearly ignored all of his stupid self-imposed rules.

What did the doctor know? Ten days was overkill. She would have totally been fine if he made her scream, let her ride him, then slammed her into the wall and wore them both out.

Lorelei scowled at herself as she had the thought. It still hurt to breathe sometimes, but that didn't matter.

"Are you going to be okay for an hour?" Vinnie asked.

Lorelei looked up and realized she never said anything after his comment about Karli. "Yeah, yeah. I'm fine."

He came closer, his gaze assessing her as he moved toward her. "Are you sure?"

"I was daydreaming about getting you naked," she confessed.

Vinnie leaped back, making it out of her reach before she got her hands on him. "You are dangerous."

"Especially when I don't know if you're a friend or foe."

His eyes softened, his entire demeanor changed with the reminder that she could have hurt her housekeeper the week before. "You will get your memories back."

Lorelei nodded, fighting the anxiety rising in her throat.

He stepped into her arms, removing her crutches and setting them against the wall while he supported her weight. "I hate that I have to leave you today."

"I'll be okay."

"I'm not sure I will be."

Lorelei snorted. "You seem like you're always okay."

"We're not so different."

"I'll have to take your word for it."

"Are you okay? You seem like something's going on."

"How would you know that?"

He shook his head. "It's just a feeling I have that you're more anxious than you have been the last few days."

"I'm fine."

He pulled back and looked more closely. "No, you're not. I'm going to call Damien and tell him I can't go in. I need more time off. He never should have demanded—"

"No!" Lorelei grabbed her crutches from the wall and fitted them under her arms.

Vinnie stopped, turning to face her and studying her carefully. "No?"

Lorelei shook her head. "You can't put your entire life on hold. Your career. I might not remember mine, but I know what I do is important, and so is what you do. You're helping people. You're saving people. What if there's another woman out there who will die if you aren't there to see what everyone else misses? You have to go to work."

"But—"

"Vinnie, I'm okay. I'm anxious, yes. I know I need to open that computer and try to find answers, but I don't know if I'm ready. I don't know if I'll ever be ready. For any of it."

"Shit," he breathed. "I didn't know that was weighing on you."

"I didn't want you to. I wanted to ignore it and pretend there was nothing wrong with me."

"There is nothing wrong with you." He cupped her jaw and lifted her lips to his.

The gentleness of his kiss was enough to make her already foggy brain even foggier. In the best possible way.

"I will go through it with you later, if you want me to," he breathed against her lips.

Lorelei rolled her lips in and eased back from him. "I might."

"Anything you want or need, you let me know. Okay?"

She nodded.

He tilted her chin up again. "I mean it. I will quit my job if you don't feel safe without me here."

She shook her head before he finished his sentence. "I will not let you do that. I've been fine. I am fine. And Karli will be here soon."

Vinnie exhaled slowly. "Are you trying to convince me or you?"

Lorelei chuckled. "Both I think."

Vinnie smiled. "It shouldn't be this hard to walk away from you."

"You'll be back. And I'll be here."

"I know." He stepped back and drew a breath. "Okay. I'm going. Keep the door locked. If you want to go anywhere, you have a key. Karli will text before she gets to the door. And call me if you need anything."

Lorelei nodded. "I will. I'll be okay."

Vinnie exhaled. "I know. I'll see you as soon as I can get back here."

"Be safe. Kick some ass out there."

Vinnie chuckled. He stepped back in front of her and kissed her hard, then he was gone.

Lorelei didn't move for a long minute, listening to the sounds of him locking the door, then walking down the hallway and down the stairs. She strained to hear him, holding her breath until the only thing she could hear was the blood rushing in her ears.

The computer glared at her.

"Dammit."

Waiting for Vinnie was the easy choice. It meant she wasn't alone. But there were still a lot of things Lorelei didn't know about herself, about the woman she was before she lost her memory.

Did she want to discover the truth with Vinnie there? Or was it better to get a peek inside her mind when she was alone?

She moved to the couch and sat down. She rested her crutches against the cushions. She considered turning on the TV, but she wanted to be able to hear any noises outside the apartment. To hear if someone approached.

It was strange being terrified of being alone. Lorelei knew it wasn't how she lived her life before. She lived alone and worked alone, going to meet an informant alone the night she disappeared, according to what she was told by others.

But she hadn't been alone since Vinnie found her. The closest was when she went to the bathroom or took a shower. And even then, Vinnie was close enough to hear if she needed help.

Now she was alone. Her thoughts, her fears, and her brand new laptop were the only things to keep her company.

Karli would be there in forty-five minutes. Maybe less. It was now or never if Lorelei wanted to get a peek into her before life without someone looking over her shoulder.

She drew a breath and picked up the laptop. She pulled it onto her lap and opened the lid. It started immediately, a lock screen preventing her from gaining access.

She touched the fingerprint scanner. A circle spun on the screen, then it unlocked and her work life flashed on the screen.

Lorelei watched as it all came up, one program after another. She leaned back and watched, letting it all come up before she picked a place to start.

"Guess this one is as good as any."

11

———

A KNOCK ON THE DOOR STARTLED LORELEI AWAY FROM THE file she was reading. She was so involved she didn't realize how much time had passed. Or that she didn't hear people walking around outside the apartment door.

"Lorelei! Open the door." The knocking resumed after Karli's shouts.

"Coming!" Lorelei called back, as much to let her cousin know she was okay as to tell her it would be a minute.

Lorelei stood and grabbed her crutches. She was more comfortable with them than when she walked out of the hospital, but she was still slow. She couldn't wait to be done with them, but at least she could handle getting around.

Lorelei unlocked the knob and deadbolt, then opened the door for Karli to walk in. Karli's worried look had Lorelei on alert immediately.

"What's wrong?" Lorelei asked.

"I thought something happened to you. I texted you when I got here but you didn't answer. I worried something happened. I'm glad I was wrong."

"I'm fine," Lorelei said, waving her hand toward the

computer. "I decided to look at the computer Adam had sent over."

"Did you remember anything?" Karli's hopeful gaze made Lorelei snort.

"I wish, but no. It's like drinking from a fire hose. There's so much, and I can't understand even half of it. I feel even more confused than before."

"Do you want to talk it out? I don't know if that's allowed."

Lorelei shrugged. "I don't know either. But it's not like you're going to help the other side."

"Definitely not," Karli said.

Lorelei locked the door, and they moved to the couch. Lorelei pulled the laptop closer. She angled it so Karli could read the file.

"What am I looking at?" Karli asked.

"That's what I'm trying to figure out. I have case files with information that's collected from anyone who's working on the case, so it looks like those are shared files. But these are my personal files. Things that were buried, but still on the network. Probably so someone could get to them if anything happened to me. Thanks *past me* for being smart enough to think of that."

Karli hugged Lorelei to her side and squeezed. It was comforting, but not the same as when Vinnie held her.

Lorelei focused on the feel of her cousin and closed her eyes. She wasn't alone. She was safe. Karli was there. It was all good.

The thought gave her the courage to keep digging into the confusing information on the computer. "Thank you," Lorelei said.

"You're welcome," Karli replied. "I know all of this is

weird, and I know I keep saying that, but I am here for you. I'm really happy you called me to be here today."

"I have no idea if you have a job or somewhere else you need to be. It's... this is all just so odd for me. Like, I know there are things missing, obviously, but I also understand the world."

Karli nodded. "You know how to walk and talk and function. You understand that people work and drive and do all these things. You just don't remember anyone."

"Yeah. I guess it's good that I know some things, but it's so strange to me the things I don't remember."

"Have you talked to your doctor about that?"

Lorelei shook her head. "I didn't think about until today. When I'm reading all of this stuff and have no idea what it means."

"Then let's look at it. Maybe I can give you some insight since I know you. Or maybe Adam needs to look at it. He might know what all of this means and you don't have to struggle with it."

"Maybe. But..." Lorelei chewed her lip and struggled to find the words.

"But what?" Karli asked. Her tone was gentle but cautious.

"I think I hid all this. I don't think anyone else knew all this information."

Karli's brows shot up. "Not even your partner?"

Lorelei shook her head slowly. "Why would it be in some kind of code if I shared it all with Adam?"

"Maybe the two of you created the code together?"

"Maybe," Lorelei said, but she knew that wasn't it. She had secrets. From her partner and now from herself. And figuring them out could mean the difference between saving a life and costing her one.

"Let's look at it. What's the first one?" Karli asked.

Lorelei pointed to the screen and the gibberish in the file.

"What the hell does that mean?" Karli blurted.

Lorelei snorted. "You said you wanted to help."

Karli chuckled. "I didn't know it was going to be that confusing."

Lorelei smirked. It was not going to be an easy day.

VINNIE REACHED for his phone to call Lorelei and shoved it away as quickly as he retrieved it. He was not going to bug her.

"You doing okay?" Damien asked, leaning against the wall next to Vinnie's locker.

They'd just come back from a raid. A stash house was the center of a stand-off and their team was called in to help after the target refused to negotiate.

The whole reason Vinnie's presence was requested was to take part in an early morning briefing about a high-profile visitor coming to the city and the need for extra security. Vinnie and the rest of his team were asked to be in charge of the operation, which meant they all had to be there.

After the meeting, there was a training session. Training was interrupted by the raid.

Now they were back, and Vinnie was itching to get the hell out of there.

"Do you need me here the rest of the day?" Vinnie asked his boss.

Damien sighed heavily. "What are you doing with this agent?"

"What does that mean?"

"It means she has her own team that can stay with her until her head is healed and she can be on her own. Why does it have to be you?"

"We talked about this last week. I thought you were okay with it."

"I... I'm just looking for a timeline here."

"Captain Patrick was going to assign someone to the team while I'm out."

"He did. And it's great to have a body, but that's not the body I need. When we're training and we're preparing for ops, we need you here. Even when shit happens and we have to go, a new guy isn't the same as someone who's been a part of this team for a decade."

"You're making me feel old."

Damien shook his head. "You and I both know this team is special. It's different. You don't get here just by being a good cop. And you don't stay here by being a good cop. SWAT isn't like everything else. We have to trust each other in ways no other group has to."

Vinnie sighed, nodding. "I know. And I am coming back."

"When?"

Vinnie scrubbed a hand down his face, thinking about Lorelei's recovery. In a few days, she'd be cleared to be alone for periods of time. In just one day, her *no strenuous activity* requirement would be lifted, which Vinnie could not think about in front of his boss.

Karli was willing to help, but it wasn't so easy with Lorelei on crutches.

"Give me the rest of this week. I'll be back next week for the high-profile op and have a plan for going forward when I come back."

Damien considered Vinnie's offer. It was clear he didn't love the idea of letting Vinnie miss out on more shifts, but it was better than Vinnie not being around at all.

Vinnie waited, knowing if he added something, it would only be to cave and do whatever his boss wanted him to do. When Vinnie tried out for SWAT, he knew his numbers weren't the highest of everyone who tested. Marcus encouraged Vinnie to do it, and with Marcus's support, Vinnie fought like hell and made it through.

But finding his spot on the team was different. Just because he was in didn't mean he was going to stay there. Being a part of a team was harder than having a partner. Being part of the team meant navigating the emotions and opinions of everyone.

Damien was the one who made that possible. He gave Vinnie a place where he could thrive, a spot on a team that was more interested in who he was and his moral compass than where he came from. Their team was a blend of legacy cops, women who worked harder than everyone else, and men who had instincts that saved all their lives more than once.

Damien was a fair leader, and he was a good man. Vinnie didn't want to lose his spot on the team, and he didn't want to lose Damien's respect.

But he also didn't want to lose Lorelei.

"Okay. But you have to finish the shift today," Damien said.

Vinnie nodded. "Deal."

"Now, tell me about this agent. She seemed like a fierce one. Was that the real her?"

Vinnie shook his head. "She's complicated. And it's harder since her memory is shot. I think she's unsure of who she is. But she's still the strongest woman I've ever met."

Damien snorted. "Don't let Molly and Hannah hear you say that."

"Say what?" Hannah asked, coming around the end of the lockers. Her shaved head and brilliant blue eyes gave her a sharp edge and a kickass look that had men and women either trying to get her number or steering far from her.

"Vinnie says that agent he's spending time with is the toughest woman he's ever met."

Hannah nodded, bobbing her from head side to side. "I don't know that I can argue that one. She was pretty damn badass when we were on that Davis Developments call. I've never seen someone take charge of a situation like she did, and get everyone out alive. That woman and her daughter were lucky to have someone like Agent Sloane there."

"I don't disagree, but you and Molly could give her a run for her money," Damien said.

"Give who a run for her money?" Molly asked, showing up behind Hannah. Molly was tall and strong and surprised the shit out of most people when they learned who she was. She had a kind face and a soft demeanor that caught most criminals off-guard when she turned around and slapped cuffs on them. Or knocked them out with one hit.

"Agent Sloane," Hannah said.

"Vinnie's girlfriend?" Molly teased.

Damien turned to Vinnie with brows high. "Girlfriend?"

"No, it's not entirely like that," Vinnie defended.

"Not entirely? That means it's partly like that. Come on, spill," Hannah said.

"I don't kiss and tell," Vinnie argued.

"Oh shit, he's making out with the agent. Hey, boss, why didn't we get to go find her?" Hannah asked.

"He didn't get to go either," Damien said. "He just left."

"Well, it's a good thing he did, or she'd be dead, and we'd all still be wondering what the hell is going on," Molly said.

"Without her memory, we're still wondering," Damien countered.

"Yeah, but a woman like her isn't giving up until she finds the answers. We'll know who's behind all of this before we know it," Hannah argued.

"I hope so," Damien said. "We need our whole team back."

"Well, we're here today. Let's grab lunch and Vinnie can share all the dirt." Molly looped her arm through Vinnie's and tugged him from the locker room. When they were in the hallway, she whispered, "I have a ton of respect for Agent Sloane, and I'm really happy you didn't get in trouble for saving her."

"Thanks, Mol."

She winked. "Don't expect me to take it easy on you later in the ring, though."

Vinnie chuckled. "Wouldn't dream of it."

"WE NEED to get out of here," Karli declared after four hours of staring at the computer screen.

They were no closer to finding answers than when they started that morning. But Lorelei was definitely more frustrated. "Where do you want to go?"

"Lunch. I need food. I'm starving." Karli put the laptop on the coffee table and stood. "Have you been outside since you got here?"

Lorelei shook her head. "The stairs aren't easy on crutches. Vinnie's been ordering groceries so we can just stay in."

Karli looked around the apartment as if just remembering Vinnie lived there. Her eyes narrowed, seeing things Lorelei hoped would have gone unnoticed.

Like there being only one bedroom.

"Where are you sleeping?"

"In the bedroom," Lorelei admitted.

Karli looked around again. "And where is Vinnie sleeping?"

"In the bedroom."

"Does he have bunk beds?"

Lorelei snorted.

"Okay, we're going to lunch. You need to tell me all about shacking up with the sexy SWAT guy."

"Oh, please, you told me about you and Cade and how he protected you and it became more."

"Exactly. I need to know if Vinnie is just some guy or if he's going to be around for a while."

"What if I don't know the answer to that question?"

Karli grinned. "All the more reason to get out of here. Clear your head. Get some food. Indian?"

"Do I like Indian food?"

Karli nodded. "Yep. Let's go."

It wasn't as easy for Lorelei, but she got herself up and out the door. She used the keys Vinnie left for her to lock the apartment and made sure to note where things were so she could check when they came back.

The stairs were a slow process, but Karli was patient with Lorelei's speed. When they made it downstairs, Karli led the way to her vehicle and opened the door for Lorelei to get in the front.

"I'm not sure I'll fit," Lorelei said.

Karli shook her head. "Try. If not, you can go to the back and I can chauffeur you around."

Lorelei laughed and positioned herself to sit in the front. She got to the seat easily enough, but getting her casted ankle in was a little tricky. But it worked, and Karli laid the crutches across the backseat before getting in behind the wheel.

Karli was quiet on the drive to lunch, something Lorelei was learning meant her cousin was trying to find words for whatever she was thinking.

"Just say it," Lorelei said when Karli parked in front of a small restaurant.

Karli chuckled. "I hate that you can still read me. You don't remember me, but you can read my thoughts."

"I don't want to have to. Just tell me what's going on. What do you want to say?"

"I planned to talk you into moving in with me and Cade, but now I'm not so sure I should do that."

"Why? What changed your mind?"

"I think your connection to Vinnie is stronger than I realized. I think you're falling for him."

Lorelei shook her head. "I barely know him. Hell, I don't know anyone. How could I be falling for him?"

Karli opened her mouth to argue, but Lorelei held up a hand.

"Let's go eat. I need food, and so do you. I know you know me better than I know myself, but a few orgasms are not going to make me fall in love with a man I've known for two weeks."

"A few orgasms?" Karli shouted. "Okay, we're going in, and you're going to tell me exactly what's been going on with you and Vinnie."

"Crap."

Karli snorted. "You're the one who said it."

Lorelei shook her head and waited for Karli to get the

crutches out of the backseat. Lorelei opened the door to get some fresh air and was surprised when she heard her name.

"Lorelei? Lorelei Sloane?"

She was trapped. And cornered. And had no way of defending herself against the woman who was coming at her. The woman who was reaching into her bag.

Was this it? Was this the end?

Was she going to kill Karli, too?

12

———

"Don't move!" Karli shouted at the woman. Or maybe at Lorelei. All Lorelei knew was they both froze.

"Lorelei?" the woman said, her blue-eyed gaze stuck to Lorelei.

"What do you want?" Karli asked.

"I... I just wanted to say hi. Lorelei saved my life, and I... I'm sorry. I didn't mean to scare you." The woman broke down, sobs bouncing out of her like they were held back and had to break free.

"Do you have a weapon?" Karli demanded.

"What? No. Why would I have a weapon?" The shock of the question silenced her sobs. Was that a trick or was that real?

"You were reaching into your handbag."

"I was going to show Lorelei a picture of my daughter. She saved us both. Made it possible for us to have a life. It's been years since I've seen Lorelei." She turned to Lorelei, her brown ponytail swinging. "Do you not remember me?"

Lorelei shook her head, hating the anguish in the woman's voice. Pain came from disappointment and sorrow.

This woman thought Lorelei would remember her. Should remember her.

"I have amnesia," Lorelei blurted. "It's not you. I don't know myself. Or my cousin, Karli." She waved toward Karli.

The woman glanced at Karli, her gaze clearing. "Wow, you really look alike." She straightened and turned to Karli. "I'm Bonnie. Lorelei and Adam saved my daughter and me from my ex-husband. He was going to sell my daughter and kill me so he could pay off his debts."

"I'm so sorry," Karli said.

Bonnie nodded, sniffing. "Thanks. Lorelei was amazing. She protected us and arrested him and took down the group that was going to buy my daughter. It was the most terrifying thing I've ever been through, but Lorelei made sure we survived."

"She's good at her job," Karli said, a genuine smile for Bonnie.

"You really don't know me? Or anyone else?" Bonnie asked Lorelei.

Lorelei shook her head and turned so she could get out of the vehicle. Karli grabbed the crutches and held them for Lorelei to stand while Bonnie gasped.

"What happened?"

"I don't know," Lorelei admitted. "I was abducted and tortured and left for dead. I was lucky. Someone found me, and I've been trying to recover, but my memories are not coming back quickly."

"Oh, wow. I'm so sorry. And I'm sorry I scared you. I know you don't know me, but I really do want to show you pictures of my daughter. Maybe it'll help?" Bonnie looked at Karli as if asking for permission.

Karli nodded, and Bonnie reached into her handbag.

Lorelei moved away from the vehicle and closed the

door. They stood at the curb to look at pictures of an early-twenties dark-haired white girl that Lorelei swore she'd never seen before.

"She's beautiful," Lorelei said.

Bonnie nodded. "She is. And smart. She's in college right now, trying to decide what she wants to study, but she's considering law enforcement because of you."

"Wow, that's a huge honor," Karli said.

Lorelei nodded. "It is. I know it's not an easy job, and I hope my current condition doesn't scare her away from it."

Bonnie smiled, her eyes kind and understanding. "I hate that you're hurt, but I know what you do is important. You're saving lives. You saved ours. We would both be dead if you and Adam hadn't helped us. If my daughter wants to do the same thing, wants to be like you, nothing could make me more proud."

"Thank you," Lorelei whispered. The compliment made her feel warm and fuzzy inside. Like her life had value. She had value.

"Are you just here to visit your cousin while you recover?"

Lorelei shook her head. "I've sort of moved here. I guess."

Karli stepped in. "It's a long story, but Lorelei and Adam came here for a case and stuck around. Adam got married a few weeks ago."

"Oh, that's so exciting! I'm so happy for him. And I feel safer knowing you are here and working to keep Niagara Falls safe. There's been a lot going on lately that has had me wondering if we should find somewhere else to live, but Lexi loves it here and I can't imagine not being close to her."

"It's a great place to live," Karli said. "And the people working to keep us safe are all working hard."

Lorelei recognized that as a diplomatic answer, one intended to stop the conversation. Was it because Karli was one of the victims? One of the people directly tied to the hell that was happening?

And why the fuck couldn't Lorelei remember any of it? Ugh. It was so damn frustrating.

"Oh, yes. I have no doubt." Bonnie smiled. "I should go. Let you get on with your day. Lorelei, it was so nice to see you. I really hope I run into you again. Hello to Adam for me. Nice to meet you, Karli."

"You, too, Bonnie. Have a good day," Karli said.

Bonnie waved and moved past them, continuing her walk down the sidewalk.

"Did you trust her?" Karli asked.

Lorelei glared at her cousin. "I don't trust myself. How the hell do I know if she was telling the truth?"

"Let's text Adam when we get inside. Make sure he knows her story."

Lorelei nodded, following Karli to the restaurant door and watching Bonnie walk away.

A server led them to a table by the front windows, and Karli immediately pulled out her phone. She typed out a message, then set her phone on the table to wait for Adam's reply.

The server came back with waters for both of them and asked if they were ready to order.

Lorelei shot Karli a panicked look, but Karli just smiled. "We need a minute, please."

"Not a problem. Take your time."

"Thank you," Karli said, smiling at the server. "What is wrong with you?" she hissed at Lorelei.

"I have no idea what I like. None of this is familiar to me."

"I will order. You don't have to freak out. What have you been eating all week?"

"Whatever Vinnie puts in front of me," Lorelei admitted. She hadn't realized how much she was relying on Vinnie until that moment. "He hasn't asked what I like, just cooked food and gave it to me. How does he know what I want to eat?"

"He probably watched what you were eating in the hospital. And he's pretty healthy, so he's making things that he likes and if you're not complaining, he's assuming you're okay with it."

Lorelei nodded. "You're probably right."

The server came back, and Karli ordered for both of them. Lorelei sipped her water and looked around. No recognition at all.

It was getting frustrating.

"I hate this," Lorelei said when the server walked away.

"Hate what?"

"Not knowing anything about myself. That woman, Bonnie, she could have been dangerous. She could have been innocent. She could have been anyone. I had no idea who she was. I walk by the mirror sometimes and wonder who is right there before I realize it's me. I am sick of not knowing what the hell is going on."

"Is that why you opened the computer today?"

Lorelei considered the question, then nodded. "I guess so. I... I want answers, but it's terrifying. The nightmares..."

"Are you still having them?"

Lorelei shook her head. "Not since Vinnie started sleeping with me again."

Karli's eyes widened. "What?"

"Not sex, just sleeping in the same bed as me."

Karli's raised brow said she didn't believe Lorelei.

"There's been no sex."

"Just orgasms?"

Lorelei's cheeks burned. "There have been a few of those."

"Okay, start at the beginning and tell me how this all happened."

Lorelei sighed heavily and grinned. "I yelled at him."

"And he gave you orgasms?"

"Basically, yeah." She told Karli the whole story about threatening to leave and Vinnie's reaction, then the aftermath and how the last few days had gone.

"And things are okay?" Karli asked.

"Of course. Why wouldn't they be?"

Karli inhaled, then let her breath out slowly.

Lorelei couldn't remember her training, but she knew that slow breath meant Karli was about to say something Lorelei was not going to like.

"I keep going back and forth, but I wish you'd come to live with Cade and me. That you were around people you know."

Lorelei wanted to argue that she didn't really know any of them, but she kept her mouth shut.

"Vinnie is a stranger. We believe he's one of the good guys, but we've thought that before."

"He knows Marcus and Frannie," Lorelei said, remembering Frannie saying she spoke to Karli. Maybe that would ease her cousin's mind.

Karli nodded. "I know. And Frannie said he's good. Said she would trust him with her life."

"So why can't I?" Lorelei asked.

Karli shook her head. "It's not that you can't. It's just that..."

"You want me to trust you."

Karli looked up at Lorelei and nodded. The pain in her eyes said it hurt her that Lorelei chose Vinnie over Karli.

"I'm sorry," Lorelei said. "I do trust you. I wouldn't be here if I didn't. I wouldn't have told you about my notes. I wouldn't have let you in. But it's hard. It's so damn hard. I fucking hate my brain. I hate that I have no idea what is going on all the time. That I'm not sure how I'm supposed to feel, who I'm supposed to turn to, what I'm supposed to do. It's confusing and aggravating and miserable."

Karli reached across for Lorelei's hand. Her outburst drew the attention of diners closest to them, but Lorelei was having a hard time caring. She just wanted to remember something. Anything.

Karli's phone buzzed, and she glanced down at it. "It's Adam." She let go of Lorelei's hand and picked up the phone. "He said he remembers Bonnie. She was a little clingy, but she was telling the truth about her and Lexi and the ex-husband. The ex is in prison, but he cut a deal to flip on the group he was going to sell his daughter to."

"Sounds like a great idea," Lorelei dead-panned. "Why would we give people deals? He was going to sell his daughter."

Karli texted back to Adam, then set her phone down. "I don't get it, but if it means someone worse goes away for longer, I guess it's a good thing."

"Maybe I'm not a very good agent. I think they should all be in prison forever."

Karli grinned. "There's that spark that drove you to become an agent. When you first told me you were switching your major, I thought you were crazy."

"I switched my major?"

Karli nodded. "You did. You were a psychology major, but one of your friends went missing. She was on her way home from class one night and disappeared. No one ever found her. You spent an entire semester searching for her in every spare minute you had, and when you pissed all off the campus officers and the local and federal ones, you changed your major so no one would ever be lost forever like she was."

"Seriously?"

Karli nodded again, her gaze full of admiration. "I thought you were the most amazing person I'd ever known. You were so strong, and so smart, and so determined. I think a part of you thought you'd find Annie one day."

"Annie?" Lorelei asked. The name didn't ring a bell, but that didn't mean it wasn't in there somewhere.

"Yeah. Annie Lake. Do you recognize her name?"

Lorelei shook her head, hating that another person who mattered to her was gone from her memory. "I hate this."

"You'll get your memories back. I know you will."

"I hope so."

VINNIE COULDN'T REMEMBER EVER BEING SO happy to be on his way home from work. He loved his job. It gave him purpose and direction at a time when he had neither. Being a police officer, and then a SWAT officer, said he was making a difference in the world.

But he had something else he was enjoying just as much. And she was waiting for him at his apartment.

Vinnie had a smile on his face as he climbed the stairs to his floor. He expected Karli to be there, but the only one he wanted to see was Lorelei.

Voices inside his apartment surprised him. A male voice blended with the female voices. More than two voices.

Tension put him on edge, but they laughed, and Vinnie tried to relax. He never said Lorelei couldn't have people over. He just hadn't expected her to have a party.

Vinnie unlocked the door and walked in to Lorelei, Adam, Raina, Karli, and Cade all in his living room. They looked up when they realized he was there.

"Vinnie! You're back," Adam said. "How was work?"

"Um, it was good. How are you? How was your honeymoon?"

Adam's smirk, followed by his shared grin with Raina, told Vinnie far more than he wanted to know about Adam and Raina. "Honeymoon was very good."

"Ew," Karli said.

"Just wait until it's yours," Raina countered.

Karli's eyes went wide.

Cade threw his arm around her shoulder. "Don't scare her off for me."

"Are you going to propose?" Raina asked.

"Not right now," Cade said. "When we're ready."

"Ooh, I can't wait!" Raina gushed.

"Lorelei was going through some of the files with me," Adam said, extracting himself from the couch and moving toward Vinnie at the door. "Sorry we all invaded your space."

"The files?" Vinnie asked, glancing at Lorelei. He thought she was going to wait for him.

Adam nodded. "Yeah, on her new computer. She used some kind of shorthand that she doesn't know and hoped I would be able to put some pieces together."

"Oh. Um, good. I hope you could." Adam was Lorelei's partner. Of course she went through the computer with him. Vinnie had no reason to be upset. Or jealous. He wasn't an agent.

"Unfortunately, no." Adam shook his head, his gaze unfocused, like he was trying to figure something out. "She and Karli were looking at everything this morning, and Karli was no help. She thought maybe I would know something, but none of it makes sense to me. Lorelei had her own investigation and code for her notes. Even Cade couldn't decipher it and he keeps notes in code, too."

"Cade? And Karli? And none of you could figure it out?" Vinnie asked. That wasn't really what he wanted to know. He wanted to know how many people Lorelei shared her notes with that weren't him.

He offered. He told her they'd go through everything when he got home. But she didn't wait for him. She shared it with her cousin and her partner. And her cousin's boyfriend.

Not just her partner, who would have access to the same information, but two civilians. Two people who wouldn't know what Lorelei knew.

She didn't want his help. Not for anything besides orgasms and sleeping.

"It's not simple," Adam continued, as if Vinnie's question was only about the complexity of the code. "We'll keep trying, though. Next time you work, Lorelei is probably going to come into the office with me so we can go through things in a place where we have access to more information."

"Sounds good. I'm going to jump in the shower."

"Wash off the day. I get that," Adam said. He returned to the couch and wrapped himself around his wife.

Vinnie walked away. He wasn't in their group. Just like when he found Lorelei, he was an outsider. In his own home.

Vinnie remembered to grab clothes before he went to the bathroom. He locked the door and turned on the shower, frustrated with himself for thinking Lorelei was there for him.

It was sleep and orgasms. She didn't think he was worthy of sharing her notes. Of confiding in about the case she was working on. Just the physical stuff.

Vinnie wanted to shout into the water, but he kept it in. It wouldn't change anything. He couldn't force her to open up to him.

The apartment was quieter when he got out of the shower. He dressed and stalled as long as possible before admitting to himself it looked weird for him to be in the bathroom so long.

Adam and Raina were gone when he walked out of the bathroom, but Karli and Cade were still there.

"We were going to go out to dinner. Want to join us?" Cade asked.

"Nah, I'm good," Vinnie said.

"Are you sure?" Lorelei asked.

Vinnie nodded. "Yep. You go have fun. Enjoy your night out. I'm not your keeper. You don't have to check with me before you do things."

"I'm not... I wanted you to join us. That's all."

"It was a long day. I'm just going to stay in. I might be asleep when you get back, so lock the door. Unless you're staying with Karli and Cade?" It was petty, but he couldn't help but ask.

"I'm coming back here. Unless you don't want me to."

"It's up to you where you want to be. I'm not going to force you to stay here."

"Why are you acting like this?"

Vinnie shrugged. "I'm not acting like anything. Just want you to do what you want."

"I... I'll be back after dinner."

"Whatever you want."

Lorelei's eyes narrowed, trying to figure out why he was being an asshole.

He couldn't explain it. But he also couldn't stop.

"I'll see you later."

"If that's what you want."

"It is," she said. She moved toward him like she was going to touch him, but she stopped. She shook her head once, then turned and went to the door.

"What was that about?" Karli whispered as the door closed.

"I wish I knew," Lorelei answered.

That makes two of us.

13

———

Lorelei's mind stayed on Vinnie all through dinner. It was supposed to be a fun night with her cousin and friends, but all she wanted to do was talk to Vinnie. To find out why he was upset. To fix it.

"Do you want this?" Karli asked, dragging Lorelei back to the conversation around them.

Lorelei shook her head, not caring about the last egg roll on the plate in front of her. She wasn't really hungry. Not after walking away from Vinnie.

"Are you worried about Vinnie?" Karli asked.

Lorelei forced a smile to her lips and shook her head again. Pretend, pretend, pretend. "No. I'm sure it's just something with work. It's fine."

"It'll be fine. And if it's not, you can just move in with Cade and me."

Lorelei smiled. She had the urge to tell Karli to quit pushing. She didn't want to move in with Karli and Cade. She wanted to be with Vinnie.

But if Vinnie didn't want her there, Lorelei needed another place to go. She couldn't isolate herself from the people who cared about her. Even if she didn't remember them.

Karli wrapped her arm around Lorelei's shoulders and hugged her tight. "I'm so happy you're here, cuz," Karli said.

Two young girls in matching jean overalls. Curly black hair in braids. Blue beads on the ends. Red shirts, white shoes, sparklers in their hands. They laughed together, spinning in circles until the sparklers went out and they collapsed together.

"I'm so happy you're here, cuz," young Karli said. She threw her arms around young Lorelei.

"Me, too."

"July Fourth," Lorelei whispered.

"What?" Karli asked.

"July Fourth. We were in matching outfits and playing with sparklers. There was a big white house and adults around a fire pit. Water. Maybe a beach? Is that real?" Lorelei looked up at Karli and found tears rolling down her cousin's face.

"You remember that?" Karli whispered.

Lorelei nodded. "You said *I'm so happy you're here, cuz,* and the memory popped up. It is a memory, right? We were young, eight or nine?"

"Yeah. The whole family rented a house for the July Fourth week. We shared a room and insisted on matching outfits for the holiday. Your mom did our braids. We loved to swing them and make the beads clack together."

"I remember that."

"You do?" Adam asked.

Lorelei nodded, feeling a piece of herself snap into place. It was the first memory that didn't terrify her. The first one that wasn't about her being attacked.

"That's amazing, Lorelei," Raina said, reaching for Lorelei's hand.

Lorelei sat with the memory, trying to conjure up more. She couldn't see her mom or remember swinging their hair, but laughing with Karli was solid.

Karli was telling the truth about being cousins.

The relief that knowledge brought was shocking. Lorelei didn't realize she was holding on to doubt about what Karli said. That she questioned if her cousin was really her cousin.

"Are you okay?" Karli asked.

Lorelei looked over at her, seeing the woman next to her in a different way. "I am. Thank you for sticking with me through all of this. For not giving up on me."

"I would never." Karli grabbed Lorelei's hand and squeezed.

"None of us would," Raina said.

Lorelei nodded, realizing she had the attention of the entire table. Adam and Cade were smiling, and Karli and Raina were wiping tears from their eyes. It was a big moment.

And the one person Lorelei wanted to share it with wasn't there.

Vinnie had been her rock for two weeks. He'd put his career at risk to save her, then continued to risk it by not going back, even though his boss demanded it.

And on his first day back, he withdrew from her.

Lorelei wasn't going to let him do that. She was going to find out what was going on and make it right. Get back to where they were before he went back to work. Be there for him the same way he was there for her.

She wasn't giving up on him.

VINNIE HEATED up a frozen meal and sat on the couch. His stomach churned, and his mind mocked him.

She doesn't want you.

You're not important.

You have nothing to offer her.

He hated that the words were truth. Lorelei was bigger than him. She was better than him. She had people around her that would be there for her, no matter what. People who cared and came running when she needed them.

He'd never had that. He was alone. The only person who ever watched out for him was Marcus. His parents... They barely earned the titles. He didn't remember his mom. The only memories he had were his grandmother telling him she was a waste of a human and she left him when he was two.

Of course, Grandmother hated his mother because she was the reason Vinnie ended up living with her. His father wasn't much better than his mother. He worked odd jobs and spent more time away than at home. He was content to drop Vinnie with his mother and disappear for weeks at a time. Something he never did until Vinnie's mother took off.

And his grandmother? She tolerated him. She let him stay because he had nowhere else to go, but if he did, she would have packed his bags for him.

Vinnie got the hell out of there as quickly as he could. He knew the only person he could count on was himself, so why pretend otherwise? When his grandmother died, Vinnie made sure she had a nice funeral, and the seven people who attended said nice things, but Vinnie only felt relief. He didn't have to think about anyone else.

For seventeen years, Vinnie didn't worry about anyone else. Didn't think twice about what anyone else was doing or if they were okay.

Then he met Lorelei.

She's too good for you.

"Yeah, I know," he told the voice in his head. Vinnie sighed and turned off the TV. He needed to do something that would wear his mind and body out. Something that would mean he could sleep.

Preferably before Lorelei got back. If she came back.

He laced up his sneakers and stepped onto the treadmill. He pushed the speed higher and higher until he had to sprint to keep up with the belt spinning beneath him.

His feet pounded the belt. He stared at the wall on the other side of the apartment, the taunts of his mind echoing in time with his pace.

Not good enough.

Not worthy.

She doesn't want you.

Vinnie ran until sweat poured off his body and his muscles screamed at him to stop. He slapped the stop button to bring the belt to a halt, accepting he'd fall if he didn't stop soon. Having her return with him crumpled against the wall was not going to change her mind about him.

Nothing would.

Vinnie stalked to the shower. He didn't want Lorelei to come back when he was in there, so he rushed through his second shower of the afternoon, then stretched out on the couch.

It was a dick move, but it was his only move. She couldn't sleep there with him. But if he went to the bed, she would crawl in next to him.

He couldn't pretend he was okay. He had to put distance between them again. She was going to leave, and she was going to leave soon. He had to protect himself from it. Leave first. Make sure she didn't have anything to hold on to.

He gritted his jaw and told himself it was for the best. She deserved more than he could offer her. The sooner she realized that, the better it would be for both of them.

Vinnie was almost asleep when he heard her key slide into the lock. He sucked in a breath and waited, not moving. He left the light on in the bedroom for her so she could see, but she would notice him on the couch.

Another voice outside told him Lorelei wasn't alone. Karli. Her family. The person who should be taking care of Lorelei. Not because he didn't want to, but because people counted on family. Or so he heard.

"Is he asleep?" Karli whispered.

"It looks like it."

"Are you sure you're okay here?"

"Yeah. He's a good man."

"I know that, but do you really want to be here? After that memory came back, you know me again."

Her memory came back? Vinnie wanted to sit up and ask her about it, wanted to find out everything.

But he didn't. If her memory came back, she would definitely be leaving soon. She would know she could trust the others and make the only choice that made sense. She would go stay with one of them.

"I do know you, but I also know him. I want to be here. I'll be fine. I promise. We'll talk tomorrow."

"Okay. Good night, cuz."

"Good night." Lorelei closed the door and locked it.

Her silence, and the tingle traveling up his spine, told Vinnie she was watching him. Trying to decide if he was really sleeping or just faking it.

He didn't move.

After a few minutes, she let out a breath and moved away from the door. The clack of her crutches was quiet and slow. Retreating to the bedroom.

A door closed, but the light didn't dim, so it was likely the bathroom. Vinnie cracked his eyelid and looked. The bathroom door was closed.

Vinnie shifted quietly, trying to settle the restlessness he felt. He wasn't one to avoid problems. He preferred to handle things. But nothing felt normal with Lorelei. He was equal parts scared of losing her and aware he would.

He fucking hated it.

The bathroom door opened. Her crutches carried her a few steps out of the bathroom, then stopped. She was watching him again.

He didn't move. Again.

"I wish you were awake so I could talk to you," she said. Her voice was a normal tone. She wasn't trying to be quiet. She was trying to wake him up. "Hopefully, I can tell you about my day in the morning."

Vinnie held his breath. He ached to hear what was going on with her. To have her tell him about her memory and her day and her cases.

But he didn't move. She chose Adam and Karli to share with. He offered to help her with her cases, and she chose them. He understood. He wasn't mad. Hurt, yes. But not mad.

The writing was on the wall. And he was going to wait it out, and let her go when she made the choice to leave him.

Just like everyone else in his life.

HE WASN'T ASLEEP. She knew he wasn't asleep. He was too still. And he was barely breathing.

But he didn't want to talk, so Lorelei went to bed. She wasn't ready to sleep yet, but with the laptop in the living room, she didn't have much to do.

She was restless and frustrated. She'd gotten used to curling up with Vinnie and talking for a while before they went to sleep. And she'd gotten used to his hands wandering her body and settling her before she fell asleep.

Lorelei replayed the memory of her and Karli over and over again in her mind. She wanted more memories. She wanted to know who she was.

Not knowing who she was... It was lonely. Like living a stranger's life. Even with others telling her who she was, Lorelei felt like she was alone. And she was starting to think it wasn't on accident.

Karli and Adam never mentioned a relationship. No one who claimed to care about her showed up. She saw no evidence of another person in her apartment, and there was nothing to suggest she had a significant other in her life.

Ever.

A stranger found her. A man she'd never met before, a man who knew her from work, went looking for her and found her. No one else did. What did that say about who Lorelei was? What did that say about her life?

She didn't want to be alone. She didn't want to lie on her couch and die. She didn't want to be taken because she didn't have anyone.

It didn't matter that she didn't know who she was before, Lorelei knew she didn't want to be that woman again. She didn't want to be someone who existed separate from everyone else in her life.

Karli had Cade. Adam had Raina. Jessica had Braden. Frannie had Marcus. Even the women Lorelei hadn't met yet had people. They were paired up. They had their person who would stop at nothing to find them if they went missing.

Lorelei had no one.

Except Vinnie.

But did she have him? Would he be there for her after she was healed? He acted like he wanted her to be there. Before, at least.

Lorelei swung her legs out of the bed and reached for her crutches. She grabbed a blanket and pillow from the bed and tucked them under her arm.

Each step was a challenge. The blanket slipped, so she stopped and wrapped it around her shoulders. The pillow fell. She thought about leaving it behind, but she knew she needed it.

One step after another, she slowly made her way to the door. Everything hurt, and not because of her injuries. Because she knew she wasn't who she wanted to be. But she was going to change that.

She moved out of the room, one step at a time. Vinnie was snoring softly on the couch, actually asleep this time. He looked peaceful, like nothing could get to him.

Lorelei was a little jealous. When she first got home, she was angry that he was pretending to sleep and didn't want to talk to her, but now she just missed him. She missed curling up next to him. It was frustrating that he was able to sleep without her by his side.

She debated. If she laid down next to him, he'd wake up. He worked all day and needed his rest.

But she needed him.

It was selfish, but she was feeling a little selfish. The

notes in her files led her to believe she didn't trust anyone. Not even Adam, who couldn't explain her shorthand.

Lorelei moved the last few feet to Vinnie. His brown hair fell over his forehead, softening him. His lips were full and parted with each breath. His lashes flickered, but his eyes never opened.

His hand was tight on the blanket he'd covered himself with. The white sleeves of his tee stretched tight around his biceps. His legs stretched to the other end of the couch, filling all the space.

Lorelei wished she understood what it was about him that made her feel so safe, but it didn't really matter. Even having a memory of Karli didn't make Lorelei want to leave Vinnie. She knew Karli and Cade would welcome her into their home, just like Adam and Raina would, or Frannie and Marcus. Others had offered. Lorelei had people who would be there for her if she needed them to be, but Vinnie was the one she wanted to be around. Vinnie was... different.

Lorelei dropped the pillow next to the couch. She unwound the blanket and let it fall on top of the pillow. She leaned her crutches against the wall, making sure they were secure and wouldn't fall during the night. She rested her weight on the arm of the couch and picked up her right leg. She'd never lowered herself to the floor, but it couldn't be that different from anything else. Just farther to fall.

She supported her weight and slid down, doing her best to go slow. The couch was the only reason she made it to the floor with a soft thud instead of shaking the entire building.

Vinnie made a noise, but he didn't wake up.

Lorelei let out the breath she was holding and positioned herself in front of the chair. Her head was close to the couch, but her body stretched away so Vinnie wouldn't step on her if he got up during the night. She shoved the pillow into the right spot and put her head on it. She twisted the blanket around herself.

The floor was not comfortable.

She turned on her side and immediately rolled onto her back again. She should have brought another pillow for her ankle, but she didn't think about it.

She closed her eyes and drew a breath. It didn't matter if she slept like shit, she had Vinnie there. He would keep her safe. He would make sure she was okay.

He groaned and moved, rolling over and letting his hand fall over the side of the couch.

She looked up at it. She reached up and threaded her fingers through his. He squeezed her hand, and she finally relaxed. He was there. She was okay.

14

VINNIE STIRRED WHEN LORELEI CRIED OUT. HIS MIND processed her call before he woke.

She cried again, a whimper.

His eyes opened, taking in the room and searching for her.

He was on the couch. The day before came back to him with sharp and painful clarity. She didn't need him.

She made another noise, and Vinnie realized she wasn't in the bedroom. She was there. Close. In the room with him.

He looked down and saw her outline on the floor.

She thrashed and flung her arm.

He reached for her, taking her hand.

She stilled immediately. A rapid breath said she woke up. She let it out slowly, as though trying to pretend she was still asleep.

Vinnie let her have the moment, not calling her on it. He rubbed her knuckles, hoping it soothed her. It usually did, but she was usually asleep when he was helping her through a nightmare. She rarely woke up.

"Are you awake?" she whispered, her voice barely audible. Unlike the night before when she spoke in a normal tone as he pretended to sleep.

"Yeah."

"I'm sorry I woke you."

"You can't help having nightmares."

She breathed in what sounded suspiciously like a sob.

"What are you doing out here?"

Her hand tightened to a fist, the air in the room thick with sudden tension. "I didn't want to be alone."

"Did you have a nightmare earlier?"

The sound of her head rubbing the pillow told him she was shaking her head. "I wanted to be close to you."

"It didn't keep your nightmare away tonight."

"That's not why I wanted to be close to you," she whispered.

"Then why?" The question came out harsher than he intended.

She was quiet for a long moment. She was still awake, but she was choosing her words carefully. "I had a memory come back tonight when I was at dinner. It was Karli and me when we were kids. Our families rented a beach house. It was so vivid and... fun. I felt alive. I was surrounded by family and happy."

Vinnie swallowed roughly. He hadn't lost his memory and still didn't have any like what she described. "That sounds nice."

"It was. But..."

"But?"

"That's not my life now. Before I lost my memory."

"How do you know?"

She scoffed. "The person who found me was a stranger. The person who took me knew if they left me in my own apartment, no one would find me until it was too late. My cousin has Cade. My partner is married. My friends are paired off. Everyone in my life has someone else. I'm alone."

"You're the least alone person I've ever known," Vinnie grunted.

"It doesn't feel that way to me. I feel like... I feel like everyone is just checking in. But none of them are my person. No one knows what my shorthand means, which says I never let them into my mind. I didn't have a significant other, or at least not one who wants to admit we were together. And the one person who came looking for me doesn't want to be around me."

"Why do you think that?" Vinnie asked.

The darkness of the room hid her from him, but he could feel her reaction to his question. Not being able to see each other meant Vinnie could ask a question like that and not worry about her seeing the longing on his face. The longing he knew he sucked at hiding.

Her friends probably laughed at the poor sap he was, begging for scraps from her. Sitting in his apartment and feeling sorry for himself while she was out with them. Enjoying life and kicking ass and surrounded by people.

"I wanted you to go to dinner with us tonight. I wanted to be close to you. I slept on the damn floor of your apartment because being in the other room was too far from you and you pretended to be asleep when I got home so you didn't have to talk to me."

"I..."

"Don't lie to me, Vinnie. If nothing else, don't lie to me."

He drew a breath and let it out slowly. "You're going to leave."

"What?"

"You're going to leave me. You're going to go back to your life and your world and I'm not going to be a part of it. I wasn't before this, and once all your memories come back, I won't be a part of your life. I know that. And I'm... I don't want to stand in your way of rebuilding that life."

"That's fucking bullshit."

"What?"

"Why... You're the one and only person I feel safe around right now. You're in my life whether you like it or not. I want to be around you. I want... to be with you. I wanted to spend time with you tonight."

"You just didn't want to share your files with me," he said, sounding like a petulant child even to his own ears.

She let out a breath that sounded half like a laugh. "That's what all this is about? Because I didn't show you the files? I'll show them to you right now." She made a move like she was going to get up.

"Don't. I don't want your pity or whatever. You..."

"I what?"

"You didn't feel like you could share that with me. I'm not going to force you to."

She laughed. "Do you know why I looked at those files when you were gone?"

He shook his head, then remembered she couldn't see him in the dark. "No."

"I was afraid I would uncover something horrible about myself. That you would see something that changed your mind about me."

"Why would you think that?"

"Because I care what you think about me. I want you to..."

"To what?"

"To want me in your life as much as I want you in mine."

"I don't have anything to offer you, Lorelei. I'm nothing special."

"That's not true."

"It is. I live in a one-bedroom apartment in a crappy complex because I've never had anything. I... I don't have any happy childhood memories. My mom left my dad and me when I was too young to remember her. My dad moved in with my grandmother, but he was barely around. My grandmother resented that she had to raise me and wasn't afraid to let me know how she felt. There were no vacations or happy times. I was a burden. My whole life, I was a burden."

"You saved my life," she whispered.

"That was doing my job."

"No. It's so much more than that. You risked your job to find me. You walked away. You could have lost your job, and you were willing to do it to find me."

"Because I knew you would be able to stop all of this. I believe in you."

"All I am right now is a burden. I don't know anything about what I'm doing. I can't remember anything about the man who took me or what he wanted to know. I've invaded your home, your life. I never asked you if it was okay. I never asked you anything. Just let you take care of me, let you put your life aside for me."

"I wanted to," he confessed. "I wanted to do whatever I needed to do to help you. That won't change."

"Then how can you say you have nothing to offer? How can you think what you're doing for me isn't significant?"

"What am I doing that is significant? That anyone else couldn't do for you?"

"No one else makes me feel the way you do."

"You can give yourself orgasms," he blurted.

She breathed a laugh. "Well, I'm happy to hear that, but I meant making me feel safe."

"Oh." Vinnie felt like a dick for going straight to sex.

"I know it doesn't make any sense. I know no one gets it. But the only time I feel like I don't have to look over my shoulder is when I'm with you. When you're right there, making sure I have everything I need before I even know I need it."

"The doctor said that'll probably change as your memories come back."

She breathed a laugh. "I don't think it will, Vinnie. Karli and I talked a lot today, and the way she talks about Cade is the way I feel about you."

"What?"

"When she was in trouble, Cade was there for her. He was the person who helped her, but he was also the one who made her feel like she could do anything." Lorelei drew a breath. "I'm terrified of what's in my mind. Of the memories. Of who I was. I don't want to go back to that person. Someone who doesn't have a person who's watching out for me. Who knows when I'm missing. Who will stop at nothing to find me. Who's alone."

"You're not alone."

"Not when I'm with you. As long as you don't shut me out."

He was quiet for a minute. Letting her in was... The thought made his chest ache. He wanted her in his life. But everyone left him. Everyone decided he wasn't worth the time and energy. He wasn't worthy of loving.

"I'll try," he said.

"Good. So will I. Not that you asked."

He exhaled a laugh.

"Now, will you take me to bed because this floor is killing me?"

"Yeah, I can do that."

WHEN LORELEI STIRRED in the morning, Vinnie was still in bed with her. His back was to her, and the steady rise and fall of his side said he was sleeping. For real.

Her ten days were up. She was feeling stronger, and she was not willing to wait another day. She wanted Vinnie.

She kissed his back and slid her hand under the tee he slept in. His skin was warm and smooth. She eased her hand to his stomach, brushing over a patch of hair before reaching his bellybutton. She kissed his neck and moved her hand up to his chest.

He'd never let her touch him, so she wasn't going to push the limits, but she wanted to feel his skin.

She lifted her shirt off her stomach so she could feel his warmth against her bare flesh. With her hand on his chest, her belly to his back, and her lips against his neck, she knew the moment he woke up.

"Lorelei?" he groaned.

She didn't say anything, just continued what she was doing.

His soft moan said he wasn't against it. He reached back and cupped her hip, pulling her body closer to his.

She slid her hand back down his body, stopping short at the edge of his shorts. She teased the soft hair she found peeking out from his waistband and dug her fingers into his flesh.

He groaned again, then flipped so fast her arm got caught between them. He tugged her close, letting her feel the way he'd responded to her early morning exploration, then kissed her hard, prying her lips apart with an eager tongue that plunged deep into her mouth and teased her right back.

When he tried to push her to her back, she stopped him.

He pulled back, looking at her with glassy, confused eyes.

"No clothes. I want to feel all of you."

"But—"

"My time is up, Vinnie. If you don't want this, I won't push, but I want you. I want to feel you inside me. I want to make you feel as good as you make me feel. I want you."

He groaned and dropped his forehead to hers. His eyes were closed, and his body tense. The only part of him that moved was his cock twitching against her hip. "I don't want to hurt you."

"You could never," she breathed. "I trust you."

His eyes opened at her words, and his breath hitched.

She cupped his jaw. "I trust you, Vinnie. And I want you. Please."

"Last night—"

"Please don't tell me no."

"I don't think I could ever tell you no."

"Then kiss me."

He lowered himself over her slowly, giving her time to stop him. She had no intention of doing so. She lifted to meet him in the middle, drawing him down to her with an arm around his neck.

His lips against hers made her sigh. He was familiar and safe. He was exactly what she wanted. She closed her eyes and gave in to the feel of his body next to hers and his lips against hers.

His hand grazed over her body, tentative and careful. He lifted her tank top and spread his hand wide on her belly. When he pulled back, she blinked her eyes open.

"I want to see you," he whispered, his gaze locked on the exposed strip of flesh. "I want to look at you, Lorelei."

"Yes," she breathed. She wanted to see him, too. All of him.

He eased her shirt up her belly, kissing the skin he uncovered. When he reached her breasts, he sat up and used both hands, slipping them under her tank top and palming her breasts. He groaned and drew a sharp breath, then pushed her shirt out of the way.

She leaned up and let him pull it off her body.

He tossed it to the side, then put his hands right back on her breasts. "When I walked into your hospital room and saw you like this, I almost couldn't walk out. You were so beautiful, even injured and unsure."

"And now?"

"Now, you've given me permission, and it's so much better. To touch you and see you. And kiss you." He leaned down and drew one nipple between his lips, swirling his tongue around the tight bud. "So good," he whispered against her skin.

Lorelei's back arched to press her breast into his mouth.

He groaned and sucked more of her into his mouth, using his hand to tease the other nipple.

"Vinnie," she whispered. She clutched his head, threading her fingers into his hair and holding him tight.

He sat up and tugged his shirt over his head, throwing it to the side before returning to her breast.

She spread her hand across his back, loving the feel of his skin under her fingertips. She was torn between focusing on his skin or his lips on her breasts. Both felt like the best thing she'd ever experienced.

Then he moved, lifting up to kiss her again. He parted her lips with his tongue and teased the waist of her shorts.

She lifted her hips to encourage him, and he groaned.

His hand slid beneath the edge of her shorts, inside her

panties. They both stilled as he worked his way through her curls to her soaked core.

Vinnie groaned and dipped a finger inside her.

Lorelei whimpered and lifted her hips, trying to get him deeper inside.

He pumped his finger into her, then he swiped his thumb over her clit, and she nearly screamed. "Get your shorts off," he ordered.

She shoved at the fabric, pushing to get it over her hips as he continued to play with her body. "Vinnie."

He withdrew his hand from her and took over the task of removing her shorts, taking extra care to get her clothes over her cast. "Are you okay?"

She nodded. "As long as you come back."

"Let me look at you."

She resisted the urge to cover her body. She had curves and rolls. She was strong, but she wasn't thin. Being surrounded by other women who sported the same general shape normalized her appearance and gave her a sense of confidence in who she was.

But with Vinnie's eyes on her, his cock twitching in his shorts, and the hungry look on his face, Lorelei knew she'd never felt more beautiful. She knew no man had ever made her feel the way Vinnie did in that moment. Like there was nothing she should change.

"Fuck, you're stunning." He crawled onto the bed again, settling next to her. His hands slid across her skin before settling between her thighs.

She shivered at his touch and parted her thighs for him.

He pressed two fingers into her and closed his eyes. "You feel so good."

"Shouldn't I be the one saying that?"

He chuckled and swiped his thumb over her clit. "I love the look on your face when you come."

She gasped. "You do?"

He nodded. "You look like you're so happy. Like nothing can bother you."

Lorelei snorted. "That's definitely not how I feel most of the time."

"Don't think about that right now."

He added a third finger, and all thought disappeared for her. He watched her as he thrust his fingers into her faster and faster. She lifted her hips and let the feel of his touching her carry her away.

"Let go, Lorelei."

She parted her lips and released an exhale. The pressure built inside her, everything swelling between her legs, and then let go. Her body shook and pulsed, her breath stopping while the orgasm crashed over her.

He licked her neck and whispered in her ear, "Again."

She drew a shaky breath and gave into the feel of his fingers, his cock against her side, his tongue on her neck. "Vinnie." She cried, she tensed, she swore she blacked out, and she came hard. Hard enough that her ankle hurt, hard enough that she didn't care.

"Fuck, that was beautiful," he breathed.

"Please, Vinnie. I want you. Please." She pried her eyes open to look at the man who made her feel like she was normal. Like she was okay.

He withdrew his hand from between her legs and licked his fingers, then shoved his shorts and briefs down, revealing a long and thick cock that she ached to feel inside her.

Lorelei reached for him, and he obliged, stepping closer to the bed so she could wrap her hand around him.

His dick twitched at her touch, and he groaned.

She wanted to draw him into her mouth, but she wanted him inside her more. She stroked him a few times, licking her lips and imagining his taste.

He pulled back. "Are you sure about this?"

"Yes." She met his gaze, making sure he knew she understood exactly what she was agreeing to. What she wanted since she stopped hurting so badly. From the day her head cleared and the painkillers stopped being the only thing she wanted, she wanted Vinnie.

He opened the drawer of his nightstand and grabbed a condom. He rolled it down his length, then positioned himself between her thighs. "Tell me if something hurts. I don't want to hurt you."

"You won't."

"I will do my best not to, but tell me. Please."

She nodded, knowing agreeing was the only way to get him to move.

And he did. He rubbed himself against her, sending shivers down her spine. He pressed into her, one inch at a time, all his muscles tense from holding back.

She hooked her good foot around his hip and pushed him forward, trying to hurry him up.

He glared at her, but he didn't fight her. When he sank all the way into her, he stilled. "Dammit, you feel good."

"Fuck yeah," she agreed. Lorelei knew she wasn't a virgin, but she didn't remember anyone else. She didn't know the feel of a man inside her. She didn't know anything could feel so good.

And when he moved, she wondered if sex had ever been so good. If she forgot about it because it was never worth remembering.

Vinnie started slow, but slow didn't last long. He

slammed into her, hooking her left knee over his forearm and opening her up wide.

Lorelei cupped his jaw and stared at him. She had no idea it was possible to feel as good as she did. To have her heart full to bursting and her body tight and tingly all over. To feel like everything happening was meant to be.

To even think being attacked was okay because it brought her to Vinnie.

He shifted his position and rubbed against her clit with his next thrust, and she exploded.

Her orgasm crashed over her fast and hard, stealing her breath and tightening every inch of her body.

He pounded harder, frantic and beautiful, as he lost his mind with her. His face twisted, his lips parting before he surged into her and let go. "Fuck!"

She closed her eyes and felt him twitching deep inside her. How could he ever think she wouldn't want him? That he didn't have something to offer?

She'd be dead if it weren't for Vinnie. And every day, he saved her all over again.

15

Vinnie stirred eggs and tried to wipe the smile off his face. It wouldn't leave.

He was happy. He couldn't think of the last time he was happy. Maybe early in his relationship with Allison. When she still wanted to spend time with him.

He pushed thoughts of his ex out of his mind. She didn't get to occupy the same space as Lorelei. Especially when Lorelei called out to him from the living room.

"What are we doing today?"

We. He liked the sound of that. "What do you want to do?"

She didn't answer until he walked out of the kitchen. Her gaze ran down his body, and his dick responded instantly. "You."

Vinnie chuckled. Four days of starting their day with sex wasn't enough. He didn't think he'd ever have enough of her. "I'm not going to argue with you on that. Is there anything else you want to do?"

"I feel like there's something I'm supposed to do. I don't know what it is, though."

"Adam didn't mention anything. I doubt you have a meeting or something on a Saturday."

Lorelei shook her head and glanced at the laptop. "I think I need to dig into that more."

"Okay."

She looked up at him. "Will you help me?"

He tried not to grin and lost. "Of course."

She smiled back and reached for the computer.

Vinnie finished making their breakfast and carried two plates out to the living room.

Lorelei had already logged into the computer and was looking at a file.

"What is this?" he asked.

She grabbed a slice of bacon and pointed to the screen with it. "It seems like this is where I made most of my notes. I have been trying to figure out what it means, though. I used a shorthand that I can't understand."

"Mind if I look?"

She turned the laptop toward him and let him take it from her lap. She picked up her plate and stabbed at the scrambled eggs while Vinnie focused on the screen.

"Are these initials?" he asked.

"That's what Karli wondered, too."

"But that doesn't make sense to you?"

She wrinkled her nose. "That seems too easy. Plus, Adam didn't know what any of them could mean. I would expect he would recognize at least some of them if they were initials."

"True." Vinnie looked at the notes and tried to make sense of what she could have recorded. Everything was typed in, so it wasn't a matter of not understanding her handwriting. It was only deciphering her code.

Pairs of letters followed by numbers. Sometimes she had

two numbers, sometimes three. There didn't seem to be an order to any of it.

"Could these be case numbers?"

"Adam said they're not."

Vinnie didn't like asking her the same questions she'd already answered. It felt like a waste of her time.

Initials made sense because there were two, but they could have been in a code. Still, there was no way to know what the code was.

So what else could they mean? Vinnie looked for patterns and repetition. One combination she had at the top and bottom of the first sheet.

"Do you know what this is?" he asked, showing her the duplicate.

"That's... weird. Why would I have put the same thing twice?"

Vinnie shook his head. "I don't know, but I'm sure there was a reason for it."

Lorelei nodded, staring off while she finished her breakfast.

Vinnie studied the list, unable to make sense of any of it.

When Lorelei set her plate on the coffee table, Vinnie handed the computer back to her. She clicked to another file, and she stopped.

"Abigail Painter," Lorelei said.

"Who is that?"

She shook her head. "I don't know, but I think she's someone I need to talk to."

"What if she's not?"

Lorelei shook her head slowly. She pointed to the screen. "LR. It's not first initials, it's the last letter in a name."

"Why do you think LR is Abigail Painter? It could be a hundred other people."

She nodded. "I know, but as soon as I saw LR, I knew her name. I don't know what case she's involved with, but I feel like I need to talk to her. Maybe I have a way to contact her."

Vinnie watched as Lorelei clicked through the computer like she knew exactly what she was looking for. Before she found an answer, his phone rang.

He glanced at her, but she was engrossed. He went to the kitchen where he'd left it plugged in overnight.

"Hey, Mol. What's up?"

"Oh, thank God you answered."

"What's wrong?" Vinnie's spine stiffened. Molly didn't call him often, and she never sounded the way she did. Scared but angry.

"I was in an accident."

"You what? Are you okay?"

"Yeah, yeah. I'm fine. But the cops are insisting I go to the hospital."

"She was wandering around and almost walked out into traffic," someone said in the background.

"Who was that?" Vinnie asked.

"Paramedic. He's trying to put me in an ambulance."

"Get in the fucking ambulance, Molly. Let me talk to the paramedic."

The phone was muffled for a second before a man's voice said, "This is Holden Cross."

"Hi, Holden. I'm Vinnie Morgan. I work with Molly. What hospital are you taking her to?"

"St. Nicholas. Will you be able to meet her there?"

"Yeah, I'll be there in ten minutes. Is she okay?"

Holden sighed. "I think she'll be fine, but she seems a bit confused. The airbag went off and probably gave her a concussion. It's better if she gets checked out."

"Do you know where her car is going?"

"It's probably going to be totaled. It's pretty bad. Someone turned in front of her. She had no time to stop. The accident wasn't her fault."

"Okay. Thanks, Holden. I really appreciate your help."

"Just doing my job. I'm glad she has someone who can get her. We should be at the hospital in ten minutes or so, so if you beat us there, just hang tight. I'll give them your name so they know to find you."

"Thanks."

"Giving you back to Molly now."

"I hate you," Molly said.

"You love me, and you know Holden's right. You'd have to be cleared before returning to work, anyway. If you get someone to clear you now, you won't have to sit out."

Molly grumbled. "I hate when you're right."

"I'll see you soon."

"Hey, Vinnie?"

"Yeah, Mol?"

"Thank you. I know you've got a lot going on right now, but I really appreciate you coming to get me."

"Anytime, Mol. I'll see you soon."

Vinnie hung up the phone and took a breath. His heart was racing. He didn't like his people getting hurt. And if the police and paramedic thought Molly needed to go to the hospital, she was hurt.

Vinnie went back to the living room, where Lorelei was still staring at the computer. "Hey. Did you find anything?"

Lorelei shook her head. "No. I wish I understood all this."

"You will. We'll figure it out." Vinnie rubbed the back of his neck. "I need to run out for a little bit."

That got her attention. Lorelei looked up at Vinnie, her gaze clearing after a minute. "Is everything okay?"

Vinnie nodded. "One of my teammates, Molly, was in a car accident."

Lorelei's eyes went wide. "Is she okay?"

Vinnie shrugged. "I think so, but the paramedics are taking her to the hospital. Her car is totaled. She needs a ride home."

"Do you want me to go with you?"

Vinnie shook his head and walked to the couch. "No, but thank you for offering. I'm sorry to run out on you like this."

"You're not. You have people in your life who need you."

Vinnie chuckled. "Molly doesn't need anyone. She's as tough as you are. She was on the call with me when we worked with you. She's a fan of yours."

Lorelei pressed her hands to her cheeks. "That's sweet. I don't feel like I'm the kind of person who should have fans."

"You are. And you do. I'm your biggest one." Vinnie leaned over and kissed her. "I hate to leave you right now."

"Go help your friend. Make sure she's okay. I'm going to keep digging into all this. When you get back, I'll share what I've learned."

Vinnie grinned. "Sounds like a date."

She snorted. "Weirdest date ever."

"Maybe, but if I promise to take you to bed afterward, maybe that'll make up for it."

Lorelei chuckled. "I like that promise."

He kissed her again, crashing his lips to hers. He didn't want to leave her, but he wasn't going to abandon Molly.

Vinnie pulled back and grinned when Lorelei didn't open her eyes right away. She bit her lower lip and smiled. "You know how to leave a woman wanting more."

"I hope not. I'd rather have you fully satisfied."

"I was... until you kissed me again and reminded me what you are capable of."

Vinnie kissed her once more. "I won't be long."

"Just make sure she's okay. I'll be fine here."

"Good. Let me know if you need anything. I'll be back as soon as possible."

"I hope your friend is okay."

"Me, too. Thanks."

"Bye."

He waved and let himself out. He locked the door, then walked away before he called another teammate to go help Molly instead.

LORELEI WAS ENGROSSED in her search for Abigail Painter. There was no contact listed, no information about the woman, just the two initials that might or might not actually lead to the woman Lorelei thought it led to.

She slapped the laptop closed and tossed it onto the couch next to her. She hated not knowing what the hell was going on. One step forward and six steps back. She got a memory, but it wasn't one that helped her solve the case. She knew a name, but it didn't lead her to a solution for the other names.

"When am I going to remember everything?" she asked aloud.

She needed to move. To get up and do something besides sit there. She grabbed her crutches, frustrated again that she couldn't just go for a walk. She slammed them down and stomped her way across Vinnie's small apartment.

Nothing made sense. And no one could help her.

Lorelei paced for a few minutes, then went back to her computer. She opened it up and wondered if there was software on it to let her search for people. Cops had that, right? It made sense she would, too.

She found something that looked like it would do the job, and she typed in Abigail Painter's name.

Within seconds, three women with the name were shown on the screen. One was local, and the other two were hours away.

Lorelei stared at the driver's license picture of the woman. She wanted to believe she recognized her, but the longer she stared, the less familiar she looked.

"This is pointless."

But it wasn't. There was an address. Two actually. Work and home.

She could go look for the woman. Maybe if she saw her in person, she would recognize her.

Lorelei debated on waiting for Vinnie, but she was going crazy sitting around his apartment all day. The address wasn't far, surprisingly. And the phone she had came with a credit card loaded onto it to use for things like getting a ride. She wasn't going to talk to the woman, just see if she recognized her when she saw her in person.

Lorelei flipped through the ride share app and figured out how to use it, then made her way downstairs. She requested a ride once she was on the ground floor, then walked outside to wait for the driver to pick her up.

A blue sedan pulled up in front of her. The license plate matched the one in the app, and the driver confirmed his name. Lorelei managed to get herself into the backseat and close the door, then told the driver she was ready.

Ten minutes later, she was standing in front of a salon on a quiet street not far from the center of the city. The building next door had bars on the windows and a cage across the front door. The one across the street was vacant, a broken window in the front and a faded sign for an old store telling the tale.

Lorelei wanted to pretend she was okay being there, but the reality was she had no idea.

"Agent Sloane?" a woman hissed.

Lorelei turned and saw Abigail Painter looking at her.

"What are you doing here?"

Lorelei opened her mouth to say something, but a vehicle came around the corner. Abigail's eyes went wide.

"He found me!"

"Who?"

Before Abigail could say anything, a man jumped out of the car. He went right for Abigail, a knife in his hand.

"No!" Abigail screeched.

Lorelei swung one of her crutches at the man, catching him off-guard. The sound of his arm breaking echoed off the buildings around them.

"Gah!" the man shouted. His knife fell to the ground. He bent to grab the knife with his other hand, and Lorelei swung again, hitting him in the shin.

"Agent Sloane, inside," Abigail shouted.

Lorelei moved as fast as she could, half-running on her good foot as she hurried to beat the man to the door.

He shouted as Lorelei made it inside.

Abigail slammed the door shut, the door locking automatically. She slid a cage in front of the door and backed away. She pulled out her phone. "How did he find me?" she whispered.

"I'm going to kill you, bitch! Come back out there. That stupid one led me right to you. You can't hide from me forever."

"Who is that?" Lorelei asked.

Abigail spun to face her, her eyes tugging together. "That's the man who kidnapped me."

"Who what?" Lorelei breathed.

"You found me. A year ago. He kidnapped me and was going to kill me. He drugged me and raped me and wanted to kill me, but you found me. Why did you come here?" Abigail asked.

"I don't... I'm sorry," Lorelei whispered.

The man hit the door, something solid connecting with the metal and the sound clanging through the whole building.

"Why are you here? You said we couldn't have contact ever again. Did you know he was back?"

Lorelei shook her head. "I don't know anything. I'm sorry. I... I thought you could help me figure out who I am. I had your name, and I thought..."

"What do you mean, help you figure out who you are?"

"I have amnesia. I was abducted and tortured and left for dead. My memories... I didn't know who you were. I don't know who I am."

"We need to call for help. He knows where I work now. He can find me. I have to leave."

"I'm sorry, Abigail. I had no idea."

She shook her head, her dark hair flowing over her shoulders. She turned her back on Lorelei and tapped out a number on her phone. "He's here."

Lorelei wondered who she was speaking to. It couldn't have been the police.

"Agent Sloane is here." Abigail glanced at Lorelei. "She doesn't know anything." Another pause, and Abigail looked away. "I can't tell if he left, but I want him put away."

"Who was that?" Lorelei asked when Abigail hung up the phone.

"It was Samuel MacNeil."

"Who's that?" Lorelei asked.

"He works for Rose Protection Agency. He and his partner, Austin Ward, kept me safe after you found me in Boston. You brought me here. Samuel was supposed to be the only person who knew my location."

"I'm sorry," Lorelei said. "I have no idea why I knew your name."

"You know Abigail Painter. That's not my real name."

"What's your real name?"

"It doesn't matter. I just…"

Abigail jumped when the man banged on the door again, letting them know he was still there, and still trying to get inside.

"How did he follow you? Did he track your car?"

"I took a ride share," Lorelei said.

"Your phone?"

"It's new. FBI issued."

"Then he must be watching your credit cards or something. There had to have been a way for him to track you."

The door rattled again, and this time, a different voice called out.

"It's me. He's gone."

"Dammit," Abigail breathed. She went to the door and unlocked it, letting two large men inside.

The first one looked around the room with a careful gaze. He was older, probably close to sixty if Lorelei had to guess. His hair was cut short, and what was left was gray. He had sharp, assessing brown eyes that scanned her, then quickly moved on. The gun strapped to his thigh, the knife on his belt, and the size of the man's arms said he was used to making shit happen.

The second man was younger, likely late-thirties. He was

dressed similarly in all black, with weapons strategically placed. His brown hair was longer, giving the man a softer look. His blue eyes added to the softness of him. He spared Lorelei a smile before he continued his observation of the room.

"Are you okay?" the first man asked Abigail.

Abigail nodded. "I saw her outside and walked out to see why she was here. She said she has amnesia and has no idea what's going on."

"She's telling the truth," the first man confirmed.

"He followed her. I don't know how, but he followed her here."

"We'll get you out of here," the second man said. "We won't let him get you."

Abigail nodded.

The first man walked over to Lorelei and stuck out his hand. "We've met, but since you don't remember, I figure I should introduce myself. I'm Samuel MacNeil."

Lorelei shook the man's rough hand. She wanted to recognize him, but there was nothing there.

"That's Austin Ward. We both work for Rose Protection Agency. We helped your partner and his wife, and our team was assigned to Dawn Patterson a few months ago."

Lorelei nodded like she had any idea who Dawn Patterson was. Karli said Dawn was going to let Lorelei stay at her house, but Lorelei hadn't actually met the woman. Not since she lost her memory.

"Sorry. I guess you don't know Ms. Patterson yet. Anyway, we need to get to work moving Ms. Painter. Do you have a ride back to wherever you're staying?"

Lorelei shook her head. "I got dropped off by a ride share service."

"We can get you back. But we need to move. Another

unit is coming to clear the place of any evidence of Abigail being here."

"Are they going to find him?" Abigail asked.

"We're going to do everything possible," Samuel said. "I promise you."

Abigail drew a breath and let it out slowly. She clearly trusted the men in the room.

Lorelei didn't get any bad feelings from either of them, but she wished she knew who they were.

"Agent Sloane saved me," Abigail said as they all made their way to the front. "She doesn't know who she is, but she saved me. Whacked him with her crutches and broke his arm. Maybe his knee. I'd be gone, or dead, if she hadn't done that."

"If I hadn't come, he never would have found you," Lorelei said.

"He would have eventually. I'll look over my shoulder until I know he's in the ground," Abigail said.

"We're not going to stop until we know you're safe," Samuel said. "Now, let's move."

16

———————

Vinnie pulled into the lot at Molly's apartment complex and found a spot near her building. He turned off his SUV and opened the door.

"You don't have to walk me up," she argued.

"It's that or you come home with me. You can have the couch."

"You already have a houseguest."

"Yep, and she's in my bed. The couch is empty."

"Ew. I don't want to hear you two having sex."

"Then you should let me walk you up."

Molly rolled her eyes and let Vinnie help her out of the SUV. She was sore, and the doctor said she'd be stiff for a few days, but she was lucky and had no major injuries.

"I hate this," Molly said.

"Everyone does. Are you sure Hannah's going to be able to stay with you?"

Molly nodded. "She's coming by after her date."

"And you're going to call me if she can't?"

Molly rolled her eyes. "Yeah, yeah."

Vinnie grinned and opened the door to her building.

Molly walked inside slowly. She had bruises on her shins from the airbags, and her shoulders and neck were sore from the impact. She wasn't cleared to return to work, but the doctor said there was no reason Molly couldn't go back in a week if she didn't feel worse. She probably had a concussion, but it was minor and there was nothing the doctor could do for it. He wasn't worried about major issues. Thankfully.

Molly's apartment was small like Vinnie's, but it was more updated. She had an elevator to get them to the fourth floor, and a quiet hallway that she constantly said was the only reason she could sleep during the day when they worked a night shift.

Vinnie wasn't so lucky, but he wasn't willing to spend his money on a nicer place. Not when he wasn't sure he'd be able to afford it forever.

Molly unlocked her door and led the way inside. She dropped her keys into a ceramic bowl on a table next to the door, then trudged to the living room and collapsed onto the couch.

"Do you want something for the pain?" Vinnie asked.

Molly refused any IV pain meds when she was in the hospital. The doctor said she could take over-the-counter meds when she got home. They wouldn't work as well, but they were better than nothing.

Molly shook her head. "I'm going to suffer through it."

"Why? Just take something. You're going to be miserable."

"I'm going to be miserable no matter what."

"Yeah, but you'll be less miserable if you take something."

Molly's grumble was enough of an answer for Vinnie to go to her bathroom and dig through her medicine cabinet.

He found generic pills and dumped four into his hand. He stopped in the kitchen and filled a glass with water, then brought both to Molly.

She smiled weakly at him and didn't argue before she swallowed the pills.

"What do you need?"

"Less bruises," Molly said.

"Funny. What can I actually get you?"

"Nothing. I'm good. You can go home and see your girl."

"She's fine. She knows I'm here. She said she hopes you're okay."

"I'm good. Now, go."

"Why are you trying to kick me out?"

"I'm not. I just don't want you to have to be here all day when you have someone you want to spend time with."

"And I'm telling you I'm good."

Molly sighed. "I wouldn't pass up something to eat."

Vinnie nodded and went to her kitchen. He wasn't a gourmet chef, but he could hold his own. He made them lunch while Molly found something to watch.

When Vinnie brought out the chicken and vegetables he stir-fried together, Molly sat up and accepted the bowl.

"How the hell did you do this with the ingredients in my kitchen?"

Vinnie chuckled. "Most of this was in the freezer. I took a chance that you weren't planning to use it for anything."

"I didn't even know it was there. It smells amazing."

"Eat. Want more water?"

"Yes, please."

Vinnie sat next to her on the couch and watched a show about people buying a house in Australia. They argued about which house the couple should get, and Molly claimed victory when she guessed the one they were going to buy.

An hour or so later, Molly began to fade. Vinnie cleaned up the kitchen and made sure she had her phone and remote close, so she could reach out if she needed anything.

"Are you sure you're good?" he asked.

She nodded. She looked a lot better with food and pain meds, but it was going to be a while before she was feeling back to normal. "I'm good. I promise."

"Okay. Offer stands to come to my place. Just let me know."

"I'd rather be home alone tonight."

Vinnie grinned. "Understood, but the doctor said no. We want you back soon."

"I'll be back before you," Molly taunted.

Vinnie chuckled. "Probably. And I'd be thrilled with that."

"Go back to your girl. Tell her I'm sorry I pulled you away for so long."

"She's all good. She was trying to learn more about her cases. Getting frustrated, but she was staying at my place all day."

"Good. Thanks, Vinnie. I... Thanks."

"You're welcome, Mol. I hate that you needed me, but I'm glad you called."

She smiled, wincing when she tried to move.

He helped her up, moving slowly so she didn't feel the need to hurry. He hugged her, then let himself out of the apartment. She locked the door behind him, and he headed for the elevator.

As soon as he was back in his SUV, he called Hannah.

"What's up?"

"Just wanted to give you an update on Molly. What time are you getting here?"

"What are you talking about?" Hannah asked.

"Molly's accident. She said she talked to you about coming over tonight."

"Molly was in an accident?" Hannah screeched.

"Dammit. She played me."

"Yeah, she did. Now, start at the beginning and tell me what the fuck is going on."

Vinnie laid out the day for Hannah, from Molly's call and the police and paramedic insisting she go to the hospital to dropping her off at home and her saying Hannah would be there after her date.

"For fuck's sake. Is she okay?" Hannah asked.

"Yeah, I think so. She's in pain and she will be for a while. I guess I should have known she called me because I'm not going to be at work for a while. I was the sucker who couldn't tattle on her."

"She's shit out of luck now. I'm already on my way."

"Do you have a date tonight?"

"Yeah, but I can reschedule. Molly's more important."

"Are you sure, Hannah?"

"Yeah. I know you have shit going on. How are things with Lorelei?"

"Good."

"Okay, good. Listen, I'll be there in five. You don't have to wait for me. Unless she's not allowed to be alone?"

"No, she can be for a little while. Not overnight, though. The doctor said it would be better if someone was there tonight, but after that she should be fine. She's mostly okay. Bruised, not broken."

"We'll see after I arrive," Hannah threatened.

"Go easy on her. She's injured."

"And she should have called me."

"I know, but—"

"I know, I know. I'll go easy on her."

"Thanks, Hannah. I should have called you earlier. I'm sorry I didn't."

"Not on you, Vin. Thanks for letting me know what's going on."

"Yep. Keep me posted."

"I will."

Vinnie hung up and set his phone in the center console. He pulled out of the lot and made his way home, anxious to see how Lorelei did all day without him.

He was getting out of his SUV when another vehicle pulled into the lot. He wouldn't have thought twice about it, but the large black SUV had tinted windows and was definitely not standard issue.

Vinnie made his way to the door, watching the SUV as it pulled to a stop at the curb. He narrowed his gaze on the vehicle.

The driver waved.

What the hell?

Vinnie stepped away from the building as the backdoor opened. He reached for his gun, just in case, and was shocked when Lorelei slid out of the SUV.

"Lorelei?"

"Hey," she said.

A man came around the back of the SUV, approaching Vinnie with an outstretched hand. "Austin Ward. That's my partner, Samuel MacNeil. We work for Rose Protection Agency."

"And why are you with her? Did something happen? Are you okay?" Vinnie did a quick scan, failing to find any injuries.

"I'm fine. It's a precaution," Lorelei said.

"She was followed today. She went to see a woman she rescued from a kidnapper a year ago. He somehow followed her and almost got to both women," Austin explained.

"Abigail Painter?" Vinnie asked.

Austin nodded.

"You found her? I thought you didn't know where she was," Vinnie asked Lorelei.

"I searched her name, and it gave me an address."

"Why did you go alone?"

Lorelei hung her head. "I was just going to see if I recognized her. I didn't plan to talk to her. I didn't know the guy was following me."

"What if he'd attacked you?"

"She broke his arm. Maybe his knee," Austin declared, a proud smile on his face.

"You did what?" Vinnie barked.

"It was fine. I'm an FBI Agent. I know how to defend myself," Lorelei snapped.

Vinnie drew a breath. "You're right. And I shouldn't have gotten upset. But you don't have a weapon. You don't know what situation you're walking into. I would have gone with you."

"I know. I didn't think it was going to be a big deal."

Vinnie sighed. "I'm glad you're safe. Is Abigail okay?"

"She will be. We're going to relocate her," Austin said.

"She's in WITSEC?" Vinnie asked.

Austin nodded. "The guy who kidnapped her was never caught. He's connected to a few other unsolved cases."

"Shit," Vinnie breathed.

"It'll be okay. But no more exploring," Austin chastised Lorelei.

Lorelei nodded, moving toward the building without looking back.

"Thanks for bringing her back," Vinnie said. He shook Austin's hand, then followed Lorelei to the building.

She didn't say anything as she moved to the stairs. She struggled to make her way up them, and when she got to his apartment, she finally looked up at him.

"I know I screwed up," she said quietly.

Vinnie unlocked the apartment and held the door for her to go in. "You didn't mean to. You had no idea she was in protection."

Lorelei shook her head. "It's not only that. Someone was following me, and I had no idea. And I went out alone. I..."

"You what?"

"I think that's why I was taken. I went to meet someone alone. Adam said two others offered to go with me, but I said it was fine. If I'd let someone else go, I might not have been attacked. I might not have disappeared."

Vinnie pulled her into his arms. She trembled against him. He wanted to take all her pain and fear away, but he didn't know how.

She wasn't wrong. If she hadn't been alone, it would have been safer. Before and now. But she was strong and capable and could do anything.

The problem was the bad guys didn't always play by the rules.

Or ever.

"What can I do?" Vinnie asked.

"Just let me beat myself up for a minute. I know I screwed up, and I need to sit with it so I don't do it again. So I don't think I'm invincible again."

"None of us are. That's why we work with teams."

Lorelei nodded. "I just need to remember that."

"You do. And you need to remember you're not alone. Come on. Show me how you found Abigail Painter. Maybe we can come up with some other names and people who aren't on the witness protection list."

Lorelei snorted. "That would be good."

THE BOSS PEERED out the window at the shitty apartment complex where Lorelei Sloane disappeared. She sure was lowering her standards for this one.

"She's almost making this too easy," the boss whispered.

"What are you going to do to her?" Nina asked.

"For now, nothing. She almost got that woman killed because she's so damn incapable," the boss said.

"It looked like she handled herself."

The boss snorted. "She got lucky. If he wasn't such a bumbling fool, it would have been a different story. How many people can't take out a woman on crutches?"

"Did you send him there?" Nina asked.

The boss looked at Nina. Her wide eyes said Nina was shocked the boss could do something like that. Why, that was a mystery.

"Of course I did."

"Why would you send him there? You don't know that woman. She has nothing to do with us."

The boss shook her head, her blonde hair cascading over her shoulders. She pushed it back and focused on Nina. "This is how I build my organization. I've lost employees lately." She shook her head. "Stupid men who can't follow orders. I need to refill the ranks."

"With a man who kidnaps and rapes women?"

The boss turned to face Nina. "He's already trained. I

don't have to do much to get him up to speed. Of course, him being on the FBI radar already could be a problem."

"Discretion is key."

"Always. You're learning."

Nina smiled under the boss's praise. One day, she might have the potential for more. She was still too innocent, too naïve. When she came to the company, to the boss, she was broken and lost. She needed a place where she felt like she was valued and contributing.

The boss gave her all of that and more. She gave Nina a home, a future. Nina was like a sister, someone she was going to take care of forever.

Everyone knew Nina was the most important person to the boss. She was the closest thing to family. Her only family.

Just like the boss was Nina's family. The only family she was allowed to talk about. The boss made sure of it.

"Hopefully he can evade capture, but if he doesn't get his head in the game, he's not going to have an option to continue his employment."

"But you told him where to find that woman. Why would you tell him if you were going to get angry at him for going after her?"

"If he'd succeeded in capturing her, killing her, he would have had the job without question. But since he failed, I don't know what I'm going to do."

"You're not going to give him a chance?"

"I gave him a chance. What would you do?" It was a test. To see if Nina was starting to understand how things worked.

Patience and understanding were not the way to run a business. Not at all.

Nina considered the question for a minute, then shook her head.

The boss fought the quirk of her lips. She was proud, but giving Nina too much praise was not good for her. She needed to always be looking for approval.

"Like you said, he didn't succeed. But also, the FBI is watching him. He's too much of a risk."

"I agree. What would you suggest we do?"

"Do?"

The boss quirked an eyebrow. "Yes, do."

"What do you mean?"

"He knows more than most people who don't work for us. He had exposure to parts of the business he shouldn't have."

"Which means?"

"You tell me. What would you do?"

Nina looked out the window. "He has to go, doesn't he?"

"Say it, Nina."

"He has to be killed," she said, her voice soft and unsure.

"Why?" the boss asked.

Nina looked up at her. Her lower lip wobbled. "Because he can ruin everything."

The boss nodded. "We can't risk that, Nina. We can't risk anyone who can destroy everything we've worked so hard for. And he knows too much."

Nina nodded, but she didn't look too happy about it.

It didn't matter. She didn't make the decisions. No one but the boss decided who lived.

And who died.

17

———

Lorelei remembered more and more about her life over the next month. The attack was still a mystery, but the events leading up to it and the other Curvy Vigilantes were people she had both old and new memories of.

The more Lorelei remembered about who she was before her abduction, the less she wanted to go back to being that woman. Alone and fiercely independent. She didn't trust anyone, including her own partner.

Lorelei never wanted to be that alone again.

And it seemed Vinnie was happy to help her with that.

"What are you thinking about?" he asked as he drove her to Dawn's house for a party.

Lorelei's cast was coming off the next day, and Karli and the others insisted on celebrating the night before with a party.

"I'm just thinking I don't want to be who I used to be. I like having people I can count on. People I can trust."

Vinnie rubbed his hand over her thigh. "It sounds like you've always had people you can trust, you just didn't let them in."

"That's true. I guess that's another thing I want to change."

"In what way?"

"I've made mistakes. The way I've treated people. I don't want to be that person anymore."

"Then don't be."

She laughed. "Just that simple?"

"Why not? You're the strongest person I've ever met. If anyone can do it, it's you."

She breathed a laugh. "I wish I had that kind of confidence in myself. That I could just decide to change and it's done."

"Why can't it be? It might take some getting used to, but it sounds like the old you never would have done something like this."

"A cast party?" Lorelei asked with a laugh.

"Yep. You're an amazing person. What you've been through and the way you took it and turned it into something positive... Most people couldn't do that."

"I hope most people don't have to."

"True, but it's not easy to go through what you went through and fight back to regain pieces of your life again."

"I can't let them win. Even if I don't know who they are."

Lorelei hadn't figured out who any of the other people in her notes were. She was afraid to try after what happened with Abigail Painter.

The man who attacked them was found floating in the river a few days later, so Abigail was safe, but Lorelei knew that didn't mean it was over. Or that going to find Abigail alone was okay.

Someone knew she was going to be there.

The FBI went through Lorelei's computer and phone

and found nothing that tracked her location. There was no explanation for how that man found them.

It didn't make Lorelei feel better.

Vinnie pulled into the long driveway that led to Dawn's impressive home. She inherited it from a man who knew she would put his wealth to good use. From what Lorelei had seen, Dawn was doing exactly that and giving back and helping the community. Including funding the Curvy Vigilantes and the others trying to put an end to the hell that started many, many years ago.

The vehicles in the driveway told Lorelei the others had arrived. Vinnie parked close to the door, in a space left open for them so Lorelei didn't have as far to go on her crutches.

Vinnie helped her out, smiling at her and kissing her softly before the two of them made their way to the front door.

"Good afternoon," Cole, Dawn's butler and the man who ran the household, said. Cole was an employee of the former owner, and Dawn wanted to keep as many people employed as possible. She said Cole was like family, even though she'd only known him a few months.

"Hi, Cole," Lorelei said. She'd been to the home a few times and understood why Dawn liked the man. He was kind and friendly and a wealth of knowledge about any subject from pop-culture to ancient history.

"How are you, Ms. Sloane?"

"I'm well, thank you. Learned anything new recently?"

The man's eyes lit up. "I was watching this brilliant documentary about food production recently. It was talking all about the way our food is grown and produced and why it's better for everyone if we strive to buy organic produce only."

"Have you switched Dawn and Gage to organic?"

"Yes, I have. They wouldn't have known, but I always make sure Ms. Dawn knows what I'm spending money on."

"You know she trust you," Lorelei said.

Cole nodded, smiling brightly. "Yes, but trust has to be earned over and over again if it's going to be maintained."

Lorelei sucked in a breath. "That's a very interesting way of thinking about it. As someone who didn't know who to trust for a while, I definitely agree. The people in this house earned my trust more than once, and never blinked about doing it over and over again."

"That's how you know they're doing it for the right reasons."

Lorelei nodded. "You're a very smart man, Cole. Thank you for sharing your genius with the rest of us."

"Thank you, Ms. Sloane."

Lorelei squeezed his hand, then proceeded down the hall toward where the voices of the others drew her.

Vinnie paused to speak to Cole, then followed Lorelei, not far behind her as she moved through the house.

The backdoors were thrown open and people were scattered around the patio and the room Dawn had converted to a casual dining room. When she and her boyfriend, Gage, moved into the house, Dawn said it was stuffy and formal, and not at all like the man who'd given her the gift of his fortune, or like Dawn and Gage. They were slowly figuring out what each room was going to be.

"You're here!" Karli said, spotting Lorelei before the others. Karli got up and hobbled over to Lorelei.

"You're in a cast? What happened?" Lorelei asked. Why didn't she know her cousin broke her leg?

"It's fake," Karli said, holding her casted leg up and unstrapping the boot. "We didn't want you to feel alone at your cast party."

Lorelei looked around the room and saw a cast on every single person's leg. Including Vinnie's when she turned to look at him.

"What? You guys are crazy. Why did you do this?" Lorelei asked, laughing. She couldn't believe they were all willing to wear casts for her.

"We figured it was your last night, and we should know what you've been through for nearly two months," Frannie said, stomping her cast on the ground in an awkward walk to say hello.

Lorelei hugged Frannie. "This is just too funny."

"It was Vinnie's idea," Karli said. "He knew you were sick of being in a cast, especially through the warmer weather. He said he wished he could wear a cast to support you, and it just took off from there."

Lorelei turned to face him. "How did you get a cast?"

"Cole stashed it for me. He handed it over when you came back here, and I slipped it on." Vinnie grinned, clearly enjoying that they pulled the whole thing off.

"Well, this better be one hell of a party if we're all in casts."

"Cast party!" Karli said, lifting her foot high in the air and nearly losing her balance. "Oof."

"Be careful. You don't want to end up in a cast for real!" Jessica said.

"Trust me, you don't," Lorelei said, hugging her cousin. "This is so great."

Karli laughed. "I agree. It's a good excuse for all of us to get together, and it's fun. Come get a drink."

Lorelei laughed and followed Karli to the drinks table set up near the patio. "This is insane. I can't believe you guys are all wearing casts."

"It's a cast party. We could have all pulled out our masks and had a masks and casts party."

Lorelei snorted. "That would have been insane. Someone definitely would have gotten hurt."

Karli chuckled. "Probably true."

"What are you two laughing about?" Frannie asked, wrapping an arm around Lorelei.

"I told her we should have worn our masks and made it a masks and casts party," Karli said.

Frannie laughed with them. "I love being around you ladies. You keep me feeling like I'm not the old lady I know I am."

"You are not an old lady," Karli insisted. "You are an inspiration to all of us."

Frannie's cheeks reddened. She waved her hand. "You're too much."

"Not even close. I don't know what any of us would have done without you bringing us together and giving us all a place to feel like we belong," Stacey said. Stacey Allen worked for Frannie, but she was also one of the Curvy Vigilantes.

"I was definitely feeling very alone and lost when I met all of you. I don't think I would be here if it weren't for you," Dawn said, joining their group. "I definitely wouldn't have created a life that makes me feel like I'm doing something good for the world."

"You are," Frannie said, grabbing Dawn's hand. "And your donation was beyond generous."

Dawn smiled. "What you do, helping women and children who have nowhere to go... It's amazing. I know you need the money, and I know you will use it to help even more people to feel safe and to start over."

"She will," Stacey agreed. "She's been talking about the

things she wants to do. You've made a huge difference for Shelter in the Storm."

"Good." Dawn smiled, looking truly pleased to hear her money was going to help people. As a former nurse, she dedicated her life to giving to others, and with billions, she was making sure her lifelong mission was felt by the community.

"Enough about all of this," Jessica said, dropping her voice, "how are things with Vinnie? He's a seriously sexy man."

"Jessica!" Karli hissed.

"Oh, please. You're not asking because she's your cousin and you already know. The rest of us want to know if things are going as well as it appears they are," Jessica said.

Karli and Jessica were college friends who reconnected years later. So many things Jessica said reminded Lorelei of Karli. Lorelei understood why they were such good friends. Adding in Raina as the third one of their group made the trio fun, hilarious, and took away any chance at a filter.

Lorelei glanced at Vinnie, where he was talking to Gage and Marcus. He looked over at her and winked. Lorelei's cheeks warmed, and the chorus of aww behind her said they were all watching.

"Let's go on the patio. So he doesn't overhear this and run for the hills," Lorelei said.

"The only place that man is running is to bed with you over his shoulder," Edie said.

Lorelei felt a connection to Edie. They'd become friends in the last few weeks. Edie had also experienced memory loss because of the abuse she suffered at the hands of the same organization. It was worse for Edie. She was held captive for months. She escaped, or she'd have died in their sex dungeon, available to whatever man paid the owners to have her.

The thought of what Edie went through turned Lorelei's stomach, but seeing the way the other woman fought back and reclaimed her life inspired the hell out of Lorelei. All the women did. Arrested, accused, left for dead, stalked and attacked, and worse. They were strong. They were survivors. And they were the reason Lorelei was alive. They were the ones who knew she left, and they were the ones who made sure others knew. Who got the word out.

If it wasn't for them, Vinnie never would have gone looking for her.

Lorelei settled onto one of the wide and comfortable chairs Dawn decorated the patio with. The summer evening was warm but not uncomfortable. The breeze floating around them offered enough to cool them down, but not so much to put a chill in the air. It was perfect.

"So, things are going well?" Jessica asked.

Lorelei smirked. "Yes. Things are going well."

"She has flat out refused to move in with me and Cade," Karli said. "We keep asking, but she's said she's not leaving Vinnie until he makes her."

"That's how I felt about Holden," Mackenzie said. "After we were snowed in, it was almost impossible to go back to a life where he wasn't there all the time."

"You were snowed in?" Lorelei asked.

Mackenzie nodded. "You didn't hear that story?"

Lorelei shook her head. "Can't say I remember that one. I thought I knew all the stories."

"That was when I showed up at the rescue center," Edie said.

"Oh!" Lorelei exclaimed. "I heard about that. I don't think I pieced it together, though. That's crazy."

Mackenzie nodded. "I never thought Holden was serious all the times he was flirting with me. But those few days it was different. I saw so much more of him."

"Me, too," Edie said.

The other women laughed. Edie winked at Mackenzie, who pressed her hands to her cheeks.

"I still feel bad we were fooling around with you right there," Mackenzie said.

"I was pretty out of it. I really don't remember anything. I just like teasing you," Edie said.

Mackenzie sighed, her shoulders sagging comically. "I wish you'd told me that before. I've been feeling guilty."

"You should! You were getting it on with the sexy paramedic in front of a woman who could have been dying," Raina teased Mackenzie.

"I'm never telling you guys anything again." Mackenzie crossed her arms and sat back in her chair, attempting to pout. Her smile messed up the effect.

"I feel honored I was there when you and Holden fell in love. Even if I don't remember it," Edie said.

"I definitely didn't know I was in love with him then. I was still fighting it," Mackenzie admitted.

"Yes, but it worked out. He didn't give up on you. Ever," Frannie said.

Mackenzie nodded. "He saved my life."

"You saved my life," Raina said.

"And mine," Edie agreed.

The three of them reached out to hold hands. They told Lorelei she was there the day they were talking about, but she hadn't regained her memory of that day.

"I thought for sure you and Adam were going to end up together," Raina admitted to Lorelei. "When I met you two, I thought there was no way he wasn't in love with you."

"Why would you think that? We've never... well, I don't think we've ever been like that," Lorelei said. "I definitely don't get those vibes from him now."

Raina shook her head. "He told me the same. That you two clicked instantly as partners. He knew from day one he could trust you with his life and that you would always be there for him."

"That's how I feel about him," Lorelei agreed. "Why would you think there was something more between us?"

Raina chuckled and looked around at the others. "Are you serious? Is she serious?"

Lorelei looked at the smiles on the other women's faces. "What?"

"You are a badass. You are smart and strong and sexy. You never seemed scared of anything. Hell, you were protecting me. I mean, I wished I was half as brave as you. What man wouldn't want you?" Raina asked.

Lorelei snorted. "I don't think I was a very good person, or a great partner, but it seems as though there weren't a lot of men beating down my door. There certainly haven't been any that came to find me when I disappeared."

"Vinnie did," Karli reminded her.

"Yeah, but Vinnie said we didn't know each other before. We weren't dating. He just worked on the task force that went into Davis Developments," Lorelei said.

"It was meant to be that he found you. And now you're in love," Raina said.

"In love? No," Lorelei argued.

The others exchanged glances, avoiding Lorelei's.

"Karli, tell them. There's no way. It's not like that. We're having fun and enjoying each other's company. We're getting to know each other and solving the mystery of who the fuck kidnapped me. I don't love him, and he doesn't love me."

"Are you sure about that? Because he's looked over here about every fifteen seconds to make sure you're okay," Jessica said.

Lorelei glanced back and found Vinnie watching her. He smiled, and her chest squeezed painfully.

"I can't be in love with him. I barely know him. Hell, I barely know myself."

"Clearly your heart didn't get the memo."

Lorelei sucked in a breath. They were right. Her heart didn't get the memo. Because she might not remember having been in love in the past, but she was pretty damn sure she was now.

With the man who saved her life.

18

VINNIE COULDN'T TAKE HIS EYES OFF LORELEI. SHE WAS
stunning when she laughed. She was stunning when she
was engaged in a conversation. She was stunning all the
time. He couldn't fathom not being a part of the world he'd
been introduced to thanks to her.

"Things are going well?" Marcus asked, leaning against
the wall where Vinnie stood.

Vinnie nodded. "Yeah. She's ready to have that cast off."

"You know I don't mean that."

Vinnie stopped and looked at Marcus. He wanted to play
dumb and pretend he didn't know what the question really
was, but it was Marcus, and that wasn't an option.

"I don't know. I think so. You know how I am."

Marcus nodded. "Always waiting for the other shoe to
drop. What if there is no other shoe?"

Vinnie shook his head. "There's always another shoe."

"What do you think it could be? What are you worried
about?"

Vinnie shrugged, but the answer was right there.

Marcus waited him out, letting the silence drag on until Vinnie had to fill it.

"She's too good for me."

"What makes you say that?"

Vinnie snorted. "You and I both know she's meant for so much more than me. I saved her life, but that doesn't mean she'll stick around forever."

Marcus chuckled softly. "You're the only one who thinks that. If you look around this room, you'll find a lot of these couples who started out in a similar way, but it was more than that. You're selling yourself short, Vinnie."

"Am I, though? She didn't know me before, and after she refused to stay with her family and close friends. She's leaning on me. As soon as that cast comes off and she can be independent again, she can drive herself around and work and do all the things she wants and needs to do, I am no longer necessary."

"There's a big difference between her needing you and her wanting you. Which would you prefer?"

Vinnie rolled his eyes. "Of course I'd rather she wants me, but that's my point. She's needed me, so she's never had to consider if she wants me."

Marcus shook his head, a smile on his face. "And again, you're the only one who thinks that woman doesn't want you. Look at her."

Vinnie looked at Lorelei, laughing at something one of the women said. She leaned in closer to Karli, then jerked upright. She turned, her gaze colliding with Vinnie's. She smiled, and every inch of him responded to the look in her eyes.

"That's what I'm talking about. That feeling right there. The one that has your breath rushing out of you, your body responding to the woman you love, and everything in you aching to go across the room to her."

"It's so not fair that you can read me so easily. No one else can do that."

Marcus laughed. "I've known you long enough that I should be able to. The only thing I haven't figured out is why you went after her."

"What do you mean?"

Marcus shrugged. "Don't get me wrong, I'm happy you did. I'm relieved you found her alive. She's an amazing person, and she's a valuable asset. But you didn't know her. You risked everything to try to find her. Why?"

Vinnie hadn't been asked directly. He wasn't sure he could explain it, not even to Marcus. But he owed the man the best answer he could give. "As soon as I heard she was missing, I had this feeling inside that she was dead. That she wouldn't be found alive, maybe is a better way to say it. She was too close to all of this. Trevor Davis and Damon Street and all the others. She was the one piecing it together. She was leading the charge, from what I could tell. Nothing against Adam, or anyone else, but Lorelei wasn't distracted by anything else. She wanted to solve this. To put away the people responsible for all this hell."

Marcus nodded, following and not disagreeing.

"We've been on some of the calls. Some of the houses that were used for these women. Not a lot, but a couple of them, and the conditions these women are in would turn your stomach. But more than that, the things they do to these women..."

"I know," Marcus said. He nodded, staring at the floor as though seeing his own horrors.

"When I heard Lorelei was gone, I worried we'd find her in one of those houses. Every life is important, but I knew if they went after her, she was getting closer than they wanted."

"I agree. And I'm sure that's exactly what it was."

Vinnie nodded, hoping that would be the end of it.

Marcus was too perceptive. "There were a lot of people looking for her."

"Yeah."

"Why you? And how did you know she'd be at her apartment?"

Vinnie shook his head. "That's the part I can't explain. I just had this feeling that's where she would be. This pull inside me to go there. To check. To see for myself if she was there."

"Intuition."

Vinnie nodded. "Yeah. After you see enough of this, you almost know their thoughts. Someone checked her apartment the day after she disappeared, but no one was sitting on it. It was too far from where she was taken. They were sitting on her hotel room, but not her apartment. It was a good place to hide her body."

"It would have been, if you hadn't figured it out."

Vinnie swallowed roughly, remembering how he found her.

"That kind of intuition is very valuable. It's the kind of thing that saves lives."

"Yeah," Vinnie said. "I trust my gut, and my team does, too."

"Don't stop. We need more cops like that."

Vinnie chuckled. "I'm not sure most of the detectives would agree with you."

Marcus shook his head. "Every job is different. A detective has to prove something. Your job is to stop things from getting worse."

Vinnie exhaled a laugh. "That's a good way to put it."

"It's true. And you're good at it. Damn good, Vinnie."

"Thanks, Marcus. That means a lot."

Marcus clapped him on the back. Gage and Braden came over and asked if they were ready to start cooking, and the men moved to the patio to start the grill.

Vinnie joined them, hanging on the outskirts. With Marcus, he felt like he belonged, but until he knew Lorelei wanted him around for longer than she needed his help, Vinnie knew his connection to the others was tangential. Getting too attached would only end badly for him.

"I CAN'T BELIEVE you threw me a cast party," Lorelei said when she and Vinnie made it home.

Home. Back to his place. She wasn't sure where home was for her. Besides with Vinnie. She hoped.

"We wanted you to know you have people who care about you."

"Are you one of those people?" she asked. What Karli and the others said about Lorelei being in love with Vinnie had been on her mind for the last two hours. She knew it was too soon to tell him how she felt, but with the knowledge in her mind, she couldn't argue with it either.

Vinnie walked up and wrapped his arms around her waist. He looked her in the eyes, his soft and caring before he nodded. "I'm definitely one of those people."

"Yeah?"

Vinnie nodded. "Yeah."

Lorelei felt the words billowing to the surface. Before they could fall out of her mouth, she dropped her crutches and pulled Vinnie down for a kiss.

Vinnie didn't waste any time wrapping her up and lifting her into his arms.

She squeaked and tried to pull back. "I'm too heavy for you."

"Not even close." His whispered words were accentuated by him carrying her through the apartment and depositing her gently on his bed.

Lorelei didn't let him go, pulling him down on top of her.

He crawled over her, bracketing her hips with his knees. He let some of his weight rest on her. Her ribs were mostly healed, but Vinnie was still careful with all of her injuries.

Too careful if Lorelei had a say. She wanted to know what he was like unfiltered. Wild and passionate and crazy for her. A part of her wondered if he wasn't that interested in her. If he'd never be that way because they were just sleeping together and she was the only one falling in love.

He nipped her lip, and she gasped. "You're getting lost in your head. What's going on?"

She shook her head.

Vinnie propped himself up. "You can tell me."

"I'm just worried about what happens after tomorrow."

His sharp intake said he'd been wondering the same. "Maybe we just take it all one day at a time."

"We can," she said, hedging his answer with her own stilted one.

"You can stay here as long as you want to."

She nodded. He wasn't asking her to stay, but he wasn't throwing her out either.

"Do you want to talk about it?" He didn't move, but his corded muscles said he was ready to if that was what she wanted.

She shook her head and slid her hand over his chest. "I don't want to talk at all."

His smile was all the promise she needed. He let her feel his weight again and kissed her until they were both breathless and writhing on the bed, desperate for more.

Vinnie climbed off her. He looked down at her, his gaze drifting from her face to her toes and back. "I love seeing you in my bed."

She smiled, hoping he still felt the same way after her cast was off and he didn't need to help her with everything. "I love being in your bed. But I prefer to have you a little more naked."

He chuckled and reached back to tug his shirt off. He tossed it toward the laundry basket, then hooked his thumbs in his shorts and briefs. Both came off at once.

Her mouth watered for him. He'd resisted for a month, but she was done letting him hide from her. She reached for him, wrapping her hand around his length. She surprised him by sliding to the floor and stretching her cast out next to him, bringing his cock to her mouth.

"Lorelei," he groaned as she sucked him inside.

She hummed, hoping he wouldn't pull back from her. Her ankle was healed, her ribs were better, and she wanted to taste him. She wanted to know she gave him something. Not as a thank you, but a memory.

She held his hips, her fingertips digging into his flesh as he started to move. His hands went into her hair, smoothing her natural curls back so he could meet her gaze.

"Fuck," he groaned. "That's the hottest fucking thing I've ever seen. Watching my dick disappear between your lips."

She groaned her agreement and took him deeper, wanting to know he was enjoying it.

"Fucking hell, Lorelei," he grunted.

His abs rippled in his attempt to hold back, but she wasn't having that. She slicked her tongue around his crown, then sucked him in deep, repeating the process until he fucked her mouth without thought to how she was handling it.

"Oh, fuck," he whispered. "Fuck, I'm gonna come. Lorelei. Fuck."

His breathless pleas urged her on. When he tried to pull back, she held on and sucked him deeper.

"Oh, fuck. Lorelei. I can't stop. I'm coming. Fuck." His words ended with a grunt and a gasp before he gave in and came in her throat.

She held on to him, loving the way he let go. His body trembled and jerked with aftershocks from his release.

As soon as he was done, he jerked her back and lifted her to her feet. She swallowed and smiled at him. "You're fucking amazing. I wasn't expecting that."

"I've been wanting that for weeks. You always stop me."

"I didn't want to hurt you."

"I feel pretty amazing right now," she said.

"Don't think a blow job means I'm done with you."

"Promise?"

Vinnie chuckled and nodded. "Fuck yeah. Your turn."

She sucked in a breath. The look in his eyes was almost as intoxicating as the way he looked at her when her lips were around his cock.

He helped her remove her clothes quickly, then eased her onto the bed again, with her legs hanging over the edge. He kneeled between her thighs. "Spread wide for me, Lorelei."

She did as he asked, moving her legs as far apart as they could go before he leaned in and licked her fully from her entrance to her clit. Her hips lifted from the bed, seeking more of him.

Vinnie didn't waste any time. He plunged his tongue into her core, swirling it around before exploring her folds on his way to her clit.

She was wet and ready and halfway to an orgasm from giving him a blow job, and with his tongue settled on her clit, she went off like a rocket. "Oh, fuck. Yes."

Vinnie chuckled, digging in harder and licking her clit until she screamed her way through a second orgasm and ran toward a third. He slid his fingers into her, and she lost her mind, grabbing his head and pulling him closer until her orgasm crashed hard over her and stripped her of all her energy.

He wiped his mouth on the back of his hand and kissed his way up her body. "You're delicious."

"Same," she breathed.

He kissed her hard, his bare cock resting next to her entrance.

She wanted to feel him without protection, but she couldn't promise him she was safe. She needed to add that to the list of things to talk to her doctor about after her cast was off.

Vinnie pulled back and grabbed a condom. He rolled it on and positioned himself, her legs propped up on his shoulders. He pressed into her, slowly at first, then slammed in hard.

"Oh, my God," she breathed, her body reacting to him instantly and finding a new reserve of energy.

"You feel so good," he grunted. His hips set a fast pace, neither of them willing to slow things down. He held her thighs and slammed into her, each stroke hitting her just right inside and pushing her closer and closer to another orgasm.

"Vinnie," she whimpered.

"Come on, Lorelei. Come with me." He squeezed her thighs and shifted his position, and she was done.

"Vinnie!" she shouted, unable to stop the shout before it fell from her lips.

"Fuck, yes," he yelled, falling right with her.

Lorelei watched him as he came, his mouth falling open in a soft O, his cheeks red, his eyes closed but relaxed. He was beautiful. And he was hers.

How did she get so damn lucky that he was the one who found her?

VINNIE HELD her hand in the waiting room at the doctor's office. When Lorelei's name was called, he stood and handed her the crutches for the last time. She said he was there with her, and the nurse let him follow them to the exam room.

A few questions and the nurse left, assuring them the doctor would be in soon.

"What do you want to do first?" Vinnie asked.

"First?"

He shrugged. "I broke two fingers a few years ago, and the first thing I wanted to do when I got my cast off was... well." He made a motion for jerking off, which was the truth.

Lorelei snorted a laugh and shook her head. "Well, I haven't been neglected thanks to you."

Vinnie leaned over and kissed her hard. He didn't mean to admit that to her, but he was happy with her response.

A knock on the door had him pulling back long before he was ready.

"Good morning," Dr. Tucker said, smiling at both of them. "I know you're ready for this."

Lorelei nodded. "I am. So ready."

"Good. Well, as we talked about before, you're still going to need to take it easy. You can walk and do all your normal activities, but it's not unusual to feel some discomfort for a while. Weeks or even months." He pulled out a sheet of paper and handed it to Vinnie. "She's going to need to do these exercises for at least a month, longer if possible, to strengthen the muscles that haven't been used for the last seven weeks."

Vinnie showed Lorelei the sheet. She reached for it.

"I gave that to him because you need to lie down," Dr. Tucker said. "I've learned it's easier when you're not watching and trying to move. My wife says they tell her the same when she gets a pedicure."

Lorelei chuckled. "I would definitely do that." She laid back, staring up at the ceiling.

Dr. Tucker started the small saw he had for cutting through the cast. Vinnie watched as the doctor zipped through the hard material like it was nothing, freeing her leg in under a minute.

"That was fast," Vinnie said.

"It didn't take long last time, either. Mark said the same thing," Lorelei said.

Dr. Tucker and Vinnie both looked at her.

"Mark? Who's Mark? Do you remember something?" Vinnie asked.

Lorelei chuckled. She nibbled her bottom lip.

Vinnie wanted to demand she tell him who she was

thinking about, but he didn't. He kept his mouth shut while she decided what she wanted to tell him.

"He was an ex. I just had this memory of getting a cast off my left arm. We... he took me to the appointment and thought it was going to be longer than it was for my cast to come off."

"When did you date him?" Vinnie asked.

Lorelei shrugged and looked at the doctor. "Um, we can talk about this later. It's not important. Are we all set, Dr. Tucker?"

The doctor nodded. "You are. Do those exercises and let us know if you need anything."

"I will. Thanks." Lorelei eased down from the exam table. She lifted her right leg and landed on her left, then put her right foot on the floor carefully.

"Everything feel okay?" Vinnie forced out.

Lorelei looked up at him and smiled. "All good."

Vinnie nodded, but he knew she was lying. Her leg might be good, but they weren't. The other shoe dropped.

And its name was Mark.

19

———

Lorelei wanted to kick herself for mentioning Mark. She should have kept her mouth shut. It just came out.

Of all her exes to remember, he was the one she thought of? It made her wonder if the others were worse. She had horrible taste in men if that was the case.

She looked over at Vinnie. She used to.

With the memory of Mark came all the things he said when he dumped her. He thought it would take longer for her cast to come off, and more time for her to want to go back to work. But that was the first thing she wanted to do when she got the cast off her arm.

And Mark was pissed. So pissed he broke up with her because of it.

It took Lorelei a few weeks, and a lot of drinks, to see that he couldn't handle her strength and independence. He wanted her to need him, to rely on him, and as soon as she didn't, he was done.

Adam helped her to see that, and told her one day she'd find a man who wasn't threatened by the things that made her who she was.

Lorelei looked over at Vinnie and wondered if he was that man.

She wanted him to be.

"What are you doing today?" Lorelei asked, hoping to smooth over the awkwardness that settled between them since she mentioned Mark.

"I have to go to work," Vinnie said.

"You do? I didn't realize that. I could have asked someone else to take me this morning if I knew you had to work."

"Mark?" Vinnie spat.

Lorelei exhaled. "Mark isn't important. Not anymore."

"But he was."

She nodded. Her cheeks warmed. Mark hurt her. A lot. More than she wanted to admit to anyone, but especially to Vinnie.

Mark was a jerk, but she was the reason things ended. She didn't see him for who he was. She never made space for him in her life until she needed his help. And when he got mad and walked, she didn't fight him on it. Just let him leave and went on with her life. She proved him right. She didn't need him, or anyone, and that truth almost got Lorelei killed.

If she'd listened to Mark a year ago, if she'd been less independent, she might not have been alone the night she was kidnapped. She might have trusted someone else.

Mark was just the first person to call her on it. He was angry at her for it. Lorelei told herself being independent was a good thing. That it was a sign of strength. It wasn't a weakness like Mark threw in her face. It wasn't something she should change.

But one year, a broken ankle, amnesia, and five broken ribs later, Lorelei knew Mark was right. Not that she needed him, but she needed someone. She wasn't an island. And pretending she was didn't do her any favors.

"Are you okay if I drop you off?" Vinnie asked, interrupting Lorelei's thoughts.

She nodded, feeling guilty for keeping him from work. Again. He'd taken weeks off to be there for her, and even after he was back to work, she was keeping him from doing his job.

She was no better than Mark, demanding Vinnie was there for her but not anyone else.

Vinnie slowed down in front of the building and pulled over behind a row of parked vehicles.

Lorelei put her hand on the door handle. "Do you know when you'll be home?"

Vinnie didn't look at her when he shook his head.

"Okay," Lorelei said. She climbed out of his SUV and moved to the sidewalk to watch him drive away.

Once he was out of sight, she looked up Adam's number on her phone and called him. "Can you come get me? I need some advice."

"On my way."

VINNIE SLAMMED his fist into the body bag in the training room. It swung back, and he hit it again. And again. And again.

Beating the shit out of the bag was better than letting out the emotions racing through him and threatening to destroy his sanity.

"Whoa. What's going on with you?" Arthur asked. Arthur was a SWAT member, but not on Vinnie's team. They did not get along. They went through training together, and Arthur was on Vinnie's heels for every exercise. Vinnie was his competition, the one he had to beat.

He never did, and the fighting never stopped.

"Move along, Arthur," Vinnie growled.

Arthur laughed, drawing the attention of the others in the training room. "Is the hero having a bad day?"

"What the hell are you talking about?" Vinnie asked.

Arthur smirked. "Even since you went and chased down that FBI Agent, everyone's saying you're a hero. You saved her life. And you're fucking her into submission."

Vinnie saw red and wanted nothing more than to watch it come out of Arthur's body. He pinned the other man to the body bag, his forearm on Arthur's throat.

Arthur's eyes went wide. He tapped Vinnie's forearm. He threw his hands wide, his gaze going past Vinnie to the others in the room.

"What the hell, Vin?" Hannah blurted. She and Molly pulled him off Arthur.

Arthur gasped for breath and held his throat like he was injured. "He could have killed me."

"Why the fuck did you go after him?" Molly asked, slapping Vinnie's shoulder.

"He's talking shit," Vinnie growled.

Arthur pushed the body bag, showing how easily he could have moved it if he wanted, then winked at Vinnie. It was all for fucking show, the asshole.

Vinnie started to go after Arthur, but Hannah and Molly held him back.

"What the hell is wrong with you?" Hannah hissed. "He's trying to get you kicked out."

"He's trying to get his ass kicked, is what he's doing," Vinnie snapped.

"And what's that going to do?" Molly asked. "You kick his

ass, and you lose your job. Do you really think that's going to win you any favors with anyone?"

"I'm not trying to win favors," Vinnie growled.

"Sure, but maybe you're also trying to not lose your job," Hannah said. "Stay away from Arthur. Let him be a dick to someone else."

"Ready to roll?" Paul asked, walking by them and pointing to the situation room.

"We got a call?" Hannah asked.

"Yeah, Damien needs everyone in there in five," Paul said. "Let's go."

Molly, Hannah, and Vinnie made their way to the locker room for a quick cleanup before they went to the situation room.

Damien was in front of the screen and nodded when the three of them joined the rest of the team. "We have a hostage situation. Local library. Domestic turned deadly. Before the cops got there and found the wife, the husband took off. Fired some shots when they came up on him, then ran inside the library. In the middle of story time."

"How many hostages?" Molly asked.

"Thirty-two," Damien said.

"Ages?"

"Toddler through seventies, from what we can tell."

"What does he want?" Paul asked.

"A way out," Damien said.

"What's our plan?" Vinnie asked.

"Get as many hostages out as possible while the negotiators handle the shooter," Damien said. "Anything else we figure out on the fly."

The team nodded and followed Damien to the truck. Hannah drove with Damien up front. The rest of them were in the back, checking weapons and getting ready for anything.

Vinnie tried to get his head in the game, but Arthur fucked with it. Vinnie knew that was the entire point, but it pissed him off that he fell for it.

They pulled up to the library and filed out, waiting for their orders. It didn't take long.

"Teams of two, make your way around the library. Recon only. Need to get eyes on the hostages and make sure everyone is okay. If you find a way to get them out, report back. Don't be seen," Damien said.

They paired off, and Vinnie and Joshua started to the right of the building. The solid brick exterior made it possible for them to get next to the building without being seen. Joshua went first, leading the way around their side of the building low, staying below the windows that let sunlight into the building on the other three sides.

Rows of shelves blocked their view of anyone inside the library. Chairs were close to the windows, but they were all empty. No one was visible between the shelves.

They kept moving along the side of the building, but had nothing valuable to report back. No hostages were visible, and neither was the shooter.

Vinnie and Joshua went back to their position at the front of the building to wait for instructions from Damien. When the other teams returned, they all reported.

"Nothing on our side," Joshua said.

"Ours was quiet," Hannah said.

"He's in the back," Paul said. He nodded to Molly. "We saw him with all the hostages in a sitting area. One gun. Can't have much left in it."

"Do you think we can breach?" Joshua asked.

Damien shook his head. "Too many unknowns. The

library has alarms that will tell him if we open the front door."

"Seriously?" Hannah asked.

Damien nodded. "It's supposed to be so employees know when someone comes in. It's a big library and if they're helping someone or in the office, they can't see the door, so they added a chime of sorts to let them know when someone walks in."

"There has to be a way we can get in there," Molly said. "What about the sides where no one saw anything?"

"That's possible," Damien said. "But if the windows are locked or sealed, we'd have to break one, and he'd hear that."

"But it's worth trying," Molly said.

"Everything is worth trying. We need a team to watch him, or create a distraction. Something to make sure he doesn't sneak up on whoever is trying to get inside."

"I'll go in," Vinnie volunteered. He looked at Joshua, who nodded.

"We'll watch the shooter," Molly said.

"Be ready to take him out if you need to," Damien said.

Molly and Paul both nodded and checked their weapons.

"Want us to create a distraction?" Hannah asked, slapping Eric, her partner, on the vest.

"Probably not a bad idea. But what kind of distraction will draw him away and not spook him?" Damien asked.

They all tossed out ideas until they agreed Hannah and Eric would be tasked with staging an accident on the road behind the library. It had to be loud, and they had to get into it if it was going to draw the shooter's attention.

Damien got approval for the plan, then they all got into position. Hannah and Eric were going first, staging the accident to get the shooter's attention. As soon as Molly and Paul confirmed the shooter was distracted, Vinnie and Joshua were going in through windows on the side.

Vinnie crouched below the windows next to Joshua. They had to test the windows to find one they could enter through. Molly and Paul were the lookouts, and with their word, it was go time. Whether they found an open window or not, the plan was set.

"Shooter is on our side. Screaming at someone. Looks like he's losing it. We need to move, boss," Molly said through their comms.

"Team one, are you ready?" Damien asked.

Vinnie shook his head. "We don't have a window to go through."

"He's swinging the gun around," Paul said. "He's gonna start shooting, boss."

"Team two, go," Damien said, giving the order for Hannah and Paul to create the diversion.

Vinnie and Joshua moved along the wall, testing windows to find one they could use to breach.

"Got a window," Joshua said. "Let us know when we can go in."

Vinnie moved to where Joshua was as soon as the crash happened on the road. Joshua pried the window open, a loud squeak making him pause.

"Stop," Paul said. "Shooter heard the window."

"Team two, get louder," Damien commanded.

Vinnie waited, his breath held, for the word that they could go. It felt like an hour before Paul's word came through.

"Go. He's at the back. This is your chance to get inside."

Joshua yanked the window, one loud squeak the only sound. Vinnie kneeled on the grass to give Joshua a boost inside, then he was gone. Vinnie hoisted himself up and rolled silently into the library.

Vinnie and Joshua positioned themselves behind shelves, knowing it would be easy for someone to see them. They couldn't see the shooter or hostages yet, but they could hear him.

"What the hell is wrong with those people?" the guy shouted.

"Diversion is working but not calming him down," Paul said.

"Team one, you need to move," Damien said.

Vinnie and Joshua exchanged a glance and moved together toward the aisle. Joshua went first, his gun pointed and his steps silent.

Vinnie watched their backs, even though the shooter was believed to be alone.

When they made it to the end of the aisle, they had no cover between them and the shooter. Half shelves filled the center of the library, and from the distance the shooter was, the shelves did nothing to block his view of Vinnie and Joshua.

Joshua signaled to Vinnie he was going to move to the next shelf. Vinnie checked the shooter, who was still watching the diversion, and nodded.

Joshua made it over, and Vinnie followed him. If they were going to get closer, they would be taking a risk with every move they made. But they had to.

Each shelf brought them closer until they had a clean shot. Joshua signaled he was going to talk to the shooter. Vinnie shook his head, but Joshua didn't back down. Vinnie was the one with more negotiation training, but Joshua had been through a class recently and wanted to test his skills.

Vinnie finally nodded. He positioned himself on the

floor, checking he had plenty of range to take a shot if he needed to put the shooter down.

Joshua stood and drew the shooter's attention to him.

Vinnie watched as the shooter realized Joshua was there. The panic in his eyes. The way he jumped. The recognition of the uniform and the acknowledgment of weapons.

He raised his gun.

Vinnie squeezed the trigger, and the shooter dropped.

"Shooter down," Paul reported.

Joshua and Vinnie moved forward, guns trained on the shooter.

The man gasped, his fingers twitching.

Vinnie kicked the gun away from the shooter while Joshua kneeled over him and put pressure on the gunshot wound that was going to kill him.

"Is everyone okay?" Vinnie asked, looking at the hostages.

They cowered in fear, hiding the children from the man bleeding to death right in front of them.

The front door opened, and medics and officers raced inside. Two medics went to the shooter, loading him on a stretcher and wheeling him out before the hostages were allowed to leave.

"Is he dead?" one woman asked Vinnie.

Vinnie shook his head. "I don't know, ma'am, but I'm sorry for what you went through."

"He said he was going to kill all of us. And if any of us survived, he was going to find us so we couldn't tell the cops what he did. He killed his wife, her parents, and her sister's entire family."

"What?" Vinnie asked.

The woman nodded. She wrung her hands and tears leaked down her cheeks. "That's what he said. He said he already killed everyone he was supposed to love, and we were nothing to him."

"Will you share that with the officers over here?"

The woman nodded again.

Vinnie led her to the detectives, who met his gaze before whisking her away to speak to her alone after they heard her report.

Vinnie looked at the space around him. It was a place that should have been happy. Peaceful. Fun. And it became a place for death. A place where a man decided no life mattered.

"Why did you shoot him?" Joshua hissed, coming up behind Vinnie.

Vinnie turned on his partner. "He was going to shoot you."

"I'm wearing a vest. There's no way he would have been that good of a shot."

"You really wanted to take that chance?"

"I wanted to talk him down. I wanted these kids to not see someone shot in front of them. Do you have any idea how this is going to affect these children? They're never going to recover from this."

Vinnie opened his mouth to defend his actions, but Joshua stalked away. He ignored everyone who tried to talk to him and slammed his way out of the library.

"What was that?" Molly asked.

"He didn't want me to shoot the guy."

"He was going to shoot him."

Vinnie nodded. He looked at the kids. The horrified looks on their faces, the tears and sobs and fear in their eyes. One recoiled when an officer tried to speak to her. A boy buried his face in his mom's shoulder and refused to turn around.

"He said he would have rather that happen than these kids see what they saw."

Molly looked at the kids. Her gaze skipped around the room, breath lifting her chest before she released it slowly. "They're never going to be the same."

"Do you think I made the wrong decision?" Vinnie asked.

Molly shook her head slowly. "You know I can't answer that. You were the one inside. I was watching, but my vantage point was different. All I could see was him raising his weapon."

Vinnie ran a hand over his face. His throat tightened. He was one of the good guys. He saved those kids.

But when they looked at him, they all hid. Buried their faces or screamed or moved behind their parents.

They were afraid of him.

20

Adam didn't push Lorelei to talk. He let her be. He distracted her with stories about their coworkers and drove around for as long as she needed before she was ready to talk.

"Find a place to park," she told him, knowing Adam would understand she wanted to talk.

He drove to Goat Island and found a spot close to the Visitor's Center and the top of Niagara Falls. They got out of his SUV and made their way toward the scenic overlook.

Lorelei leaned her forearms on the large metal railings that separated sightseers from the deadly drop to the bottom of the Niagara Gorge. She stared at the water and let the breeze drift around her, cooling her skin as the sun warmed it.

"What's going on?" Adam asked after a few minutes.

Lorelei turned to face him. "I remembered Mark this morning."

Adam groaned. "Of all people."

"I said something with Vinnie there."

"Okay?"

Lorelei scrunched up her face. "I didn't tell him why we broke up."

"Because Mark was an insecure dick who thought you were a bitch because you didn't need him?"

Lorelei snorted. "Pretty much. How am I supposed to tell Vinnie that? That the last relationship I was in was with a man who didn't want me because I'm too independent."

"You're not the same person you were, Lore. You've changed. Even more in the last two months. I didn't want you to go through all the shit you did, but I'm not disappointed you changed a few things about how you live your life."

"Like not being so independent?" Lorelei asked.

Adam laughed. "Something like that." He nudged her with his hip. "You're strong and smart and capable. There's nothing wrong with that."

"Unless it means I'm alone my whole life."

"If that was what made you happy, then no, there would be nothing wrong with that. But I don't think it is, and I know you're not alone. You have a lot of people who care about you."

"I just don't have that one who'd do anything for me."

Adam turned and leaned his hip against the railing. "Did you miss the part about Vinnie risking his job to save you? About him skipping town and not telling anyone where he was going? Or him letting you live with him and taking a leave so he could be there with you? Or all the things he's done since you disappeared?"

Lorelei fought a smile. "Okay, I guess he has proved a few things."

"Listen, I love you. You're an amazing partner and a great friend. I would do anything for you. But the way Vinnie is, the way he looks at you and how he cares for you, that's how I feel about Raina."

Lorelei nodded slowly. "Karli and the other girls were saying the same thing last night."

"I think he's in love with you. Don't let something dumb like Mark ruin things with Vinnie."

Lorelei snorted. "Yeah, you're right. I..." She shook her head. "I don't know what I was thinking."

"You were thinking you're scared. Because you don't know for sure that he's in the same place as you. At some point, you have to ask him. You have to tell him how you feel or risk letting a stupid misunderstanding ruin what you could have. It's not worth letting him walk away."

Lorelei nodded. "Thanks, Adam. I appreciate it."

"Any time. What are you doing to celebrate getting your cast off?"

She shrugged. "Vinnie's working so I don't have any plans."

"Come back to our place. Raina was worried when you called. She knew if it was work she couldn't be here, but she wants an update."

"Let's go see her. I'll invade you guys for the day and go from there."

"Sounds good."

VINNIE WAS NOT in a hurry to leave work. After learning the shooter died on the way to the hospital, he had to answer questions about why he took the shot. He knew he was in the right, but it was policy to question everyone. It was a long fucking day.

But after the way he acted that morning with Lorelei, he wasn't in a hurry to get it over with.

He was finally cleared for duty, and the higher-ups verified that he was within his rights to shoot the man who was pointing a gun at his partner, especially with civilians, including children, in close proximity. Vinnie didn't like ending a life, but he knew it was part of the job. His least favorite part, but still a part of it.

Night had arrived by the time he made his way to his SUV, and he felt guilty leaving Lorelei for so long. They needed to talk. And if he was honest with himself, he wanted to see her. It was the longest time he'd spent away from her since the day he let himself into her apartment and found her.

He drove home, practicing his apology on the way. When he pulled into his complex, he knew words weren't enough, but he didn't want to turn around and go find something else.

He raced up the stairs to his floor, then let himself in without thinking about how dark the apartment was. Not a single light was on.

Vinnie set his bag down near the door and locked the door. He let his eyes adjust and scanned the room. Lorelei wasn't on the couch or in the kitchen. He turned a light on to make sure nothing had been disturbed.

The apartment looked as though she'd just walked out.

He went through the rest of it, finding her things where they'd been that morning.

"Where is she?"

He pulled out his phone and debated texting or calling her and decided on a text.

Are you okay?

He tapped the side of his phone while he waited for her to reply. He started dinner, since he was hungry and it was late, and tried not to panic that she was gone.

> Visiting with Adam and Raina. Karli, Cade, and Jessica came over. I'm going to stay here tonight. We've all been drinking.

Vinnie breathed an angry laugh. She went out drinking. With her friends. And didn't even bother to tell him.

She was done. She didn't need him. She didn't even want him. She didn't invite him to join her, or suggest he pick her up. She just left.

Vinnie finished cooking his dinner, then forced himself to eat it. He turned his phone off and fought against all the things he'd always told himself he was.

Not smart enough.

Not desirable enough.

Not interesting enough.

Unworthy.

He'd been telling himself for weeks she didn't need him. He didn't want her to need him. Not really. A relationship like that wouldn't last. None of his others had. As soon as the women realized he wasn't going to be there for every little thing, they left, thinking it would wake him up and send him chasing after them.

Been there, done that. And it only prolonged the pain. The anger. The frustration.

He wasn't going to do it again.

Lorelei never needed him, but she said she wanted him. Marcus said the same. But it was all fuzzy. As soon as the cast was off, Lorelei was gone.

Vinnie couldn't remember feeling the way he did. Stupid for how wrong he was. Angry for how he let himself fall for her. And yeah, sad because she wasn't ever going to be his. Not the way he was hers.

He went to bed, hoping sleep would grace him and he could ignore all the shit rolling inside him. After three hours of tossing and turning, he decided he couldn't just ignore it. He had to do something.

He threw the covers off the bed and got up. He stripped the sheets and carried all of it to the washing machine. He shoved everything in and started the machine, washing her scent off his sheets.

Then Vinnie went to the bathroom. He turned on the light and saw all her products. Skin care, hair care, medications. He gathered all of it onto the coffee table in the living room.

The bedroom was next. Clothes from the floor, drawers, and hamper. He put the dirty clothes in the washing machine when he moved the bed linens to the dryer, then grabbed her suitcases and bag.

One item at a time, he removed her from his apartment until all that was left were three pieces of luggage full of the possessions of the woman he loved and would never be worthy of.

He carried himself back to bed and fought for sleep until his alarm went off far too soon. He took a cold shower that did nothing, then made a pot of coffee.

Vinnie glared at the luggage by the door as he drank his fourth cup of coffee. He scribbled a note and left it on top, then grabbed his keys and hoped like hell she was gone by the time he got home.

Jessica offered to drive Lorelei home when they all got up. Being the two without a significant other in the room, Lorelei took her up on the offer.

"How is it not having the cast on?" Jessica asked as she drove away from Adam's house.

"I think good. So far. I was a little sore yesterday after Adam and I went to the Falls, but it was okay after a little rest."

"I've never broken anything, but I imagine you figure out in a hurry what you can do."

Lorelei chuckled. "Yeah. Not my first broken bone, unfortunately."

"Are you remembering more stuff?"

"Yeah. It's weird what comes back and what doesn't. I know there are big holes in my memory. Things that feel like they're right there, but when I reach for them, they scatter."

"Maybe you're not ready to deal with those yet."

"Probably, but the longer it is, the more worried I'm not going to remember. The attack... I don't want to relive it, but I know it's important. I know there's something from the time I am missing that will make a huge difference."

"Have you thought about hypnosis or something like that?"

Lorelei nodded. "Yeah, but trusting people is still hard."

Jessica inhaled deep. "I know that feeling."

"I still can't believe this one case has affected so many people in the same group."

"We know each other, so we have connections that were vulnerable. That were taken advantage of."

"I guess that makes sense."

Jessica pulled into the apartment lot and parked.

"Do you want to come up?"

Jessica shook her head. "No, but thanks. Braden should be getting home soon."

Lorelei grinned. "I know you're anxious to see him. Thanks for the ride. I know I'll see you soon."

Jessica hugged Lorelei. "I hope so."

Lorelei said goodbye and got out, heading up to the apartment. Her ankle was sore by the time she made it upstairs, but she was happy to be home.

Vinnie's home. But close enough. Lorelei decided after her talk with Adam the day before that she was going to tell Vinnie how she felt. That she was going to let him know all about Mark and why things ended and how she threw herself into work after that and tried to prove him wrong but only ended up getting herself kidnapped. How Vinnie was—

Lorelei stopped at the door. Her bags were packed. Literally. Sitting just inside the front door and ready for her to go.

"No," she said, closing the door and locking it before stomping through the apartment to find Vinnie.

He wasn't there, of course. She knew he wasn't there when she walked in.

She went back to the living room and stared at the luggage. A note was tucked into the handle of one of the suitcases.

Lorelei didn't want to read the note. She didn't want to see his dismissal of her. She wasn't done with him. She couldn't believe he was done with her.

Lorelei stared at the note like it was going to attack her and dug in her handbag for her phone. She glanced away from the note long enough to pull up Karli's name and tap.

"Are you okay? I thought Jessica was taking you back to Vinnie's," Karli said as she answered the phone.

"She did. But Vinnie's at work and all my stuff is packed."

"What? He packed your things?"

Lorelei nodded. "Yeah. I came home, here, whatever, ready to tell him I'm in love with him, and he's ready to push me out the door."

"Don't let him."

"What do you mean? It's his apartment."

"Sure, but that doesn't mean you have to make it easy. I'll come get you and we'll get together with everyone. Come up with a plan. Make sure he knows he can't just end things without a conversation."

"I don't know."

"Get your ass downstairs now. I'll be there in ten."

"Okay."

Lorelei hung up the phone and sighed. Was she wrong? She thought Vinnie felt the same.

She shook her head and walked out, leaving her bags packed by the door, the note still on top. Whatever he had to say, he was going to say it to her face.

Karli was alone when she pulled into the lot, which Lorelei was grateful for. She liked Cade, but she needed her cousin for this one.

"Frannie said to come to Shelter in the Storm. We're all going to meet there. It's quiet today."

Lorelei nodded, trying to make sense of her jumbled thoughts while Karli drove across town to the shelter. Karli parked on the street close by, and they walked two blocks. Frannie welcomed them in, guiding them to a living room at the front of the old house turned shelter.

Jessica, Raina, and Dawn were already there when Karli and Lorelei arrived. Mackenzie and Edie showed up as

Stacey walked down the hallway from her office, then they all turned to Lorelei.

"He packed your things?" Edie asked.

Lorelei nodded. "I didn't go through the apartment, but that's what it looked like."

"Are you sure he wasn't packing to take you on a trip?" Mackenzie asked.

"With only my suitcases?" Lorelei replied.

"Yeah, probably not," Raina said.

"What did you guys talk about the last time you saw him?" Stacey asked.

"My ex-boyfriend. I had a memory come back about him, and I mentioned him," Lorelei admitted, picking at her nail beds.

"You didn't tell me that," Karli said.

Lorelei shrugged. She looked up at Raina. "I called Adam yesterday about it. He knew the guy. Told me I was better off without him. Mark wasn't right for me. He was... too neat."

"It's bad to be neat?" Dawn asked.

Lorelei shook her head. "No, but it's bad when his clothes had to be perfectly pressed and he didn't like me doing my job."

"Why would he not like your job? You're a badass," Karli said.

"Thanks, but it seemed he wanted to be the strong one. He wanted me to need him. I broke my arm and went right back to work when my cast came off. He dumped me because I didn't need him anymore, and he liked me relying on him for everything." Lorelei's throat tingled with shame.

"He wasn't worthy of you," Frannie said. "But Vinnie isn't like that. Do you know about his family?"

Lorelei nodded. "He told me his grandmother raised him."

"Did he tell you how he met Marcus?"

Lorelei tried to remember the story but came up blank. She knew they had history, but Vinnie never shared the story.

"Vinnie is a good man. One of the best. But he's never had anyone who wanted him in their life. He's always done what you just said and thrown himself into work. When things get hard, he digs into his job. He's smart, and he's capable, and he has a bright future, but there's a reason he's single. And it's not because he's not a good man."

"You can only push someone so far," Stacey said to Frannie. "If he's not willing to try to make a relationship work, it shouldn't be up to Lorelei to do the work for both of them."

Frannie shook her head. "No, it shouldn't. I agree. But I also think Vinnie's scared. I think he heard about an ex and assumed there was more there. That he immediately saw himself as not good enough. And he panicked. Especially since you didn't go home last night."

Lorelei's eyes widened. "He thinks since I don't need him that I don't want him."

Frannie shrugged. "That would be my guess. We're always looking for signs around here, for warnings that a man is not going to treat you the way you deserve, but I've known Vinnie for a long time, and he's the most loyal, dedicated, kind man I've ever known."

"That's what I thought, too," Lorelei admitted.

"Then don't let him get away. Fight for what you want. And if he's done, you'll let him go, but I don't think that's what going on here. It just stinks you have to be the one to push back."

"She's good at that, don't worry," Karli said with a wink at Lorelei.

"I better be, because I'm not ready for things to be over between us."

21

VINNIE WALKED INTO WORK WITH A CHIP ON HIS SHOULDER and a fire in his gut. He needed to beat the shit out of something. Forget about Lorelei and the shooting the day before and everything except wearing himself out until he couldn't lift his arms.

"Yo, Morgan! Wanna go a round?" Arthur shouted as soon as Vinnie stepped foot in the gym.

Vinnie stopped his path toward the body bag and looked at Arthur, leaning against the ropes in the ring, a confident smirk on his shit-eating face.

Vinnie changed course, heading for Arthur.

"It's a good day to kick your ass," Arthur taunted. "Always is, but today feels especially fun."

Vinnie glared at Arthur as he tossed his bag to the side. He grabbed his boxing gloves and strapped them on, tapping them together before climbing into the ring.

Arthur smirked. "Need to warm up?"

Vinnie shook his head. "I'm always ready to beat your ass."

"Bring it," Arthur said.

Vinnie held his hands up and watched Arthur's movements. Arthur liked to dance around on his toes and avoid shit more than he liked to throw punches. Vinnie was more than happy to land a few blows and get out the anger he was full of.

Arthur jumped forward, and Vinnie swung, landing a jab to his side.

Arthur jumped back, chuckling, but his face told the truth. It hurt.

Vinnie was light on his feet and ready for the next time Arthur made a move, landing another jab to Arthur's chest. Arthur didn't move away fast enough, and Vinnie knocked him off his feet with an uppercut to the jaw.

"Whoa, Arthur. I thought you were going to kick his ass," another guy on his team said. "You realize you're the one on the ground, right?"

"I kicked your ass, Hector."

"True. You got lucky. Won't happen next time. I'll be ready for your dirty moves."

"I'm not dirty," Arthur shouted. He scrambled to his feet, facing off with Hector. "You gonna come up here and say that to my face?"

Hector chuckled and shook his head. "I'll let Vinnie say it for me."

Arthur turned back to Vinnie, as if he forgot they were in the middle of a fight.

Vinnie wasn't going to fight dirty and catch him off-guard, but he wasn't going to give him extra time to get ready either.

Arthur came at Vinnie, unfocused and wild. He swung, leaving himself wide open for Vinnie to return a punch.

Jab to the chest, uppercut to the jaw.

Arthur backed up, hands up to protect himself.

It was on.

Vinnie landed jabs to his ribs, alternating sides. Arthur hit the ropes, and Vinnie kept going. Ribs, arms, kidney, uppercut. Over and over as the blood rushed through his ears and all sound beyond his gloves hitting flesh a muffled hum.

"Vinnie!" someone shouted, yanking him off Arthur.

Vinnie fought them, shrugging them off before he heard his name again.

"Morgan!"

Shit. Vinnie dropped his hands, all the fight gone as he realized he fucked up. Bad.

"My office. Now," Damien snarled at him.

Vinnie glanced back at Arthur, who was fighting off his teammates. They were trying to help him up. Blood poured from Arthur's nose. The way he twisted to the side said his ribs were injured.

Fuck.

Vinnie ducked between the ropes and followed Damien down the hallway to his office. As soon as they were both inside, Damien closed the door. Hard.

"What the hell is wrong with you? You do know Arthur is a member of this team, right?"

"He's not on our team," Vinnie spat.

"He's a fucking SWAT member," Damien growled, getting in Vinnie's face. "You don't do that. You don't lose your shit and wail on anyone until they can't fight back. What the hell is wrong with you?"

Vinnie opened his mouth to defend his actions and shook his head. It was better if he kept quiet.

"You don't want to tell me, fine. You can work patrol for the day."

"What? But I—"

"You beat the shit out of a teammate. You were ruthless and violent. You killed a man yesterday, and today you looked like you wanted to do it again, but this time with your bare hands. So unless you can tell me what the fuck is going on with you, you're on patrol."

Vinnie glared at his boss. He hated patrol. Not because it wasn't valuable work, but because Vinnie fit in SWAT. He liked kicking in doors and taking down assholes like the fucker who killed seven people the day before.

"I'll get my head on right, boss. I won't fuck up again."

"You're right. You won't. Or you'll be on patrol for good."

"You're really going to send me down to patrol?"

"Get the hell out of here, Morgan. I don't have time to babysit. You want to act like that, they can deal with you."

Vinnie slammed his fist against the wall and yanked the door open. He stomped to the locker room before he remembered his bag was still in the gym.

Vinnie retreated and stomped his way to the gym, the halls clearing ahead of him whenever someone saw the look on his face.

Vinnie grabbed his bag and turned to head back to the locker room. He was almost there when Molly caught up to him.

"You're going to patrol today? What the hell happened?"

"Nothing," Vinnie barked. He wasn't in the mood to talk to anyone. At least on patrol he could ride alone or ignore whoever he got sidelined with.

"That's bullshit. You hate patrol. You beat the shit out of Arthur for a reason."

Vinnie spun on Molly and got in her face. "Do I need a reason? He's a cocky son-of-a-bitch who doesn't deserve to be here. He threw down a challenge and couldn't live up to it, and I'm the one who's the asshole?"

Molly raised one eyebrow. "Back the fuck up. Right. Now."

Vinnie froze and realized he was towering over her. If he saw someone in his position over another person, he would have thrown them against the wall. Vinnie took a step back and shook his head. "I apologize. I was not trying to get in your face like that."

"I know, which is why I didn't kick your ass for it. What is wrong with you?"

"Nothing." Vinnie pushed past her and went into the locker room.

Molly followed. "Is this about the shooting yesterday? Are you still messed up about that?"

"No. I'd do the same thing again if I were in that situation. I know I did what needed to be done. Not that I liked it, but there's no telling what he would have done if I hadn't put him down."

"I agree. So what's up your ass? Did something happen with Agent Sloane?"

"It has nothing to do with her," Vinnie growled through clenched teeth.

Molly was silent while Vinnie shoved his SWAT uniform to the side and reached for the patrol uniform in the back of his locker. He tugged it on with jerky moves, fighting each item the whole way.

When he was done, he looked up at Molly.

"What happened with her?"

"Nothing."

"You're lying."

Vinnie snorted. "No, I'm not. Nothing happened. She wasn't at my place when I got home last night. Went out with her friends and stayed out all night. Didn't come back to my place at all."

"Okay. And?"

"And what?" he barked. "She leaned on me for two months. Needed me to help her with everything. And the day her cast comes off, she's gone? I'm just discarded trash that was only useful when she needed me."

"Are you really that dumb?" Molly asked.

Vinnie did not like being called dumb. Almost as much as he didn't like being told he deserved more than he knew he did.

Molly shook her head. "You came in here with a stick up your ass yesterday. She probably didn't want to deal with you when you got home. And you're pissed."

"She was talking about an ex. Some guy who helped her last time she broke something."

"And?"

"And apparently it's her pattern. Pair up with a guy who's around until she's healed, then skip out."

"How do you know that? Do you really think that's who she is?"

"You don't know her."

Molly laughed. "You're right. I don't. I've never had a conversation with her. But you have. For two months, you've been caring for this woman. For two months. You dropped everything here to go find her. From the way you told it, she jumped at the chance to stay with you. You were the only one she trusted. She had family and her partner and other friends who were all willing to let her stay. All kinds of people who would have taken care of her. Do you really think she was just using you until she was better? That it was worth it to her to stay in your fourth-floor walk-up one-bedroom apartment when she could have stayed with a billionaire who has more bedrooms in her house than your entire building?"

"She didn't know them," Vinnie defended.

"She didn't know you! You were a stranger, too. There's no reason she wanted to be with you except she wanted to be. She didn't know any of you, but she chose you. She didn't do it because it's a pattern. Are you really this oblivious?"

"What are you talking about?"

Molly tilted her head to the side. She looked at Vinnie long enough that he shuffled his feet uncomfortably.

"Why are you looking at him like that?" Hannah asked.

"Because he has no idea that Agent Sloane is in love with him," Molly said.

"Really?" Hannah asked, her lips lifting into a grin.

"See? She thinks you're crazy, too," Vinnie said.

Hannah snorted and turned to him. "Oh, no, sweetie, that wasn't because I agree with you. It was a surprise that you hadn't figured it out by now."

"She's not in love with me," Vinnie argued.

"Really? She's just been living with you for two months. Sleeping with you. Making a home with you. Her memories are coming back, and she never went to stay with anyone else. She's suffered through stairs and one-bedroom and a tub that could not have been easy to get into on crutches. And the real kicker? She's put up with you."

Vinnie growled at Molly.

"She's right," Hannah said. "There's no way in the world that woman is not in love with you. Now, if you don't feel the same, that's a problem for you to solve, but she's gone."

She's gone. Shit. She was gone. Or she would be when she got back to his place and found he'd packed all her stuff.

"What's that face for?" Hannah asked, circling her hand around Vinnie's head.

"I packed all her stuff last night."

"Oh, shit," Molly said.

"What does that mean?" Hannah asked.

"Agent Sloane stayed with a friend last night. Didn't come home before he left this morning. And while she was gone, he packed her shit," Molly explained while Vinnie pulled out his phone.

"And I left her a note."

"What did the note say?" Hannah asked.

Vinnie shook his head. "Nothing good. Fuck. I need to tell her I was wrong."

"So you love her?" Molly asked.

Vinnie sighed. He glared at his friends while they grinned like fools at him.

"Yeah, he loves her," Hannah said.

Vinnie let out a laugh and shook his head. "Yeah, but I messed up, and she's going to hate me."

"Then change her mind."

"How the hell do I do that?"

"You tell her you were wrong and that you love her and that you'll never, ever, be so stupid again as to think you know what's going on in her mind," Molly said.

Vinnie snorted. "Will that work?"

"No," Hannah said. "But lots of orgasms usually do the trick."

Molly nodded. "She's right."

Vinnie shook his head and scrolled his phone to find Lorelei's number. He tapped it and listened to it ring. And ring. And ring. Then her voicemail picked up.

"Call her again."

"Morgan!" a man called from down the hall.

"Shit. I gotta go," Vinnie hissed.

"Keep calling her. And when you get her, tell her not to read the note and that you're sorry."

"Always say you're sorry," Molly agreed.

Vinnie nodded. "Thanks. I love you guys."

"We love you," they said together. "Fix things so you can come back to SWAT next shift."

"I will. Thanks!" Vinnie took off, calling Lorelei again. Still no answer.

He would talk to her. He had to. He had to make everything okay.

VINNIE WAS twitchy the entire shift. He never got in touch with Lorelei, so as soon as he was off, he went to Karli's house.

Where no one answered the door.

"Dammit!" Vinnie shouted as he went back to his SUV. The house looked dark, so he guessed they really weren't home and not that they were all hiding from him.

He fucked up. In a big way. He pushed Lorelei away because he was afraid of loving her. Of wanting her and her rejecting him.

And he probably lost her because of it. A self-fulfilling prophecy.

What an idiot.

He could go to Adam's or Dawn's or maybe find one of the others, but would any of them want to help him get her back?

Probably not.

Vinnie drove by Adam's, but it was dark, too. Even though Molly pointed out that Lorelei could have stayed with Dawn, he doubted she'd be there. Lorelei would choose Karli or Adam. And both offered so there was no reason to think she would have gone somewhere else.

Like she chose to do when she moved in with him. She chose.

He was so blind.

Vinnie went home, making a plan to track Lorelei down on his first day off. He had two more days on shift, then he was going to find her. No matter where she ended up. Even if she went back to Boston.

He let himself into his apartment and stopped short when he realized the lights were on. The TV was on. Someone was in the kitchen.

"Lorelei," he breathed. "You're here."

She turned on him, a hand on her hip. "Yeah, I'm here. You don't get to kick me out. I'm not done with you, Vinnie Morgan."

"You're not?"

She shook her head. "No. I'm not. But I am mad at you. How dare you pack my shit? How dare you assume you know what I want?"

"I was an idiot."

"You're damn right you were. My ex did that. Mark? Who you freaked out about? He dumped me because when I got my cast off my arm, I didn't need him anymore. He thought I was going to stay home and require his help forever. That I was going to turn into some alternate reality version of myself. He told me I was too independent for him. You know what I did?"

Vinnie shook his head.

"I tried to prove to myself that being independent was good. That I didn't need anyone else. I was so set on being independent, I stopped sharing things with my partner. I stopped reaching out to friends and family. And I made the worst decision of my life and met with an informant alone and almost got myself killed."

Vinnie sighed and took a step toward her.

"And then I met you. And you didn't need me. I needed you, but you knew who I was. More than I did. You were here for me, in every possible way. And then you decided it was too much. But you don't get to decide that, Vinnie Morgan, because I'm in love with you. And if you don't feel the same, that's fine. I will go if you really want me to, but you don't get to throw me out without telling me to my face that you don't love me."

Vinnie took a step forward, then another, and another. He didn't stop until he cupped her jaw and lifted her face so he could see only her. "I am the biggest idiot on the planet. I convinced myself you didn't need me. You didn't want me. I have never had anyone who wanted me because of who I am. It was always what I could do for them. My grandmother got extra money from the government for taking care of me. My dad got to leave and have a better life without me. All my exes wanted the cop or the man who took care of things, but it wasn't about me. No one ever wanted me."

"I did. I do," she whispered.

Vinnie nodded. "I want you, too. I am so sorry I packed your stuff and left you that note. I never should have done either. I—"

"I ripped the note up and never read it," she confessed. "And I moved all my stuff back in."

Vinnie breathed a laugh. "Good. On both."

"Are you sure?"

"More than I've ever been about anything. I love you, Lorelei Sloane."

"Thank God. It took you long enough to say it. I thought I was going to have to re-pack all my stuff and ask Karli if I could move in with her."

"Please stay, Lorelei." He cupped her jaw and tilted her face up to meet his gaze. "Let me prove I'm worthy of you."

"You honestly think you're not?"

He shook his head. "No one is worthy of you. You're... amazing. And I'm the lucky one you chose to be with. I want you to know you will always be the one I choose. I will always want a place in your life. I will always want to take care of you."

"I have a lot of needs."

"I promise to fulfill all of them."

"Can we start now? Because it was really lonely sleeping without you last night. I missed you a lot."

He slid his hands down to her ass and squeezed both cheeks. "How much is a lot?"

"So much that I don't think it'll take any work at all to get me to come."

"Oh, yeah?"

"Yeah. Make love to me, Vinnie."

He growled at her words and lifted her. She wrapped her legs around his hips and kissed him while he carried her to the bedroom. He set her down inside the bedroom door and they worked together to yank clothes off, leaving them in a puddle for later.

He rolled a condom on as she laid on the bed, then he positioned himself between her wet thighs. In two strokes, he was fully seated in her.

"Fuck, you're wet."

"I've been hoping we would end up here. I've been thinking about all the ways I was going to convince you to love me."

He shook his head. "I'm sorry I was such an idiot. That I tried to push you away."

"You're not going to do that again," she said, reaching up to cup his jaw.

"Never." He kissed her palm, then her wrist. He withdrew his hips and slammed hard into her.

"Yes," she breathed.

He reached between them and pressed down on her clit, already there and needing to feel her come on his cock.

"Vinnie," she moaned. "Oh, yes."

She came softly, her eyes locked on his and her body pulling him over the edge with her.

He rolled to the side and pulled her with him, holding her tight and knowing he was never going to let her go.

22

THE NEXT NIGHT, LORELEI WAS WAITING FOR VINNIE TO GET home from work when her phone rang. She didn't recognize the number, but she knew there were likely people whose numbers she never saved, so she answered it.

"Hello?"

"Lorelei?"

"Yes. Can I help you?"

"I hope so. I wanted to meet with you again. You said to call if I had new information. I have something to share with you. Something you're really going to want to hear."

Lorelei closed her eyes. The memory came back in a rush, too fast for her to capture it all. Too much.

"You were there," Lorelei breathed.

"Where?" the woman asked.

"I... I was kidnapped," Lorelei admitted.

"What? When?" she gasped.

"I... When we met before. My memories have been slowly coming back."

"Wait, you have amnesia? You don't know who I am, do

you? Oh, God, how do I know they didn't flip you? You could be working for the other side."

"I'm working for the FBI. I'm not a double agent."

"Isn't that what anyone would say? I never should have called you."

"You said you have information. That it's something I would want to hear."

The woman was silent. Her soft breath was the only sound coming through the phone.

"Are you still there?"

"How do I know I can trust you?"

"I was the one who was kidnapped. How do I know you weren't involved?"

She gasped. "I would never." A soft sob came through the line. "I went to you because you said you would always fight for the right people. That you wanted to stop the people who've been killing and kidnapping others."

"I do. I'm still trying to do that."

"You don't even know what you're looking for."

"It sounds like you do."

The woman sucked in a breath, letting it out slowly.

Lorelei waited. She knew this was the informant she spoke to the night she was taken. More memories were trying to fight to the surface, but she needed to set a meeting with this woman. She needed her to trust Lorelei.

If she was involved, she could lead them to whoever was in charge. If she wasn't, she had information that could help. Either way, Lorelei needed to meet with the woman.

"You can tell me what you want to say over the phone," Lorelei prompted. It was never a good idea, and it wasn't something she'd ever advise anyone. If they were sharing information, there was a chance their phone was being monitored by someone. But if the woman refused to meet, Lorelei was willing to take the chance.

"You said never to do that. Always meet in person. Never share information that could blow up an investigation over the phone."

"Then we need to meet."

"Fine, but it has to be tonight. I don't want the people who took you to come after me."

"Neither do I. Where do you want to meet?"

"Do you remember where we met last time?"

Lorelei drew a breath and closed her eyes. She saw flowers, big red ones. Water ran by, not too fast but steady. There was a building, glass. Like a greenhouse or conservatory. Lorelei knew the place. "Yes. I know where we met."

"Two hours," the woman said, then hung up the phone without another word.

Lorelei sucked in a breath and lowered the phone. She kept her eyes closed and replayed the conversations with the woman. The one that just ended, then the one they had when Lorelei was at the wedding.

"I need your help. That case you're working on. I have information for you, but someone's been following me."

"Can you get to our usual spot? I can meet you in an hour."

"Yeah, I think so."

"Are you sure?"

"Yeah. You'll be there, right?"

"Yes."

"Thank you."

Lorelei hung up and headed for the exit. Mackenzie and Dawn stopped her and asked where she was going. She knew the informant. They'd met before. It was safe.

Lorelei went to the hotel where she'd been staying. She

changed out of the dress she wore to the wedding, swapping the satin and heels for jeans and sneakers.

Meeting an informant alone was something she'd done a million times. She didn't need backup for it. She was fine alone. Even though this meeting was more important than any other one she'd ever had in her career.

Lorelei parked her car and walked down the path toward the large glass building. The dome seemed to sparkle in the black of night, the inhabitants sleeping. A cluster of trees in front hid a bench that was perfect for quiet conversations. It had become a spot Lorelei used for meeting informants more than once.

The woman crept out of the dark when Lorelei arrived. Her jeans and black shirt made her almost invisible until she moved.

"Were you followed?" the woman asked.

Lorelei shook her head. "Were you?"

"I don't think so. Not tonight."

"Who's been following you?"

"I don't know. I've seen the same vehicle parked outside work three nights in a row. And it was down the street from my apartment before that."

"What kind of vehicle was it?"

"A black SUV. Tinted windows and black roof racks."

Lorelei fought the eye roll that ached to come out. Black SUVs were a dime a dozen and could have been a different one every time. "How do you know they were following you?"

"When I would leave, the SUV would follow me."

Lorelei nodded. That was something. But the informant was paranoid and frequently thought someone was after her, even though Lorelei had never found any evidence of it.

"You said you had information for me?"

The woman nodded. "There's a house down the street from my apartment. One of those women who was on the news was there. Edie something."

"*Edie Warren?*" *Lorelei asked.*

The woman snapped her fingers. "That's the one. It was a few months ago, and I didn't know who she was then. I just figured she was looking to score, but then I saw the news and I remembered seeing her there."

"What's the address?"

The woman recited an address Lorelei wasn't familiar with, but she typed it into the notes on her phone.

"Did you see any other women there?"

The woman nodded. "A few, but none of them were on the news."

"Can you describe any of them?"

Her nose scrunched. "They looked like they'd been on drugs. Vacant eyes and hollow cheeks. Clothes that barely covered them or that were so tight they were asking for a UTI."

"If they were being held captive, I don't think the people who had them were worried about their health."

The woman shrugged.

"Is there anything else you can tell me?"

"Do I get paid now?"

"Not until we recover something. But you'll get credit for giving me the information."

"And then I'll get paid?"

Lorelei nodded. "Yes, then you'll get paid. But first, the information needs to be validated, so it might be a little while."

"If I have something else, I get more, right?"

"Do you have something else?" Lorelei demanded. She wasn't running a fucking charity. She was looking for women who were kidnapped and forced into sex slavery. Piecing out information was not okay.

"No. But if I do, I can call you again?"

"Yes, please call me again if you have new information."

"Okay. I will. And you'll let me know when you can pay me?"

"Of course."

The woman nodded, then slipped back into the darkness.

Lorelei stood there for a few minutes, waiting to hear a vehicle or some other indicator of how the woman got there. There were homes not far, but the woman lived in the city.

Lorelei recorded her notes from the meeting, then returned to her vehicle. It unlocked with a beep, but a noise behind her had Lorelei turning.

And coming face-to-face with a fist.

Lorelei's eyes popped open.

She gasped. She didn't see the man who was behind the fist, but she knew it was the same one she had dreams of when she was in the hospital and shortly after. The one who held her.

A key in the lock had her screaming before she processed what was going on.

Vinnie rushed in, his gaze going right to her. He locked the door and dropped to his knees in front of her. "What's wrong? It's me. Are you okay?"

Lorelei nodded, her breath rushing out of her in pants of fear. She couldn't get the words out. The rush of it all was too much. Too much.

VINNIE HELD A TREMBLING Lorelei in his arms and rocked her. She shook with fear, but he didn't know what she was afraid of. It didn't matter, he wasn't going to let anything scare her.

"I got a call from the woman I met the night I was taken," she whispered.

"What?" Vinnie pulled back to look at her.

She worried her lip and nodded.

"Who is she? What did she want?"

"I don't know her name. I know she was someone I'd spoken to more than once, but I don't know her name. She asked if we could meet tonight."

"Tonight?" Vinnie barked. He jerked his emotions back. Lorelei was an FBI Agent. She was strong and smart and tough. His desire to protect her was because he loved her, but she didn't need his protection, and he needed to remember that.

Lorelei nodded and looked at the phone in her hand. "In an hour."

"Are you going to meet her?"

Lorelei nodded. "I have to. She said she has information for me." She looked up at him, her eyes wide as though really seeing him for the first time since he walked in the door. "Will you come with me?"

Vinnie nodded quickly, fighting the relieved sigh that filled him. "Yes. Of course. We should probably call Adam, too."

Lorelei shook her head. "No. She's easily spooked. If she even sees you, I think she'll take off."

"What's her story?"

Lorelei stared off at the coffee table. "I don't know. From what I remembered, she is paranoid and always thinks someone is after her. The night I was taken, she thought someone was following her."

"She called you about that?"

"No, she called me because she saw Edie at a house down the street from her apartment."

"She what?" Vinnie gasped. As far as he knew, Edie Warren as at Adam and Raina's wedding the night Lorelei disappeared.

"She said it was months before, but that she didn't know

it was Edie until after she was out. There were other women there, Vinnie."

"Adam needs to know about this. Do you know where that was?"

Lorelei nodded. "She told me the address. It was in my phone, but obviously, they didn't let me keep that. Apparently, it wasn't backed up before it was destroyed."

"Neither was the woman's contact information, or they would have talked to her. No one ever knew who you met that night."

"Then I think it's time we go find out."

LORELEI DROVE, not wanting the woman to know someone was with her when she arrived. Vinnie hid in the backseat when they pulled into the parking lot, making sure he wasn't seen by anyone who might be there.

Lorelei's heart raced as she got out of the SUV and made her way around the building to the bench under the trees. The plan was for Vinnie to follow her after two minutes and to hide in the shrubbery that surrounded the building. It would give him a view of the meeting but would also keep his location concealed.

Five minutes after Lorelei sat down, the woman came out of the darkness like she did before. Her jeans and black tee were similar to what Lorelei remembered before. Her dark hair was tied up in a ponytail. Her face was pale, almost ghostly in the darkness.

"Are you here alone?" the woman asked.

"I made sure I wasn't followed. I want to protect you."

"But you don't remember me?"

Lorelei shook her head. "Not entirely. What new information did you have to share with me?"

The woman didn't speak for a moment, staring at Lorelei with her head tilted to the side. Studying her. "Where were you taken?"

Lorelei sat up straighter. "Excuse me?"

"Where did he take you? Was it to one of the houses where they keep the other women?"

"What...?" Lorelei had a flash of memory. She saw half a dozen women in a room. Mattresses on the floor, a bucket in the corner. The door was wide open, but none of them were trying to get away.

"What did he do to you?"

"You set me up," Lorelei whispered.

"You weren't supposed to survive," the woman said. "You won't this time."

"What?" Lorelei jumped up as she heard a noise behind her.

"Lorelei, watch out!" Vinnie shouted.

Lorelei moved just before a bat hit the bench she was sitting on. The wood splintered.

The woman's eyes went wide. She scrambled backward.

Lorelei was not going to let her get away. She went after the woman into the darkness, knowing Vinnie would take care of whoever had the bat.

The tree cover was thick, and the darkness didn't help. Lorelei stopped for a second, listening for a sound to tell her where the woman went. A twig snapped to her right, and she turned to go that way.

The woman ran toward the parking lot. It was empty when Lorelei and Vinnie got there, and she didn't hear any cars pull in.

The sound of fighting behind her made Lorelei pause and think about turning back to help Vinnie, but she had to find the woman. Needed to know why she handed her over. Who she was. What was going on.

The woman turned the corner of the building and was out of sight for fifteen seconds when Lorelei heard a gunshot.

Lorelei crouched low, unsure which direction the shot came from or who took it. Behind her were footsteps. Did the woman somehow get behind her? And who was shooting?

"Lorelei!" Vinnie shouted.

"I'm here," she replied.

He was close, the footsteps she heard. "Was that you?"

Lorelei shook her head as he cupped her jaw and ran his hands over her body. "I don't have my gun. I don't know who fired."

"You're not hit?"

"No. I'm good."

Vinnie pulled his gun from his holster and handed it to her. He took his second one and nodded to her. "Let's go."

Lorelei took the lead, feeling a mix of relief and gratitude that he was still going to let her lead. They were side-by-side when they came around the edge of the building.

The woman was on the ground. Blood poured from her head. Her vacant eyes stared up at them.

"They're getting away," Vinnie hissed, moving around Lorelei.

She looked up and saw a vehicle driving along the edge of the parking area. A man ran toward the silent SUV with a splintered bat in his hand. The door opened, and he jumped in, and the SUV took off before Vinnie or Lorelei could get close enough to see anything.

"Dammit!" Vinnie shouted.

"What the hell just happened?" Lorelei asked.

Vinnie sighed and shook his head. "I don't know, but if we're lucky, she can tell us something."

"She's dead, Vinnie."

He nodded. "Yeah, but that doesn't mean we can't find out everything there is to know about her."

LAW ENFORCEMENT SWARMED the park within minutes. Adam, Marcus, Pryce, and a few other familiar faces were there. Vinnie and Lorelei told their stories to all of them, and then were left alone while the cops gathered evidence.

"I can't believe I didn't know she was the one who handed me over to them," Lorelei said when she and Vinnie sat down. "How did I not see it?"

"She gave you information. Why would you think she was playing both sides?"

Lorelei shook her head. "I don't know. I just..." Lorelei looked at the body covered in a white sheet. The medical examiner wasn't there yet, so the woman was simply covered. "It's my job to be able to read people."

"She was good."

"Yeah, but I should have been better."

"You were better."

"No, I wasn't. She surprised me. Again."

"But this time you weren't alone," Vinnie said.

Lorelei drew a breath. He was right.

"You aren't the same person you were when you met her before. When you thought being independent was the best way. You've learned that sometimes you need your team. Sometimes going at it alone isn't the right answer."

Lorelei hugged Vinnie. "Thank you for being here for me. If you hadn't come, I'd be gone again. This time for good."

"I'm not going to let that happen."

23

———

THE BOSS SAT BEHIND HER DESK AND LISTENED TO THE REPORT. It was not a good report. Not even a little. It was a fucking disaster.

"Do you know how many chances I typically give people, Benjamin?"

He shuffled his feet and shook his head.

"That's because the answer is zero," she growled.

His gaze snapped to hers. He knew his days were numbered. "It wasn't my fault. She wasn't alone."

"And you should have known that." The boss slammed her fist onto the desk as she stood. "You should have been prepared for that. Both of you should have known she wouldn't come alone again."

"Sonya said the agent didn't remember anything."

"She remembered enough to know where to meet! She remembered! How fucking stupid are you?"

"Sonya was the one who set this up. She said—"

"Sonya's not saying anything ever again. We made sure of that. You won't either if you don't take care of that fucking agent like I told you to do the first time. She shouldn't have survived long enough to be found in Boston. And now you let her get away again. Her memories are returning. It's only a matter of time before she remembers everything." She curled her fingers against the desktop, her nails scratching the surface. Bile rose in her throat. Fear. She swallowed it down. There was no space for fear.

"I'll take care of her. I promise."

"You better. You aren't getting more chances."

Benjamin nodded and raced out of the room.

She let out a breath and fought the tears building. Crying was a weakness. Emotions were a weakness. She'd had that beat into her many times. Letting it out now wasn't an option. There was one option.

End the threats against her. All of them.

"Are you okay?" Nina asked, snapping the boss out of her thoughts.

"No. Did you hear what Benjamin said?"

Nina shook her head. "I didn't. I heard him leave, and I was worried about you."

The boss glared at Nina. The sniveling bitch thought she was so smart. So intuitive. That she knew what was going on. "Do you think I can't take care of myself? I'm so weak that I would let anything happen to me?"

"No," Nina rushed to say. "I know you wanted things handled. And Benjamin isn't doing what he's supposed to do. I don't like when you're not getting the results you expect."

The boss eased the fist she clenched. Nina was pushing more and more lately. Acting like she had power. She didn't. There was only one person with power.

"I always get the results I expect. And when someone fucks up like Sonya and Benjamin, they are handled."

"Sonya?" Nina asked.

"She's dead. She didn't do her fucking job, so I had Jonathan put a bullet in her head before he brought Benjamin back here to update me."

Nina's eyes widened. Fear crossed her face.

Good. She needed to know her place. All of them did. The boss wasn't fucking around. She was a goddamn leader. And if they didn't want to follow, they could eat a fucking bullet.

And would.

Nina wiped her lashes, catching a tear before it spilled onto her cheeks, but the boss saw the move and smirked.

"Aw, you cared about her. Was she your friend?"

Nina shook her head.

The boss crossed the room, stopping right in front of Nina. "Did you think the two of you would ever get out of here? That I'd let you go? You know too much, Nina. You'll never leave me. Will you?"

Nina wiped another tear and shook her head again.

The boss grabbed the bitch's red hair and yanked.

Nina yelped.

"Are you going to leave me, Nina?" the boss demanded, tugging her hair again.

Nina shook her head. "No. I'm not going to leave you. Why would I?"

"There's no reason for you to even consider it."

Nina nodded.

The boss let go of her, shoving Nina away and turning to go back to her desk. "Get out."

Nina scurried for the door.

As soon as it closed behind her, the boss sank into her chair. She stared at the wall, remembering the day she took over. The day she walked in and put a bullet in her father's head because he thought her brother was a better choice to take over the family business.

The boss made sure her father knew what happened to his precious son before she shot him. Her father begged her not to kill him.

She hadn't shed a tear that day, and she wasn't going to shed any now. She was in charge. She earned it. And she wasn't going to lose it.

Lorelei woke with a start, sitting upright in bed as memories flooded back to her. Dreams? Memories? She didn't know the difference.

For three days, since her meeting in the park, she'd been waking up in the middle of a dream. She was brought into a mansion, gray stone with a wide front staircase that led to a solid wood door. She was dragged through the house, a maze of hallways and doors before she was shoved into a room.

A room lined with plastic.

She wasn't supposed to live through it. They intended to kill her. She wouldn't have been the first.

"Another dream?" Vinnie asked, sitting up and kissing her shoulder.

Lorelei nodded.

"I'll go start coffee." He grabbed his shorts from the floor next to the bed and padded out of the room wearing only those shorts.

Lorelei hated that she was ruining their sleepy mornings with memories, but she couldn't stop them. Not even Vinnie's presence was helping her sleep anymore.

Lorelei closed her eyes and tried to go back to the house.

To see more details. She knew it was gray stone, but she didn't know where it was. How far away. What was around it.

Or if it was real.

Vinnie asked her the first morning if she wanted to talk about it, but she shook her head. It didn't feel real. Like it was a place she constructed. After three days with the same dream, she wondered if it really was where she was held.

Lorelei grabbed Vinnie's tee, then used the bathroom before she joined him in the kitchen. She slid her hands up his chest and pressed her cheek to his back.

He grabbed her hands and squeezed, pulling them away so he could spin in her embrace and hold her to his chest. He held her without a word, letting her decide what she wanted to say.

"I keep seeing this house. A mansion, really. I was led inside and dragged through hallways and dumped in a room lined with plastic."

Vinnie sucked in a breath.

"I know they asked me questions and tortured me. I don't remember any of that yet, but when they tired of me, they stashed me in a room with other women."

"Oh, God," Vinnie exhaled.

"I don't know if any of it is real, though. If the place is real or if the women were real. It all feels fuzzy."

"Do you remember anything else about it?"

Lorelei shook her head. "Not really. It was huge. I didn't go upstairs, but I saw a staircase when I walked in. There were a lot of rooms, but most of the doors were closed. I heard yelling in some. Crying, screaming."

"You think they were operating their sex trafficking out of the house?"

"It's possible. Sonya said she saw Edie at a house near her apartment. It makes sense they'd have others."

Vinnie nodded. "It's possible. Especially since there was so much evidence at that house of others being there."

Lorelei nodded, resting her head on Vinnie again. If she hadn't been taken, they might have found some of those women. Instead, when the house was searched, it was empty. Stained mattresses and torn clothing were only small pieces of the evidence they found that led to the conclusion it had been used for exactly what they all feared.

"This house was huge, though. I haven't seen anything like it around here."

"You remember the outside?"

"A little. Gray stone. Lots of it. A huge front staircase that curves at the edges and leads to a solid wood front door."

"Gravel driveway?" Vinnie asked.

"You know it?" Lorelei breathed.

Vinnie nodded. "I think I do."

Lorelei pulled back and walked out of the kitchen.

"Where are you going?"

"We need a meeting."

"A meeting? I didn't know you were in AA."

She shook her head. "Not that kind. A Curvy Vigilantes meeting." Lorelei tapped her screen and listened to the phone ring. "I remembered where I was held. Vinnie knows the place. We need to meet. Now."

"I'll call everyone," Frannie replied. "Get here as soon as you can. Bring Vinnie."

"We'll be there soon." Lorelei hung up the phone and looked up at a confused Vinnie. "We need to go to Frannie's shelter. They've been running a secret investigation team to find out what the hell is going on. We need to tell everyone about this and put an end to this for good."

"Let's go."

VINNIE PUT his hand on Lorelei's as they waited for everyone to arrive at Shelter in the Storm. Anxiety radiated off her, flooding him as well and making the entire room tense.

Marcus and Pryce were the last to arrive, with an anxious Edie staring at the door until they walked in. When they did, all eyes turned to Lorelei.

"Since the park, I've been having a dream about where I was kept. I didn't think it was a real place, but Vinnie thinks he knows where it is," Lorelei said.

"Oh, my God," Edie breathed.

Pryce wrapped his arm around her and kissed the side of her head.

Vinnie hoped like hell this was the end. That women like Edie who were held captive and people who loved her would finally get the closure they needed. They deserved.

"Where is it?" Marcus asked.

"There's an old mansion out on the edge of town. We've never been able to get close. It's owned by a corporation, from what I know. I went there once, years ago, on patrol. A neighbor reported hearing gunshots."

"What did you find?" Marcus asked.

Vinnie shook his head. "Nothing. We weren't allowed on the property. As soon as we turned onto the driveway, we were stopped by private security. They said the shots were target practice. That the property is a hundred acres and they have always been able to host private functions that included target practice."

"And you didn't question it?" Mackenzie asked.

"We did. Absolutely. But the corporation is private, and

they had an answer for what happened. Showed us a live feed of their security system with a group firing at targets set up behind the house," Vinnie explained. "It matched up with the neighbor's report."

"So, you left?" Edie asked.

"We had to. They refused to give us access to the property, and without the owner's approval, we had no right to be there. The neighbor heard gunshots, and the owners provided an explanation."

"They're allowed to fire guns on their property?" Stacey asked.

"As long as they are five-hundred feet from any dwelling, then yes," Marcus said.

"Were they?" Stacey asked Vinnie.

Vinnie nodded. "The property was massive. A hundred acres is more than enough for them to legally fire guns."

"They had documentation ready to show you?" Edie asked.

Vinnie nodded. "Said it happened a lot. Neighbors called it in all the time. Nothing we could do, and I didn't think much of it. Until Lorelei described the house. We could see it from the driveway. It was built close to the road, relatively speaking. Couldn't see anything else, but I saw the house. Just like she described."

"Could you find your way back there?" Marcus asked.

Vinnie nodded again. "Yeah. But it's not like we can go knock on the door. It's a fortress. Cameras and fences all over, armed security. And if it's where she was, that's not all."

"What do you mean?" Pryce asked.

"There were guards all over the inside, too," Lorelei said. "At every door, in every hallway. Not an inch of that place is unprotected."

"Then it sounds like exactly where we need to go," Marcus said. "But we can't do this alone."

"I'll call Liam," Adam said. "Get F-BOMB involved."

"I'll reach out to Rose Protection Agency," Gage said, already calling. Dawn followed him out of the room to talk to them.

Marcus, Pryce, and Vinnie exchanged a glance.

"Who do we want with us?" Marcus asked.

"Foster is on vacation," Pryce said. "Otherwise he'd be here."

"My team can help," Vinnie said.

Marcus nodded. "I was thinking that. I don't know how many people we need. How many we should have."

"As many as we can," Pryce answered. "This is it. This is our chance to end this. We have concrete evidence."

"Do we?" Marcus asked. He looked around the room at the people left. "We have the faulty memory of a woman recovering from amnesia and the corroboration of someone who's never been more than a dozen feet onto the property, a decade ago."

"It's more than nothing," Frannie said.

Marcus nodded. "It is, but I don't know if it's enough for a warrant."

"Then we don't get one," Wray Allen said. "We just go in."

Marcus shook his head. "If this is all going to stick, we need a warrant. We need to do this by the book. Make sure whoever is in that house doesn't get away with all the things they've done."

"Then you have some work to do," Frannie said. "Go convince a judge we're right."

Marcus nodded and looked at Pryce. "Let's go. Two of us are better than one." Marcus turned to Vinnie. "Expect a call from Damien. I'll let him know we have a raid to do so he can call all of you in."

Vinnie nodded. "We're going to end this today."

"Yes, we are."

Lorelei wrapped her arms around Vinnie's waist. He kissed the top of her head and knew this was the end. This house was it. This was going to stop all the hell their city had been through.

He just hoped they survived it.

WHEN VINNIE'S PHONE RANG, Lorelei knew it was the call that would take him away from her. He didn't let on to his boss that he was expecting the call, just agreed to report to work ASAP.

He hung up the phone and took her hand, leading her to the front of the building where they could be alone. "I have no idea what my assignment is going to be or where I'm going to end up, but I will be there."

Lorelei nodded. "I know. I wish you could go in with us, but I know your team needs you."

"And I need you. Be careful. Whatever you do, be careful."

Lorelei swallowed roughly. She was not looking forward to returning to that house. To seeing the place her mind had blocked for more than two months. She was scared, but she knew she had to be there.

"I love you," Vinnie whispered against her lips. "And I will see you later."

Lorelei kissed him, letting herself get lost in the goodness she found with Vinnie. He was the person she'd always hoped to find. And she wasn't going to lose him. "I love you. Next time I see you, this will be over."

"Yes, it will."

Vinnie kissed her again, then let himself out the front door. Lorelei watched him until he got in his SUV and drove away.

She returned to the dining room where everyone had gathered and sat down to wait. She didn't know how long it would be, but she knew it was the right move to do this the right way. With a warrant and a team that couldn't be overpowered by whoever was hiding in that house.

Word came through that they were ready, and Lorelei watched as the women in the room with her transformed. Every single one of them stood and moved toward the door. They were willing to sacrifice themselves for this. To take down the people who'd affected their lives. To end this hell.

"You guys can't come," Lorelei said. "You're civilians."

Frannie chuckled and shook her head. "You're wrong, Lorelei. We're vigilantes, and we're not letting you go in there alone. We will be there, no matter what." Frannie slid a black mask onto her face, and all the others followed suit.

Lorelei remembered the mask Frannie gave her. She'd never worn it, but it was in the handbag she had slung across her body. Lorelei pulled it out and put her mask on, looking at the other women.

They all nodded and walked out together. The Curvy Vigilantes.

24

———

Lorelei sat in the SUV and let her instincts settle around her. For months, she'd been doubting them, telling herself her instincts were wrong and that she needed to know and understand things in order for them to make sense, but that was bullshit. That was the amnesia and the uncertainty talking.

She knew who the fuck she was. And nothing was going to stop her from going into the fortress of a house and taking back what was stolen from her.

Lorelei knew Vinnie was going to be there, but she didn't know what his team was doing. It was no longer her case to lead since her memory hadn't fully returned, but Lorelei was happy to follow Adam's directions and knew her partner would run a flawless operation.

With the search warrant in hand, the SUV parked beyond the gate with all the other vehicles. They were prepared for a fight. It wasn't going to be an easy mission, but they were going to come out of it victorious. Lorelei had to believe that.

When it was time to move, Adam and Marcus led the

way to the front. Their vehicles were surrounded before they made it to the house that Lorelei remembered with such clarity she had no doubt it was where she was taken. Where she was held. Where others likely still were.

The shootout started before anyone got to the mansion. It didn't matter that they expected it, it clicked everything into place.

This was real. People were going to try to kill them. As many as possible. And someone was going to try to get away.

Lorelei moved with the other agents as a unit, working their way closer and closer to the door. As soon as they picked off one shooter, another took their place. The guy beside her fell, someone in front did, too, but the rest of the group kept moving.

They couldn't stop.

When they made it to the door, they fanned out. One group went left, one right, and Lorelei went with Adam straight ahead. She knew that was the direction she'd been carried and demanded that as her path. Adam couldn't refuse her.

The pop of gunfire echoed through the house. Screams of people in fear and the telltale sound of flesh hitting the floor added to the carnage. This level of security didn't exist unless they were protecting something valuable.

Or someone.

Lorelei wanted to search her memory for the name. Something told her it was there. She knew who the boss was.

But she didn't. So she kept pushing forward.

As her group followed the twists and turns of the hallways, it got down to Lorelei and Adam. They barely had to speak as they went deeper into the hell of the house that held more secrets than all the FBI combined.

Lorelei's heart raced. Her body pumped with adrenaline. Sweat poured from her, soaking the clothes she wore beneath her bulletproof vest.

They didn't stop. They kept moving, searching.

"Freeze," Adam barked at a pair at the end of the hallway.

The two people stopped. One cried out, a female.

Lorelei followed Adam down the hallway, their guns locked on the two people. It didn't matter that the woman seemed to be fighting to get away from the man, they were both there, which meant they were both threats.

Adam shined his flashlight on the woman, and as soon as he did, the man shoved her at them.

Unsteady on her heels, the woman tripped and landed on Adam, knocking him to the floor while the man took off down another hallway.

Lorelei didn't move, her gun on the woman. She was barely clothed, her dress torn, no bra, and heels that cut into her red flesh.

Adam pushed the woman back, moving her easily. "I got her. Go."

Lorelei stepped over Adam and the woman, knowing she wasn't a threat. The woman sobbed and held her hands out for Adam to cuff her. She was more scared than anything and relieved to be arrested instead of carted off with the man Lorelei went after.

Lorelei moved through the halls, the air changing the farther she followed the man. It grew damp, like they were underground. The sound of gunfire was softer, too.

Where was he going?

Lorelei barely wondered before she heard a sound. She stopped, listening again.

An inhale. Quick. Close.

Lorelei turned toward the sound. She took a step forward.

He growled. A two-by-four came out of the darkness and slammed into her shoulder.

Lorelei stumbled backward, catching herself on the wall. Her gun clattered to the floor, skidding away from her as the man charged forward.

"Gah!" he yelled as he ran.

Lorelei blocked his attempt to get to her and landed a quick kick to his crotch.

"You bitch," he hissed.

Ice cold fear ran down her spine. She knew that voice. She'd been taunted by that voice. In her dreams, yes, but before that, in the very house they were in.

"It was you," she breathed without thought of her words.

"You remember me? I'm touched," the man said. His grunt as he stood brought reality back to Lorelei. "Too bad you won't be able to tell anyone anything about me."

"Why's that?"

"Because you're not going to make it out of here again. I'll kill you right here."

He smiled, his white teeth catching the little light in the darkness. He raised his arm and didn't hesitate to pull the trigger.

The searing pain as the bullet grazed her arm was enough to send her running. She took cover around the corner, spotting her gun a few feet from her, in plain view of the man who was trying to kill her.

Run and hide or fight back? Lorelei knew she didn't have time to debate her options. She put the mask back on, knowing the other Curvy Vigilantes were somewhere in the house, sneaking out the women prisoners and saving as many people as possible.

Lorelei wasn't going to run. She was going to fight back. Because she was a Curvy Vigilante.

Footsteps drew closer, and Lorelei knew she was out of time. She took a breath and ran for her gun. She grabbed it just as another bullet sliced through her, this one splitting her side.

She didn't stop, just turned and fired toward the man, hoping she slowed him down enough to get a better shot.

His grunt and string of curse words told her she hit her target.

"Lorelei!" Vinnie shouted.

"Vinnie!" she called back.

Help was coming. She was okay. And the man who took her was never going to hurt anyone else again.

When Vinnie's team breached the back doors of the house, he focused solely on his task. He and Molly moved through the house as one, clearing rooms and sending presumed innocents out for the FBI to interrogate. Their job was to take down as many people as possible.

Vinnie and Molly found Adam with a crying woman in his arms, the woman barely able to walk. She was scared, high, and injured.

But all Vinnie cared about was where Lorelei was.

"She followed the assailant down the hall," Adam reported, his words immediately followed by the echo of a gunshot.

Vinnie didn't wait for Adam to say anything else, he took off down the hallway. Vinnie knew Molly was with him, not hesitating to move deeper into the unknown.

Another gunshot echoed to the right, and Vinnie called out to her.

When she replied, he almost collapsed with relief.

He and Molly followed the sound of Lorelei's voice and spotted her on the floor, covered in blood.

"Lorelei," Vinnie breathed.

"Stop," she said. "We're not alone." She pointed to the hallway that separated them.

Vinnie and Molly moved into position, Molly covering Vinnie so he could move around to Lorelei.

He made it across the hall without incident, and Molly followed a few seconds later.

"No one's there," Molly reported.

"What? He has to be. I shot him." Lorelei tried to get up from where she'd propped herself against the wall, but Vinnie put a hand on her shoulder.

"Stay here. We'll go check."

Molly went first, and Vinnie followed. They moved down the hallway nearly a hundred feet and found no one. The darkness prevented them from seeing much, but there was definitely not anyone there.

They returned to Lorelei and found her passed out.

"Lorelei!" Vinnie shouted. "Don't leave me. Come back to me, beautiful."

Her eyes blinked open. "Help me."

"Lorelei."

"Please," she whispered. Her lips were a breath from his. Every inhale brought her chest into contact with his. Every exhale took her away from him.

No one was going to take her away from him again. Not now. Not ever. She was his.

Vinnie scooped her up and nodded to Molly. Without a word, she moved with Vinnie, making sure Lorelei got out of there safely. They would send a team for the man who shot her. All that mattered was getting her help.

"WHERE ARE WE GOING?" Nina asked.

The boss nearly turned and slapped the whiney bitch. She'd almost had enough of her questioning everything. "We're getting the hell out of here. Do you want me to leave you here?"

Nina didn't answer. Good. Maybe she wouldn't argue so much after almost being arrested.

As soon as the alarm went off to let them know someone was on the property, Fernando was in the room and getting them out. He led the private security team that made sure no one ever touched her. Including her own people.

A grunt sounded to the left, and Fernando stopped them, putting himself between the women and the noise.

"It's me," Benjamin barked.

"What the hell is wrong with you?" Fernando demanded.

"That bitch agent shot me."

"Did you shoot her back?" the boss asked, stepping around Fernando to get in Benjamin's face.

Benjamin stood upright, the pain on his face drawing her gaze to the blood soaking through his clothes.

"Is she alive?"

"Yeah. That fucking SWAT guy came."

"And you ran away? Like a weak fucking piece of shit?"

"I—"

The boss didn't give him a chance to defend himself. She grabbed Fernando's gun from his holster and fired three silent rounds into Benjamin's chest.

Nina squeaked, but she smartly kept quiet.

"Let's go," the boss said, stepping over Benjamin's face-down body and continuing down the hall toward the underground garage that led to a series of tunnels and would get them off the property miles from where the cops thought they had them surrounded.

When they got in the SUV, Nina wiped tears from her cheeks and turned to the boss. "Why did you kill him?"

The boss glared at her. She was becoming more of a nuisance. More... compassionate. There was no space for that. No room for someone who thought what they were doing wasn't okay.

"He fucked up. He had too many chances, and he fucked them all up. He wouldn't have died if he'd done his fucking job."

"You just left him there."

"Yeah, because the cops will find him. And everyone will know what happens if you don't do what I said."

"But—"

"Do you want to be an example? Because I'm happy to make you one, too."

Nina closed her mouth and turned toward the window.

She better fucking keep her mouth shut.

LORELEI WOKE up in the hospital the next morning with a weird sense of déjà vu. The pain in her side and shoulder were frighteningly similar to what she felt the last time she was in the hospital. But her ankle didn't hurt, and it wasn't as hard to breathe.

"You're awake," Vinnie said.

Lorelei smiled. That was the one thing she was happy hadn't changed. "Hey."

"Are you okay? Do you need anything? How are you?"

"I love you," she whispered.

A relieved breath rushed out of him. "Yeah? So you know who I am?"

She stared at him, pretending to be unsure for a second.

His smile faltered, returning when she grinned.

"Yes, Vinnie. I know who you are. I know everything."

"Everything?"

Lorelei nodded. "Yeah. I think being back there... Memories are flooding back in. Did you get the man who shot me? He was the one who kidnapped me."

"He's dead. They found him farther down the tunnel from where you were. It looked like he was trying to get to an underground garage."

"Garage?" Lorelei breathed. It made sense. That was how they were able to move people and product without anyone noticing.

Vinnie nodded. "There was a network of tunnels that led back to the streets, way outside where we were looking."

"So we didn't find the boss?"

Vinnie shook his head. "No, but we saved a lot of lives. That's what we need to focus on."

"How's everyone else?" Lorelei asked, remembering the massive team that went in, including her friends.

"Everyone is okay. A little beat up, but alive. We lost two cops."

"Shit."

Vinnie nodded. "Their lives weren't in vain. There were seventeen women there, and we took some of the operators into custody. We will find answers."

"When can I get out of here?"

"Soon," Vinnie said.

"Good, because I'm ready to be anywhere but in a hospital."

Vinnie kissed her softly and nodded. "Me, too."

A few hours passed before the doctor told Lorelei she could leave. Her gunshot wounds grazed her skin and she would be in pain for a while, but there wasn't much they could do for her. With the promise she would take it easy, Vinnie agreed to make sure she followed orders, and they left the hospital.

As soon as they were in his SUV, Lorelei called Adam to get a report.

"We're at Stacey and Wray's. Come over. We know we have work to do, but we're celebrating bringing home so many innocent victims. People who get to have a life again thanks to you and what you remembered." Adam sounded happy. Relieved.

Lorelei wasn't sure, but Vinnie said they should go. Lorelei chewed her lip the entire time, anxious about ruining the mood. But she knew she needed to tell them everything she remembered.

No more keeping secrets. No more thinking she could do it alone. She was going to rely on her team, just like she did in that house.

Vinnie parked on the street and led the way to the Allen's front door. Wray opened it for them, hugging both of them before welcoming them into the house.

"Where is everyone?" Lorelei asked.

"What's going on? I thought we were celebrating," Wray said as he led the way through the house.

"I remember everything. I need to tell everyone."

Wray sucked in a breath, his face serious. He opened the back door and led them onto a deck surrounded by a wide yard. Kids ran in the yard, chased by Braden and Holden. The others were relaxing on or near the deck.

When they saw Lorelei, everyone came over to say hello. She greeted them all, hating that she was dragging down the mood. But it wasn't over. Not until they took down the one in charge.

"What's wrong?" Frannie asked. "You look like you're going to be sick."

"She remembers everything," Wray provided.

"Everything?" Jessica asked.

Karli took her hand. "Oh, Lorelei, I'm so sorry."

Tears popped into Lorelei's eyes. She had fought so hard against the memories. The pain and fear she felt swamped her, and she ached to push it all away, but she couldn't. She couldn't let them win.

Which was exactly what would happen if she didn't tell everyone what she remembered.

"Do you want to talk about it?" Stacey asked. As the therapist, it didn't surprise Lorelei that Stacey asked the question.

What did surprise Lorelei was her nod. "I think that's probably a good idea. But today, I need to tell you all the part that matters."

"It all matters, Lorelei," Adam said.

Lorelei nodded. "Yeah, but most of it is my own healing. I will get there. For now, I need you all to know who we're after."

"You know who's behind all of this?" Marcus asked, moving closer.

Lorelei nodded. "There's a boss. She's pulling the strings. She's leading everything."

"She?" Raina asked.

Lorelei nodded again. "Her name is Gwendolyn Lennox."

Frannie gasped and reached for Marcus. "No," she breathed.

"Do you know her?" Adam asked.

Frannie looked up at Marcus. Tears rolled down her pale cheeks. He helped her sit. She closed her eyes and shook her head. She was quiet for a few minutes, then whispered, "Oh, God, it's true, isn't it?"

Marcus kneeled in front of Frannie. "Wow. I hate it, but yeah."

"What's going on? What are we missing?" Pryce asked.

Marcus sat next to Frannie. He held her hand and waited for her to speak.

Frannie pulled herself together and met the gazes of everyone there. "Gwendolyn Lennox was my best friend when I was in my early twenties. She ran a club for her father. The club where I got that mask. Gwennie was with me the night I witnessed Damon Street kill a woman. And because of Gwennie, and her twisted statement to the police, Damon was never arrested. He walked free for years."

"No," Raina breathed.

Frannie nodded. "She was right there for years, and I never saw it. Right there."

Lorelei stared as Frannie crumbled, breaking down into sobs that echoed across the entire yard.

The truth was finally out. But it was worse than Lorelei feared. So much worse.

Gwendolyn Lennox watched the news report and seethed. Her compound had been seized. Her fortress searched by the police. Invaded.

It was only a matter of time before they connected her to it. Before they connected everything.

She needed a plan.

Her father never would have let this happen. She could hear his taunts now.

I told you that you weren't good enough. Always said you'd fuck up and lose it all. What are you gonna do now? How do you think you're going to save everything I worked my entire life to build? I'll come back and kill you myself if you don't fix this.

"Shut up!" Gwendolyn shrieked.

"I didn't say anything," Nina said, her voice scared.

Good. She should be afraid. "I wasn't talking to you."

Nina looked around the otherwise empty room. "No one else is here."

"I was... talking to the TV. How dare they go into my home? Who do they think they are?"

"The police. And they said they had a reason to be there. This is getting close, Gwendolyn."

"I'm handling it," Gwendolyn barked.

"Are you? Because it looks to me like the cops are closing in. Maybe you should turn yourself in. Get out ahead of it. Blame someone else. Benjamin? Maybe Trevor and Damon?"

Gwendolyn turned on the little bitch she kept around to keep her sane. Sane? What a fucking joke. Nina was there because Gwendolyn needed someone she could trust.

And the bitch wanted her to turn herself in.

"Do you really think that's a good idea? That I should just walk into the police station and say I was forced into it. I'm too weak of a woman and I let the people with dicks in my life control me. Is that who you think I am?" Gwendolyn grabbed Nina's hair and yanked.

"No! I'm sorry. I was just—"

"Just what? Just trying to get me out of the way so you can take over? You don't have what it takes. You'll never be strong enough to lead. You're weak."

"I don't want to lead, Gwendolyn. I never—"

"You're right. You'll never." Gwendolyn tossed Nina to the floor. A kick. A punch. Another kick.

The bitch needed to learn her lesson. She needed to know who was in charge. And who was the fucking help.

Gwendolyn ignored Nina's cries and beat her until she was too tired to keep going. She left Nina on the floor and stalked to the bed, pulled back the covers, and climbed in.

Tomorrow was a new day. A better day. A day where Gwendolyn would figure out what was next.

Without someone trying to convince her she was wrong about the choices she made. She was never wrong.

FAITH IS AVAILABLE NOW...

Nina spent almost every day for the last twelve years regretting running away from home. The choice to give her brother his life back seemed so easy, but Nina didn't realize what hell she was running toward. What hell Gwendolyn would put her through. But now that Nina knows, she has to stop Gwendolyn from taking anymore lives. And protect her brother and the man she's loved forever.

PREORDER FAITH TODAY!

Everyone deserves justice. Even when they're no one.

Witnessing a murder was not on Frannie's bucket list.
Marcus had to find out what the curvy dancer knew.
They made a deal. She would help him, and he would find
the murderers. No one would know she was involved. She
hoped.

**Frannie and Marcus's story is available only to
subscribers.**
Sign up at https://dl.bookfunnel.com/y9ms2k2dq8 to get
FORSAKEN now, and meet Gwendolyn for the first time.

TURN the page to read chapter one of FAITH.

FAITH

CHAPTER 1

Nina Rose sat in the chair she was assigned to and glared at the sleeping bitch across the room. Gwendolyn Lennox was evil. She was mean and dangerous and not worthy of the air she breathed.

Nina imagined what it would feel like the plunge a knife into the heart of the heartless bitch who took her in twelve years ago and never let her leave. If Nina had known what she was running toward all those years ago, she never would have left home.

She stood and walked across the room. Gwendolyn almost looked human as she slept. Her blonde hair stretched over the pillows. Her mouth opened slightly. Her pink lips parted with each breath she took.

She would never stop hurting people. Nina touched the black eye Gwendolyn gave her just a few hours earlier. When she decided Nina's suggestion to turn herself in was unacceptable.

Nina was going to die in Gwendolyn's house, like so many other women. Women Gwendolyn lied about and told Nina were going to live better lives. Women Gwendolyn sold into slavery and traded for favors. Women who would never be seen again because of the monster that Gwendolyn was.

Nina shook her head, fighting tears. She was so stupid. She believed all the lies Gwendolyn told her. Thought Gwendolyn was looking out for her like the sister she claimed to think of Nina as. But Gwendolyn just wanted a pet. Someone to complain to when she was in a mood and a punching bag when she was angry.

It was the last time Nina was going to be anyone's punching bag. And if there was a weapon in the room, it would be the last time Gwendolyn used anyone for a punching bag.

Instead, it was the night Nina finally decided to reclaim her life.

She was getting the hell out of there.

She walked to the door that led to the hallway. They weren't in Gwendolyn's favorite house since the police and FBI raided it, but Nina had been with Gwendolyn long enough to know all the houses. All the routines and habits and ways out.

Nina sucked in a breath and erased all the thoughts in her mind. The guards Gwendolyn hired were as ruthless as she was, and they could sniff out a lie in a second. If they didn't believe Nina's story, they'd wake Gwendolyn up and Nina would be dead.

Her life depended on her being able to convince them she was running an errand for Gwendolyn. It wasn't the first time, so Nina hoped it worked. It had to.

She opened the door quietly, spotting Fernando immediately. He gazed past Nina to the bedroom, nodding when he saw Gwendolyn sleeping.

Nina closed the door as quietly as she'd opened it and turned to Fernando. "Is there a driver who can take me on an errand?"

Fernando glared at her. "What errand?"

Nina pointed to her eye and grimaced. "I upset her. I was going to get her some of those candies she likes so much."

Fernando glared harder. "You know better than to challenge her."

Nina nodded, letting her tears well up. It would sell the lie. "I know. And I'm sorry. I wasn't thinking. I wanted to protect her."

"What did you do?"

"I said she should think about turning herself in. Blaming Damon and Trevor and Benjamin. Tell the police she didn't know what they were doing with her company money."

Fernando's small smile was one of approval instead of dismissal. "Not a bad idea, but she'd never do it. She didn't get to where she is to play the dumb blonde."

Nina swallowed roughly, her throat sore from Gwendolyn choking her. "I know. I shouldn't have suggested it. I was worried. We were in the house when they came in. She could have been caught."

Fernando shook his head, the dark stringy ponytail he wore flopping over his shoulder. "She'll never be caught. We won't let it happen."

Nina nodded, hoping he thought it was in agreement.

"Let me see who's available. You go to that convenience store in the city, right? Close to that F-BOMB place?"

Nina nodded. It was working.

Fernando called someone and told them to get the car ready. When they questioned him, he said, "If I have to come down there, you won't be able to drive anything."

Fernando hung up and nodded to Nina. "They'll be ready."

"Thanks, Fernando," Nina said, pressing her lips into a smile. She walked away and hoped like hell she'd never see him again.

The SUV was waiting for her when she arrived. Parked under the structure, a dozen vehicles waited for whatever Gwendolyn needed them for. Decoy, transport, anything. She was the queen of her domain, and she made sure everyone knew it.

Nina didn't recognize the driver, which wasn't a bad thing. She climbed into the backseat and ignored him, watching the house disappear into the darkness as he drove away.

Fifteen minutes later, he pulled into the parking lot for the convenience store. He slid the vehicle into park and met her gaze in the rearview mirror. He jerked his head to the building.

Guess he wasn't going in. Worked for her.

Nina climbed out of the SUV and wrapped the shawl around her neck, looping it up over her face to hide as much of her appearance as possible. Gwendolyn hated when Nina let anyone see her hair. The red color was distinctive and drew attention. Attention Gwendolyn never wanted on Nina.

It took Nina way too many years to understand why.

Nina walked inside, nodding at the clerk. The man barely acknowledged her, which was just as good. If he wasn't paying attention, he wouldn't be able to tell Gwendolyn anything when Nina didn't go back out.

Nina worked her way through the store, choosing an aisle toward the back of the store so the driver wouldn't be able to see her. She got to the end and knew there was a gap. If he looked up at the right time, he would spot her, but if she was lucky...

Nina sprinted across the half-dozen feet of space, letting out a breath when she made it to the other side and saw the driver with his nose in his phone.

The rest was easy. Get to the office in the back, the one that was never locked, and call the one man she knew would save her.

Zeke Donovan stood in the bullpen at work and listened to his boss share the rest of the rundown from the last few days. It was a fuck-ton of information. FBI Agent Lorelei Sloane had pieced together more than every other person out there.

And the fuckers who took her almost killed it all with her.

But they didn't. Lorelei was safe, and she gave them what they needed to invade the stronghold of Gwendolyn Lennox's organization.

The next step was dismantling the entire fucking thing, but that wasn't what Rose Protection Agency was doing. Their involvement was limited.

Which suited Zeke just fine.

"What's up next for us?" Austin Ward asked. Austin and

his partner, Samuel MacNeil, were an odd couple that worked like ice cream and brownies. Good on their own, but better together.

"We have cases we've been working on, and a new one that just came in. Local PD might want us to protect some witnesses, especially if there are a few women who want to stick together. Most of them will go through rehab, so it might be a few months of steady work helping them out." Montgomery Rose was Zeke's oldest and closest friend. Also the man Zeke owed his life to, many times over.

Zeke knew that score was balanced, though. Zeke had saved Mont just as many times. But their scoresheet would never be even. Zeke would spend the rest of his life making up for the mistakes of his past. Working with his best friend and keeping Montgomery safe was Zeke's penance.

Mont hadn't been the same since his sister disappeared. Nina was Montgomery's favorite person in the world, and Zeke let her vanish.

He'd never forgiven himself for it. And never would.

"We're good for whatever you need. Just happy we finally know who everyone is chasing," Samuel said.

The others in the room murmured their agreement.

"When all this is done, everyone should take a few days off," Montgomery told the room. "Go to the beach or something."

Zeke snorted. "Are you taking time off?"

"He never takes time off," Berkeley said, walking into the bullpen like she owned the place. As the executive assistant, and all-around alpha male wrangler, she had every right to act the way she did.

"That's why I'm asking," Zeke said. "Come on, Mont. We all need a break. Even you."

"I'm not interested in a beach bunny or any other kind of bunny."

"Fuck, man, I didn't say that. Go skydiving or SCUBA diving or something. Get the hell out of here for a little while."

Montgomery cast a side-eye at Berkeley, who only raised one dark eyebrow at him. She was always telling him the same thing.

Zeke's phone rang, interrupting whatever Montgomery was about to say.

They all stopped, waiting for Zeke to answer the phone. In their business, when someone called, they answered. No matter what.

"Donovan," Zeke barked into the phone, locking his gaze on Montgomery's. He didn't need words to communicate with his boss.

"Zeke?" a voice whispered.

Every inch of Zeke responded to that voice. One word, and he knew exactly who it was, even if it had been twelve years since he heard her. He glanced at Montgomery. Why was she calling Zeke instead of her brother?

Zeke tore his gaze from Montgomery's. He was wrong. He had to be. It couldn't be her. And he couldn't tell his best friend it was or Mont would be crushed all over again.

They'd all lost hope, and having it back, even for a few seconds, was worse than never having it at all.

"Yeah?"

"I don't have long. I need you."

"Where are you?" Zeke was halfway to the door, moving toward the front of the building and ready to go.

"The convenience store we always hung out at when we were kids. Do you remember?"

"I'm on my way. Don't move."

"Please hurry. Park in the back."

"I'll be there in two minutes," Zeke said.

She hung up.

Zeke felt like he'd been punched. Twelve years. It had been twelve years since he heard her voice. Twelve years since the woman he loved walked out of the house and never came back. Twelve years.

His heart pounded. His palms were sweaty. Every inch of him said he would never see her again if he didn't get there soon.

He couldn't let her disappear again. He couldn't.

"Who was that?" Montgomery asked, surprising Zeke.

"Just a client. Needs me to go get her." Zeke never kept anything from Montgomery. Brothers in every possible way. The look in his best friend's eyes said he knew there was more to the story, but he also knew if Zeke wasn't sharing, there was a reason for it.

"Are you okay to go alone?"

Zeke nodded, trying to calm his racing heart. If it really was Nina, he would bring her to Montgomery so he could see his sister. Know she was alive. Twelve years was a long time to assume she wasn't, and false hope would crush him.

Which was why Zeke said, "All good. I'll check in later. How long are you here?"

Montgomery looked at his watch and shrugged. "Another hour, at least. Are you coming back?"

"Possibly."

Montgomery tilted his head. When they picked up a client, they took them somewhere safe. That rarely meant the office. "Are you sure everything's okay?"

Zeke nodded. "I think so. I'll try to be back soon."

Montgomery nodded, even as his face betrayed his confusion.

Zeke was cutting it close and had to go. He wasn't far from the convenience store, but he didn't want to risk her leaving. He raced to his SUV and cranked it up, pulling out of the lot without bothering with a seatbelt. She was more important.

A black SUV idled in front of the store. The man behind the wheel glanced up, then returned his focus to his phone. The rest of the parking lot was empty. The store appeared to be as well, except for the clerk behind the counter.

Zeke pulled in from the other side, where the man in the SUV and the clerk wouldn't see him. He eased his SUV to a stop next to the door that said Employees Only.

Leaving the engine running, Zeke got out. He went to the door, pulling the handle. Hope was a motherfucker, but Zeke was full of it.

The door creaked open, and there she was in the dark hallway. Standing in front of him like she'd been twelve years ago. She was older, but no less gorgeous. Her figure had filled out, giving her curves, curves, and more curves. The possessive alpha in him roared with desire, wanting to throw her over his shoulder and never let her out of his sight again.

"You came," she whispered, looking up at him. Until he saw her eyes, he had his doubts, but that gaze was seared into his brain. It was the gaze he saw in his dreams, the one he'd been chasing for most of his life. The one he never thought he'd see again.

"Holy fuck, it is you." Zeke reached for her, ignoring the flash of panic in her eyes. He couldn't wait another second to have her in his arms. He lifted her off her feet, holding her to him until she melted in his embrace and sank into him.

She sighed, then inhaled a shaky breath.

He pressed his nose to her neck and whispered, "Don't you ever fucking walk out on me again."

"Okay," she whispered.

Zeke let out a breath and stepped outside, checking that no one else was there. "We need to go."

She nodded and followed him, startling when she saw his SUV. It was shockingly similar to the one parked in front of the building.

"It's mine. Get in. Lie down in the back so no one sees you." He opened the door for her and waited, praying she hurried up but knowing he couldn't rush her.

She took two steps forward, then threw her arms around his neck.

He inhaled deep, closing his eyes and ignoring her body odor. She was alive. Not just that, but she was back. She called him. She was going to be okay.

"Thank you for coming to get me, Zeke."

Zeke cupped her cheeks and got a closer look at her in the bright light of the parking lot. She'd lost her childish features and grown into a beautiful woman. Curves in all the right places and that same red hair that always hinted at the spark she hid from most people.

But that wasn't all that was new. She had a black eye, handprints around her throat, and more bruises on the skin exposed by her way too small dress.

Zeke's blood boiled. Someone put their fucking hands on her. Beat her and hurt her and she was so scared, she called him in the middle of the fucking night.

He had half a mind to pull around to the front of the store and put a knife in the throat of the man who was waiting for her. But one look in her eyes, that gray-green that mesmerized him when he wasn't supposed to be in love with his best friend's little sister, and he knew that wasn't the answer.

"Let's go," he whispered.

Nina nodded and crawled into his backseat. She laid down on the floor, curling herself up tight and making it impossible for her to be seen.

Zeke closed the door, then slid behind the wheel. He watched his mirrors as he navigated the city, making more turns than necessary to confirm no one was following them. When he was confident, he breathed a little easier.

"Who was that?"

She was quiet, but he knew she understood what he was asking. "He was the driver. I don't know his name."

"Is he the one who did that to you?"

"No."

Zeke wanted to ask more. To demand she tell him everything, but the quiet answers she gave him said she wasn't ready to talk yet.

"Where are you taking me?"

"To my house. Let you shower and change, then we're going to see your brother."

"He's here?" she gasped, as though she expected something different.

Zeke glanced in the mirror, but he couldn't see her. He looked at the floor where she laid and hated he hadn't been able to provide her with more than the floor of his SUV to hide.

But she was alive.

"He never stopped looking for you."

"He didn't?" she breathed.

Zeke shook his head, then focused on the road. He drove to his home, assuming she'd want a shower and new clothes. He had something she could wear, nothing like what she was wearing, but he didn't think that dress was her choice.

He pulled into the driveway of his duplex and sighed when he saw Montgomery wasn't home yet. They didn't like the idea of having places far apart, and when the duplex was listed years ago, they jumped on the idea of having each other next door but still maintaining privacy and independence.

Something neither of them wanted for a long time after Nina vanished.

Zeke closed the garage door and let Nina out of the backseat. He helped her out, noting how fragile she seemed. He led the way around his SUV and opened the door into his house.

And was immediately met by a less than happy meow.

Nina gasped. "You have a cat?"

Zeke bent down to pick up Gene, a black and white cat with only three paws. "I have two, actually. This is Gene. He was hit by a car and lost his leg, but don't tell him because he has no idea there's anything different about him."

"He's precious," Nina whispered, petting Gene's head. She laughed, a husky, rusty sound, when Gene purred loudly.

"He's needy."

Another meow, softer and more patient, tentative followed.

Zeke turned and spotted Franklin on the kitchen counter. He nodded toward him so Nina would see the tabby. "That's Franklin. He thinks rules don't apply to him and never listens."

Nina went to Franklin and let him sniff her hand. He bumped her knuckles with his forehead, then rubbed his head under her hand, flopping on his back and exposing himself on the counter.

"Jesus, man, have some decency. She just got here," Zeke said, shaking his head at his cat.

Gene meowed, as though agreeing with Zeke.

Nina laughed again. "They're wonderful."

"They're pretty great, yeah."

The silence stretched between them. Zeke had a million questions, but he didn't think he could ask her any of them.

"So, um, the bathroom is upstairs. I'll show you where everything is and get you some clothes to change into. Montgomery lives next door, but he's not home, so when you're cleaned up, I'll find out where he is and we can go see him."

Nina nodded, patting Franklin on the head, then following Zeke up the stairs.

The cats followed along, winding between Zeke and Nina's feet and making her laugh. Zeke fought all the emotions rising up, knowing he had to keep it together until he handed her over to her brother. Zeke didn't know why she called him and not Montgomery, but it didn't matter.

She was back.

He went to his bedroom and grabbed the smallest pair of shorts he had, ones with a drawstring, and a dark tee. He didn't have underwear that would fit her, but he hoped the clothes would be enough for now. He'd buy her an entire fucking store tomorrow. Anything she needed.

She followed behind him, barely two feet away the whole time. When he showed her the bathroom off his bedroom, she sucked in a breath. "Wow."

"Take your time. I'll be downstairs. Whenever you're ready to come back down, you can, but there's no rush."

"Zeke?" she whispered.

"Yeah, Nina?"

"Thank you for getting me."

"Thank you for calling me."

Nina smiled, then turned.

Zeke left the bathroom and closed the door. He closed the bedroom door, too. He wanted to sit in the room and wait for her, but she needed space.

And so did he.

Zeke went to his kitchen and poured himself a glass of water. He downed it, wishing it was something stronger. But until he talked to Montgomery, he had to make sure his mind was clear.

Zeke alternated between staring at the ceiling and wondering if she was okay and staring at his phone and trying to figure out what the fuck to say to Montgomery.

Hey, Mont, your sister's here. In my house. No big deal. She just called me instead of you after twelve years.

Not an option.

But Zeke was going to have to figure something out.

The shower turned off, and his heart thudded hard. She would be back downstairs soon. And he would have to take her to Montgomery.

Zeke couldn't sit still. He paced the house, listening for Nina.

But he didn't hear Nina. He heard Montgomery.

The garage next door opened, but it didn't close right away.

A door opened upstairs.

Someone knocked on the front door, then a key slid into the lock.

Zeke stood still, watching as brother and sister both moved into the room.

"Hey, Zeke. What was that call you got...?" Montgomery froze.

Nina stopped halfway down the stairs.

"Nina?"

"Hi, big brother," Nina said.

Montgomery's jaw dropped. His gaze scanned his sister. Then swung to Zeke. "What the fuck did you do to her?"

Zeke didn't have time to defend himself before Montgomery charged him. Fists first.

READ FAITH TODAY!

ABOUT THE AUTHOR

USA TODAY Bestselling Author Mary E Thompson spent most of her childhood wishing she had a few less curves. She hid in the pages of books because her favorite characters never cared what size her clothes were. Now, neither does Mary, and she writes stories that celebrate women like her. Real women who have curves, chase dreams, and find love, because we should all be happy, no matter our dress size.

Mary spends her non-writing time with her husband and two kids, watching too much TV, cheering for her hometown football team (Go Bills!), and hiding chocolate from her family.

Visit https://MaryEThompson.com/ to sign up for Mary's newsletter, **Romancing the Curves**. Subscribers get free ebooks and other fun stuff, like exclusive, members only content and giveaways, plus are the first to know about new releases and sales!

www.ingramcontent.com/pod-product-compliance
Lightning Source LLC
Chambersburg PA
CBHW060653190726
48289CB00002B/397